Shifters' Haven

The author did a good job bringing the grief and pain, as well as the guilt that Nate continues to suffer across realistically... With Nate's Deputy, the author introduced some new twists to the underlying sub-plot... ~ *Literary Nymphs Reviews*

Ms. Lewis has once again given us a story of strength of character with a true sense and demonstration of what fated mates feel; the bond they share not only with each other, but also their new found family... This reviewer highly recommends Gregory's Rebellion. ~ *Dark Divas Reviews*

Total-E-Bound Publishing books by Lavinia Lewis:

Shifters' Haven Volume One
Luke's Surprise
Cody's Revelation

Shifters' Haven Volume Two
Kelan's Pursuit
Aaron's Awakening

SHIFTERS' HAVEN
Volume Three

Nate's Deputy

Gregory's Rebellion

LAVINIA LEWIS

Shifters' Haven Volume Three
ISBN # 978-1-78184-506-6

Interior text design by Claire Siemaszkiewicz
Total-E-Bound Publishing

Published in 2012 by Total-E-Bound Publishing, Think Tank, Ruston Way, Lincoln, LN6 7FL, United Kingdom.

Total-E-Bound Publishing is an imprint of Total-E-Ntwined Limited.

NATE'S DEPUTY

Dedication

This book is for everyone that has read and enjoyed Shifters' Haven to date. Thank you for your continued support and for the lovely emails you've sent me telling me how much you like the characters and world I've created. I appreciate you all more than I can say.

And as always, Mam, this is for you. I miss you. Dad, you're the best father I could have hoped for. Thank you for being you.

Chapter One

"I'm sorry, Mr Stanford, but there isn't anything I can do. There was another bid on the property—a substantially higher bid than yours."

Nate lowered his gaze and twirled the Stetson in his hands. "My family has lived on that ranch for over four generations."

This *couldn't* be fucking happening. If Nate had known the ranch was in trouble, he would have gladly handed over the money his brother Rick was short to buy the property when the owners put it up for sale. When they hadn't been able to pay the mortgage and the house hadn't sold, the bank had foreclosed. Nate had waited six excruciatingly long months for the legalities of the foreclosure to be settled, before the bank put the property back on the market. The good news was that the property was being offered at a fraction of the original cost, but the lower price had attracted new interest, and now Nate found himself in the middle of a bidding war. Why the hell hadn't Rick contacted him? Nate would have helped.

Okay, so Nate supposed he *knew* the reason Rick didn't get in touch. Before he was killed, it had been two years since they'd last spoken. Two goddamn long ass years of them each holding a grudge after a damn stupid argument that never should have happened. Nate swallowed the lump in his throat that thoughts of his brother always produced.

He hadn't had time to tell Rick he was sorry for the things he'd said, and now he would never get the chance. His brother was gone, and Nate hadn't even been able to say goodbye. By the time Kelan Morgan had tracked Nate down on a farm in Montana to inform him of Rick's death, he'd already missed his brother's funeral. What pissed Nate off most was that his own sister Lucy hadn't even had the decency to let him know. Sure, she had a problem with Nate being *queer,* as she put it, but their baby brother had died. How could she be so heartless? To add insult to injury, it looked as though the house they'd grown up in was going to be sold out from under his nose.

Fortunately, Kelan had seen fit to give Nate a job and a place to live on his ranch until he could buy his childhood home. It was damn good of Kelan to help him out, especially after what Rick had done to Kelan's family.

Nate still couldn't believe Rick had kidnapped Luke Morgan and then handed him over to Ethan Walker like he was nothing more than a fucking commodity that he could make a few bucks from. When Kelan first told him what his brother had done, Nate hadn't been able to believe it, even though he knew Kelan would never lie. To have done that to Luke for money was despicable. Rick had to have known Ethan wanted to harm Luke, so why had he done it? That didn't sound like something his brother would have done—not the brother Nate knew at any rate. The brother Nate remembered would never have stooped so low. Had Rick really changed that much in the two years Nate had been gone, or had he merely been desperate enough to make a God-awful decision? It was pointless chewing it over, because Nate would never know Rick's motivation now that his brother was gone, and that ate him up inside.

Something that continued to surprise Nate was the way that Kelan treated him like one of the family. He didn't hold Nate responsible for his brother's actions and he hadn't once said a bad thing about Rick…not to Nate's face anyhow, but he must have been thinking it. If only Nate could be as forgiving. He was so close to hating his brother for what he'd done, but mostly he hated himself. If he hadn't distanced himself from Rick, if he had been there when his brother needed him, then maybe Rick would still be alive.

"I'm afraid it's out of my hands," the Realtor said, dragging Nate out of his morose thoughts. "That is, of course, unless you can *up* your offer on the property?"

A low growl started to form in Nate's chest but he kept it inside. The Realtor, Rodney, was human, and like the other humans in town he didn't know a thing about the wolves that lived among them, even though the wolves outnumbered the humans practically two to one. The last thing Nate needed was to expose their secret and send the guy screaming for the hills.

Rising stiffly from the chair, Nate gave Rodney a sharp nod. "I'll see what I can do."

"You need to move quickly. The person that made the offer is in a good position to move forward with the sale and time is running out. You only have another five days before the cut-off date for bidding."

Nate grunted and pulled open the office door. "I'll be in touch."

It was noon when Nate stepped out of the Realtor's office and strode across the street to his truck. The sun was already high in the azure, cloudless sky and about as hot as blue blazes. Nate squinted and slipped on his dark grey, felt Stetson, pulling it low to shield his eyes. Most other cowboys Nate knew wore straw cowboy hats, which were cooler in the heat, but Nate had never taken to them. He supposed he was old-fashioned at heart.

The weather had been cooler in Montana, decidedly so. Although he'd got used to the lower temperatures, Nate had always loved the heat and stickiness of a Texan summer. He'd missed it—hell he'd missed home—but if his bid on the ranch wasn't successful, there would be nothing left for him in Wolf Creek to call home. No reason at all for him to stick around.

"Nate, that you?"

Nate stopped walking and turned to see who had addressed him. Pete Johnson, a cowboy Nate had spent some time with several years ago, stood grinning back at him—his own cowboy hat tipped as low as Nate's. Pete was one of Kelan's betas. He had a few years on Nate but he'd kept himself in shape. He looked good. His dark hair was longer than Nate remembered and hanging loosely around his shoulders. His frame was the same as before though—large, muscular, and damn fine.

"Well, I'll be damned, I wondered when I was going to run into you. Howdy." Pete dipped his hat in greeting, a warm smile playing on full lips. "It's been a while."

Nate nodded. "Has. How you been?"

"Good. I was sorry to hear of the trouble at the Crazy Horse. Kelan told me you were shot."

Nate frowned. Thinking about the night Cary had been kidnapped by those losers from town several weeks ago always made the fine hairs on the back of his neck stand on end.

"Cary is a good kid, been through a lot. He could have been killed that night."

Pete grinned, the action exposing his perfectly straight, white teeth. "You haven't changed I see."

"Huh?"

"Always putting other people first. I asked about you getting shot but your first thought was for that young panther shifter."

Nate felt a blush creep up his neck, but it was more from shame than embarrassment. If Pete knew the truth about him, about how he'd let his brother down, he might not be so quick to praise. He waved a hand dismissively at his chest.

"Was nothing. 'S already healed. You still working as foreman for old man Walker?"

"Naw, the old fool fired me about a year ago."

"Fired you?" That came as a surprise. Pete had always been a damn hard worker, one of the best.

"Let's just say he caught me in a *compromising* position with one of the hands." Pete's eyes sparkled with mirth and Nate couldn't hold back his chuckle. That sounded exactly like the Pete he remembered.

"Couldn't keep it in your pants, eh?"

Pete's grin broadened, and he shrugged his shoulders. "Something like that."

"So, where you working nowadays?"

"You haven't heard?"

Nate shook his head. "Don't listen to gossip, and don't get into town much."

"I'm working at Jessie's Dancehall, manage the place now."

"You? Manage a honky-tonk?"

Pete nodded. "I enjoy it, more than I thought I would."

"You don't miss being a cowboy?"

"I'll *always* be a cowboy, but do I miss the animals or working the land? Can't say as I do. I never was one for this damn heat, and ranching in the middle o' summer just about killed me. Jessie is thinking of selling, matter o' fact, and I've a mind to buy him out. I'm headed there now to open up if you wanna come grab a beer."

Pete raised his eyebrows in query and his mouth curved up into a seductive smile. Interest flared in his dark brown eyes. Nate considered the offer. It had certainly been a long time since he'd socialised, but based on their history together he had a feeling Pete was offering more than a friendly drink for old time's sake. With all his worries over the ranch, the last thing on Nate's mind was hooking up, so it wasn't fair to lead Pete on, no matter how tempting the man was. And Nate *was* tempted.

Pete's rough and somewhat rugged exterior appealed to Nate. He'd always been attracted to strong men even though Nate was no puny little thing himself. But it didn't matter how long it had been since Nate got any relief from a hand other than his own, he couldn't bring himself to say yes.

"Thanks," he said at last. "But I've got to be getting back to the Crazy Horse. Got some work to finish for Kelan, and I'm already late."

"No worries. How's it going there?"

"Good. Kelan's a fair boss."

"Yeah, he's a good man that one and a good leader, one of the best."

"You still one of his betas? I haven't seen you around the ranch."

Pete nodded. "Yeah. He calls on me from time to time, but I've been so busy managing Jessie's and some other things I have going on, I haven't been as involved as I should have been. I told him he might want to look for someone else that can fully commit."

"Bet he'll be sorry to lose you."

Pete shrugged. He shuffled his feet uncomfortably then looked up and met Nate's gaze. "You know, I was real sorry about what happened to Rick."

Nate lowered his head to stare at the ground and felt the familiar lump begin to form in the back of his throat. He didn't talk about his brother—ever. Hadn't since he'd learned of Rick's death. Cary had tried to talk to him about Rick a few times, but Nate always managed to change the subject and the kid hadn't pushed.

"Thanks. I'd better get going. Good seeing you again, Pete."

"You too, and Nate…?"

Nate reluctantly lifted his head to meet Pete's gaze.

"If you ever want to stop by for a…drink, *or* anything else, you'd be more than welcome."

Nate tipped his hat and strode back to his truck without another word to his old friend.

* * * *

"Have you been drinking again?" Jared grabbed hold of his brother's arm and waited for him to meet his gaze. After a moment, Tristan raised his head. His pale blue eyes were bloodshot and he seemed to have trouble focusing.

"No. Christ, will you give it a rest? I'm tired of your nagging."

"Don't lie to me Tristan," Jared fumed, trying to keep his anger in check. He was sick and tired of having the same damn argument with his brother. "I can smell it on you."

"Jesus, I had one beer...*one*."

Jared narrowed his eyes and pressed his lips together. "It's the middle of the day."

"Will you give a guy a break? I'm going out."

"Where are you going?"

"Out!" Tristan pulled out of Jared's grip, grabbed his wallet from the nightstand and strode out the door. "Don't wait up!" he called over his shoulder.

Jared jumped when the bedroom door slammed shut, and he bit back a growl. Tristan's drinking was getting out of control. He wished he could do something to help his brother, but sometimes there was only so much you could do. A person had to want to help themselves, but Tristan refused to admit he had a problem.

Their father dying had hit Tristan hard, Jared knew that. Hell, he was struggling to hold it together himself. But if his brother wasn't careful, he was going to wind up in jail...or worse. It wasn't only the drinking that was the problem—it was Tristan's anger. Jared had been called over to Jessie's dancehall on three separate occasions when his brother had shot his mouth off to some locals and they'd retaliated. One of these days Tristan was going to mess with the wrong person, and Jared didn't want to think about what could happen then. He already had nightmares of finding Tristan in a ditch somewhere, and he didn't want his waking hours to be consumed with such thoughts too.

Jared sat down heavily on the twin bed by the window and gazed around the sparsely decorated room. He knew their living arrangements weren't helping matters—if anything, they were making things worse. The small bedroom they shared at Marnie's Guesthouse was basic, but until Jared was able to buy them a house in the area, they would have to make do. He'd be the first to admit how stressful it was living in such close quarters, but he seemed to be coping with the situation far better than his brother.

Most of their belongings were still in storage in Lubbock. Jared knew that was only a small thing, but he suspected his brother would feel more at home in Wolf Creek when he had his possessions around him. Tristan had to be tired of living out of a suitcase. Jared sure was.

The drinking binges had started back in Lubbock but the problem had become exacerbated when they'd moved to Wolf Creek. Jared knew Tristan wasn't happy about the move, but there was no way he could have turned down the job as a deputy in the sheriff's office when they'd offered him the position. He'd applied to practically every office in the state when he'd got his business degree, and Wolf Creek was the only place he'd been successful.

In a few months' time Sheriff Ferguson would be up for retirement, and if Jared could put down roots and build some support within the community, then there was no reason he wouldn't get elected when the position became available…as long as he could keep his sexuality a secret, of course. If people around town found out he was gay then he likely wouldn't have a hope in hell. Not that Jared had anything to worry about on that score. It had been months since his last sexual encounter and he didn't envisage that situation changing anytime soon.

Getting laid was the last thing on Jared's mind. His brother had to be his top priority, as well as finding them a place they could call home. When they were settled, Jared hoped Tristan would quit his drinking and maybe think some more about his future. Tristan was great with his hands—always fixing things, especially cars—and there had been a time in the not so distant past in which he'd talked about becoming a mechanic. Maybe he could find himself an apprenticeship here in town.

In Lubbock, Tristan had been working in a grocery store to make ends meet after he'd dropped out of college when their Pop died. But as soon as he'd started drinking, Tristan had quit his job and had been coasting ever since, hardly seeming to be interested in anything…other than getting wasted.

They'd had money to live on for a while, sure, but it wouldn't last for very long the way Tristan was spending it, and they needed everything they'd inherited from their father in order to purchase a home so they could have somewhere to call their own. That basically meant that everything Jared earned went to support Tristan too. Jared didn't mind looking after his brother one little bit—he saw it as his responsibility now that their Pop wasn't around to do it anymore—but that wasn't the point. Tristan was twenty-one now—a man. It was time he took on some responsibility, time he grew a pair.

Jared checked his watch. He didn't have long to wait to find out about their housing situation. In exactly fifteen minutes, the Realtor's office would be calling to let him know if he'd been successful with his bid on a ranch a few miles out of town. Jared had never been so nervous. This house could be the catalyst that his brother so desperately needed to make some changes in his life, and to start thinking about his future. They *had* to be successful. Their whole future in Wolf Creek depended on it.

* * * *

After bolting the door to the stall, Nate carried Misty's saddle back to the tack room. It had been a long, strenuous day already and it wasn't even lunchtime. Nate was looking forward to a relaxing shower to clean away the grime and sweat he was covered in. The Realtors had promised him a call at exactly one thirty to let him know the results of the bidding. Nate was hoping the hot shower would help ease his nerves as much as his tired muscles. He hung up the saddle and harness and made his way out of the barn. He was halfway across the yard when Aaron appeared at the bunkhouse door.

"Nate! Phone call!"

"Fuck." Nate sprinted across the yard and up the porch steps to the door. "Who is it?"

Aaron shrugged and ducked back inside the house. "Don't know," he threw over his shoulder. "Didn't say."

Nate frowned and walked through to their shared kitchen to take the call. It was only twelve-thirty, so it couldn't be the Realtor yet, could it?

"Nate," he said into the receiver.

"Ah, Mr Stanford. Sorry to call so early, but I've had news about the ranch and I thought you'd want to know right away."

Nate held his breath. He'd managed to talk the bank into lending him forty thousand dollars to add to the inheritance money he'd been holding on to since his mother's death. He'd got more money when Rick was killed, a substantial amount split between him and his sister, but he hadn't wanted that money at first. He'd just wanted his brother back. But the best way to honour Rick's memory, he'd decided, would be to buy their family farm. Nate had placed the largest offer he could, leaving barely enough for running costs for the first few months until he started to recoup his losses. He only hoped it had been enough. His whole life rode on this decision.

"I do, thank you."

"I think it would be best if I cut right to the chase. It's not good news, I'm afraid. Your bids were all too low. The ranch has been sold to someone else."

Nate clenched the phone in his hand, feeling his wolf begin to stir as his anger rose to the surface. "Thank you for letting me know," he choked out. He ended the call and slid the phone back into its cradle.

"Fuck!"

He stared around the bunkhouse kitchen, rubbing a hand along the back of his neck. His face grew hot and his ears burned from the humiliation of losing his family's home.

"I'm sorry, Rick," Nate whispered. "I'm so sorry I let you down."

Chapter Two

Nate took a seat in one of the wooden chairs that surrounded the kitchen table and closed his eyes, fighting to keep his wolf in check. Whenever he was upset or angry, his wolf grew restless—pacing within him and desperate to be set free. Even though Nate hadn't lived at the ranch for the last two and a half years, he still considered it home. It was where he'd grown up, and he'd naïvely believed he would always call it home, but there was no chance of that now. Someone else would soon have the privilege of using that title.

What in the hell was he going to do now? Maybe it would be best if he went back to Montana. He didn't relish the thought of moving back there, but he couldn't hang around Wolf Creek watching strangers take up residence in the place he'd called home for the biggest part of his life. That would kill him as surely as anything.

Problem was, Nate also had his father to consider—not that the old man ever recognised Nate when he went to visit him in the nursing home. His father was suffering from a type of dementia, common in older wolves, so he'd been placed in a special nursing home for shifters. It was a two hundred mile round-trip from Wolf Creek. Nate tried to visit him as often as possible, but it was getting more and more difficult to see his father like that—a mere shadow of the man he used to be. Nate knew his sister made regular visits because the nurses had told him, but that was beside the point.

"Nate? Everything okay?"

Nate looked up and met Cary's gaze. The young panther shifter was hovering near the door, chewing on his bottom lip.

"Yeah, kid, everything's fine."

Cary crossed the room and took a seat in a chair opposite Nate. "Are you sure? Because you don't look fine."

Nate sighed. Trust Cary to be so direct...the kid didn't miss a beat. Nate knew there would be no point in unloading his troubles on the young panther because he couldn't change his circumstances, no matter how much he wished he could. Besides, Cary had had the troubles of ten men in his young life. He didn't need Nate's problems dumped on him.

"Just wondering on some things is all. Was thinking about moving back to Montana."

Cary sucked in a sharp breath. "What? But why? Don't you like it here with us?"

"Yeah, kid. I like it here just fine, but sometimes a man's gotta do what's best for him, you know?"

Cary's eyes were wide. "But I don't want you to leave," he whispered. "Is it because of me? Because of what happened the night you got shot?"

"Now you listen here. That night has absolutely nothing to do with my reason for wanting to go, understand? *Nothing* at all. You've got to stop blaming yourself for what happened. Those men were crazy."

Just thinking of the night Cary had nearly been killed made Nate's anger rise. Yes, Nate had been shot, but he'd been able to save Cary's life in the process. He'd go through it again...and gladly if he had to.

Nate watched Cary's throat bob when he swallowed. The kid might have stopped jumping at his own shadow, but he could still be a nervous little thing.

"You got something on your mind, there's no sense in lettin' it fester. Spit it out."

Cary nodded. "Is it because of Aaron? I get the feeling you don't like him very much. It's just that you can be...*snappy* with him sometimes."

Nate sighed. Had he been snappy with Aaron? He hadn't meant to be. How in the hell was he going to explain this? He took a deep breath before he spoke, more to give himself time to think than anything else.

"Didn't realise I'd been doing that, sorry. I don't *dislike* Aaron, quite the opposite in fact."

Cary scrunched his eyebrows together in confusion. "Huh?"

"Aaron is a nice kid—I can see that, and I've seen the difference in you since he's been around, too. You've got a sparkle in your eye now that wasn't there before. You seem...*lighter*, if that's the right word. Like all your worries and cares have disappeared."

Cary cocked his head to the side as though he were considering Nate's statement. "I guess they have. I know I'm happier now than I've been in a long time...probably ever."

"I'm glad you found someone that makes you feel that way."

"So you *don't* have a problem with him."

Fuck. Cary wasn't going to let the subject drop, and it was on ground that Nate didn't want to venture onto, but he supposed the kid deserved an explanation.

"No, I don't have a problem with Aaron. But it's difficult to be around him sometimes because he reminds me so much of my brother, Rick, when he was younger." There…Nate had said it, and it had been less difficult to admit to than he thought it would be.

Cary's eyes widened and his hand flew up to cover his mouth. "Oh God, I'm sorry. I didn't know…must be real hard for you to be around him then."

"Yeah, but don't worry about it, kid. It's my problem, not Aaron's. I never wanted to make him feel uncomfortable. I'll watch my behaviour around him in future, okay?"

Cary nodded. "Okay."

"Seems I've got an apology to make to Aaron, too."

"If you could," Cary said quietly, "that would be good. Aaron thinks he did something to upset you."

Nate sighed. He didn't fucking need this shit right now, but it was his mess—up to him to clean it up. "I'll talk to him, kid. Set him straight."

"Will you reconsider leaving, too?"

Nate sighed. "I'll think on it. Wasn't a definite anyway, just something I was chewing over."

Cary nodded, seemingly satisfied. Nate only wished he could be as happy with the answer himself.

* * * *

The minute he stepped into Jessie's dancehall, Nate spotted Pete chatting to a customer at the bar. The wolf looked good. Nate might not want a relationship with Pete, but a mutual orgasm or two before he left town couldn't hurt any, could it? In any case, a relationship would be the last thing on Pete's mind, too. Wolves rarely did relationships—they did casual hook-ups until they found their destined mate…at least that's what sensible wolves did. Nate had heard a tale or two about wolves falling in love and then *wham*—they meet their mate and someone ends up getting hurt. It just wasn't worth it.

Pete's head turned in Nate's direction. Their eyes locked, and his friend's face broke out into a wide, wolfish grin that got Nate smiling, too.

"Nate!" Pete greeted when Nate approached the bar. "Finally got you here. You change your mind about that drink?"

Nate nodded and took a seat on an empty barstool. "I'll take a beer, please."

Pete grabbed a bottle from a large fridge behind the bar, cracked it open, and placed it on the counter in front of Nate. "On the house."

"Thanks." Nate raised the bottle in a toast then took a long swig.

"So what made you reconsider?"

"Had me some bad news today—thought I'd come and drown my sorrows."

Pete nodded. "I can get behind that, but if you're looking to forget your troubles, I can think of better ways to distract you."

Nate grinned, thankful Pete hadn't questioned him about his news. He'd thought he might have to sweet talk Pete into bed but it looked like they were of the same mind. "That a fact?"

Pete crossed his arms over the bar and leant forward until he was inches away from Nate's face. "Sure is."

It occurred to Nate to check the room to see who was watching them but if Pete didn't care, he didn't either. He had never hidden who he was and he wasn't about to start now. "What time do you get off?"

Pete turned and glanced at the clock behind the bar. "I'm working the early shift today, so another couple of hours. You gonna wait for me, Nate?"

Nate grinned and picked up his beer. "Keep 'em coming and you got yourself a deal."

"Oh, *great,*" Pete groaned, glancing over Nate's head to the entrance.

"What's up?"

"Trouble, that's what."

Nate swivelled on his stool in time to catch a young, slender man enter the bar and stagger across the room. As he got closer, Nate picked up on his scent. He was a wolf—a slightly inebriated wolf.

"Seems like he's already wasted," Nate said in an aside.

"Probably is…think the guy has a drinking problem. He's in here most nights and he often stirs up trouble. Believe it or not, his brother Jared works for the sheriff's department. I've had to call him down here a time or two."

"Hope the kid doesn't start anything."

"You and me both."

The young man practically fell upon the bar and perched himself on the stool next to Nate. "Beer, please Pete," he slurred.

"Looks as though you've had one too many already, Tristan."

Tristan narrowed his eyes. "I haven't been drinking."

Nate snorted. He could smell the booze on the kid from where he sat and would have been able to without his wolf sense of smell, that was for sure. The kid reeked of it.

"One beer," Pete said, "and if you start any trouble today, I'm calling your brother to come get you, and you won't be welcome back here."

Tristan's eyes glazed over as he waved off Pete's concerns. "No trouble, just a beer."

While Pete retrieved the kid's beer from the fridge, Tristan turned to Nate, and he swayed in his seat a little while his eyes tried to focus on Nate's face. "Who are you? Haven't seen you in here before."

"Don't come in here, that's why. Name's Nate." Nate reached out his hand to Tristan. The kid grabbed it clumsily and shook it, his wrist flaccid. His hand felt tiny in Nate's much larger paw.

"You from around here?" Tristan asked.

Nate nodded. "Born and bred."

"What do you do?"

Nate was surprised when his mouth curved up into a smile. "Nosy little thing, aren't you? I'm a rancher. Work for Kelan Morgan, over on the Crazy Horse."

"Alpha Morgan?"

"One and the same."

Tristan smiled his thanks when his beer was put in front of him. He lifted it to his mouth and downed half in one long, greedy gulp before placing it down on the bar. He didn't let go of the bottle.

"Where you from, kid?"

Tristan turned and fixed his glassy eyed gaze on Nate. *Jesus.* Just how much had the kid had to drink, exactly? Wolves had fast metabolisms, so Tristan must have consumed a truck load to be this wasted.

"Lubbock."

"Whatcha doing down here?"

Tristan screwed his eyebrows together and pursed his lips as though he were trying to remember. "My brother, Jared," he said at last, "got a job down here. Works for the sheriff."

"And you don't like it here?"

Tristan shrugged. "Not really."

"Don't you have family you could have stayed with in Lubbock?" Nate normally kept to himself, didn't strike up conversations with people, especially strangers. He wasn't sure why he was asking Tristan so many questions, but something drew him to the kid. Nate didn't know where the thought came from but he was certain that beneath the messed up exterior there was goodness, bubbling just beneath the surface. Could be the kid was a little lost at the moment and needed someone to put him on the right path, and there was something about his scent... Nate couldn't put his finger on it but the kid smelt like...*home*.

Tristan straightened and pulled his shoulders back. "Nope. Just me and my brother. We stick together, only family we got."

Nate nodded and did his best not to think about Rick. Out of all the family he had, Rick had been the only one to really accept him for who he was. Nate's sister was older and mated to a pastor. She'd turned her back on Nate when he'd come out at eighteen and it had been at least ten years since he'd last seen her or her husband. It upset him sometimes, but her disapproval of him had been intense and incredibly vocal. He'd hoped she might come around but he knew many people *never* got over their prejudices, and when she hadn't even contacted him to inform him of Rick's death, *that* had told him all he needed to know. Nate supposed he was as dead to his sister as was his brother Rick.

Their mother had died a few years back. She'd been ten years older than Nate's father and although his parents hadn't disowned him when they'd found out he was gay, they had never been able to fully accept him either. Nate took a swig of his beer and used the liquid to swallow down the lump in his throat. Rick had been his only ally and he'd let a dumb fucking argument get in the way of their relationship. How could he have been so stupid? He suddenly didn't feel very sociable anymore. Would Pete be upset if Nate cut out on him?

The bar door swung open and Nate's head shot up when he heard Pete's expletive.

"Aww, fuck."

Nate spun around in his seat to see who had rattled Pete's cage this time. Three mean-looking young men breezed into the room, grinning and elbowing each other when they set eyes on Tristan. The kid showed no indication he'd heard them enter. He was still hunched over the bar, sucking down his beer.

The men crossed the room and stood behind him. Nate inhaled deeply to catch the men's scents—they were all wolves.

"Now I'm telling you the same thing I told him," Pete said, nodding in Tristan's direction. "I don't want any trouble. If you've come in here to make any, you can leave now or I'll call the sheriff."

The wolves were young. Nate would put the oldest at around twenty-two. He was the bulkiest, too, and obviously the ring leader because he took a step forward, puffed out his chest and sneered at Pete. There was real hatred in his eyes and it made Nate shiver.

"Yeah, why don't you call his brother so he can come down and save the little faggot's ass again?"

Nate flinched at the derogatory term and turned to gauge Tristan's reaction. The kid didn't say anything, but his gaze was fixed on the mirror behind the bar, and Nate saw his hand grip the bottle he held tighter, his knuckles white from the applied pressure.

"I'm warning you, Neil, do *not* start anything," Pete said.

Neil ignored Pete and continued to stare at the back of Tristan's head. Nate realised what was going to go down about five seconds before Neil struck. He waited for Tristan to take a drink of his beer then shoved his elbow into Tristan's back. The bottle cracked against Tristan's teeth, and the amber liquid spilled down the front of his top.

"Oops!" Neil and his friends began roaring with laughter.

When Nate turned to meet Tristan's gaze, the inebriated, glassy, and somewhat distant look in the wolf's eyes had disappeared to be replaced by a sharp awareness. Quicker than Nate thought the kid was capable of in his present condition, Tristan slammed the bottle down on the bar, swivelled in his seat and threw a punch, his fist landing square between Neil's eyes. Crying out from what must have been both shock and pain, Neil stumbled backwards into the outstretched arms of his friends, his hand lifting as if by instinct to cover his injured nose.

Calmly, Tristan got up from his seat and faced the three young men head on. Blood was pouring from Neil's nose and although he held his head back, trying to stem the flow, his gaze never left Tristan's.

"He bwoke it!" Neil accused. "He bwoke my fuckig nowse."

Jesus Christ. This was about to get ugly. Nate lifted himself from the stool and stood next to Tristan. He hated fighting—hated the beastliness of it, the way it turned grown men into nothing more than animals—but they *were* animals...partly...and right now the unpleasant side to their natures was about to be exposed.

If there was something Nate hated more than fighting, it was goddamn fucking homophobes. Besides, three against one wasn't a fair fight, and in Tristan's defence, he hadn't done anything to provoke the other men. At least, nothing that Nate knew of.

Even if it hadn't been an unfair fight, Nate felt as though he needed to look out for the kid, even though he had no clue why he was doing it. He held his place at Tristan's side. Nate looked around the room, but kept all four wolves in his peripheral vision. There were a group of men on the far side of the room watching the action with marked interest. They finished their beers and got up from their seats, but somehow Nate doubted they were going home. If he didn't get the situation under control, it was going to escalate pretty damn quickly. The last thing they needed was a bunch of humans getting involved in a fight with wolves. It could turn into a damn bloodbath. He shifted his gaze around the rest of the room. There were a few men sat around tables and a couple of women around the jukebox, but no one in the room was talking or drinking. They were all watching the action at the bar, and most of them looked eager to get in on it.

"Call the sheriff," Nate told Pete.

He turned back in time to see Neil's body tremble, his skin literally pulsating before Nate's eyes. The kid was about to change and with all the humans in the bar...

"Aww, fuck, get Kelan down here, too. Tell him to hurry."

* * * *

"Let me get this straight. You're saying someone *stole* your cow?"

Joe Walker's eyes practically bulged out of their sockets. *"My bull!* Jesus Christ, did you hear a word I just said, boy?" the old man fumed. "He was my prized, black Aberdeen Angus *bull!* Cost me near on ten thousand dollars."

Jared nearly swallowed his tongue. Ten thousand bucks, for a piece of meat? "You're shitting me."

While Jared watched, the vein in Joe's forehead pulsed. "No, I am not *shitting* you. Someone stole him. What ya gonna do about it?"

Joe's face was puce. Jesus, if the man wasn't careful he was going to have an aneurism. Jared needed to calm him down.

"How do you know he was stolen, sir?" Jared asked. "Are you sure he didn't escape? Wander into one of the neighbouring properties maybe?"

Well shit, that didn't work. Joe's eyes got even wider. "Where the hell is the sheriff? I can't deal with you. You're as dumb as a box of hammers."

Jared tried to ignore the old man's insult. "Sheriff Ferguson is busy on another call. If you want matter investigated, you're going to have to deal with me. Okay, can you tell me how you know the cow…uh…bull was taken?"

Joe threw up his hands. "There was no hole in the fence," he said very slowly as though he were addressing a young child. "The gate was open. Someone took 'im."

"Are you sure the gate wasn't left open by accident? Maybe by someone that works here?"

"What sort of operation do you think I'm running here? I've been in ranching my entire life. The cowboys that work for me are experienced men. Not a one of them would be as damn stupid as to leave the gate open. You need to go and question them Morgan brothers. Them boys have got it in fer me."

Jared wrote the name down on his notepad but there wasn't a lot he could do with it. "Do you have any reason to suspect these Morgan brothers?"

The old man stiffened. "Had me a few crossed words with them over the past year is all."

Jared sighed. That didn't help him much. "You can't go around accusing people without proof, sir."

"It was them, I'm telling you. Talk to them, look on their land. I know they've got my Dipsy."

Dipsy? What the hell name was that for a bull? Jared had to stifle a chuckle. "Do you have a first name for these brothers?"

"Of course, there's Kelan and Co—"

"Kelan, *Kelan* Morgan?" Jared interrupted. "As in *Alpha* Morgan?"

Joe's face paled. "Well, I'm not saying it was *him* exactly, but I wouldn't mind betting it was Luke or that ass-bandit he's shacking up with. He's got it in for me since I fired him. I'm telling you, it was him."

Jared felt his anger rise but he tried to tamp it down. This was the exact reason he couldn't let people find out he was gay. There were too many haters in a small town like Wolf Creek. Too many people who would never accept him for who he was. Jared needed to ingratiate himself into the community if he wanted to be elected sheriff. He couldn't afford to get on the wrong side of folks in town, and he certainly didn't need to get on the wrong side of his alpha.

Now that Jared came to think about it, he was sure he'd heard about the trouble between Alpha Morgan's youngest brother, Luke, and Joe's son. What was his name again? Ethan. That was it. Seemed Joe was holding the Morgans responsible for their son's incarceration…although from what Jared remembered of the story, Ethan had been the one at fault.

"This is the third bull gone in a month…*third*! I'm telling you someone has it in for me, and it's got to be that faggot."

Jared winced at the term then pursed his lips. While he stared at Joe, trying to think of a way to placate him, his cell started vibrating in his pocket.

"Yeah. It was him," Joe continued. "Him or Luke anyways."

The phone kept buzzing. *Shit.*

"Has to be one of them. No doubt in my mind, and I wouldn't rule Kelan out, either."

Jared pulled the cell out of his pocket and held it up. "I'm sorry, sir, but I'm going to have to take this. It's important."

Joe huffed out a long sigh and fixed Jared with a cold, mean stare, but thankfully he didn't say anything. Jared walked a few feet away from the old man and answered the call. "Jared."

"Jared, it's Pete. You'd better get down here. There's trouble."

Jared cursed under his breath. "Is it Tristan again?"

"Yeah. Wait a minute…*aww fuck*!"

Pete's voice cut off as Jared heard glass smashing in the background. "Pete? Pete? What's going on?"

The line was dead. Jared quickly walked back to Joe. He had to get to the bar before the situation down there got worse. "Right, well I've got everything I need from you at the moment, sir. I'll check out the lead you gave me and I'll be in touch."

"What? That's it?"

"For now, sir. I'll contact you if I need anything else."

Joe nodded. "Call me as soon as you find anything."

"Of course."

Jared tipped his hat and strode to his car. As he was making his way down the drive, he passed a sleek, black sedan with tinted windows making its way towards Joe's house. It slowed down as it passed as though the person inside was watching him. Jared shivered. He didn't like that he couldn't see the driver but they could see him. It was creepy. He dimly wondered who it could be. You didn't see cars like that in a town like Wolf Creek every day.

Five minutes later Jared was pulling up in the lot outside Jessie's Dancehall. He couldn't believe he'd been called over again. What the hell had Tristan got himself into this time? Jared wasn't sure how much more he could take.

He killed the engine and grabbed his hat from the passenger seat. He only had one foot out of the cruiser when the door to the dancehall opened and a young man came bursting out of the building backwards and landed heavily on his ass.

"Goddamn it!" Jared slammed the car door and ran in the direction of the floored man. He hadn't made it five feet before another five or six men burst through the open door. Everyone was shouting and trading insults with one another and while Jared looked on, fists started flying. It was absolute chaos.

Jared made it to the young man on the floor. He remembered him from a couple of other times he'd been called out. Neil Rafferty. He was a nasty piece of work—a troublemaker. Lived out on a ranch the other side of town with a bunch of other young kids. Dried blood covered his face and he was groaning loudly, clearly in pain. When Jared bent down to check if he was okay, he noticed the kid's eyes and teeth had shifted. *What the fuck?* It was the middle of the day and there were humans around.

"Neil, can you hear me? I need you to calm down. You *cannot* shift here, you understand me?" Jared put a hand on the kid's shoulder to try and calm him but it only served to infuriate him. He growled and bared his fangs. "Neil! I'm warning you, do *not* shift!"

When Jared looked up, he saw his brother just outside the bar door. Tristan pulled his hand back and threw a punch. There was a large man standing at his brother's side. He grabbed hold of Tristan and pinned his hands behind his back. Jared watched as one of two men that stood in front of Tristan shifted his hand into a claw and drew his arm back. Jared saw red. He left Neil's side and sprinted across the lot.

"Tristan! Look out!" Jared dived for the man, hoping to knock him out of the way before his claws caught Tristan's throat, but he wasn't fast enough. The young man struck out and Jared screamed out his frustration. But a second before the razor sharp claws made contact, the man holding Tristan pulled him out of the way and got caught in the face himself.

The man roared and let go of Jared's brother. Instantly blood began oozing out of the deep gashes along his cheek and he fell to his knees, his whole body trembling. Jared made to help the man but the young wolf raised his hand to strike again. Jared's gaze flickered to the man on the floor and for a second their eyes met. A shock like a thunderbolt hit Jared and an adrenaline rush unlike any he'd ever known swept through his body like a tidal wave.

What the hell?

Jared didn't have time to process what he was feeling. He charged the young wolf before he could strike again, knocking him from his feet so that they landed on the hard, dirt floor with a thud. They scrambled for dominance until Jared was able grab hold of the wolf's arms and pin him to the ground. All around them the fighting continued. Sounds of fists hitting flesh and low growls tore through the otherwise quiet evening air. The reek of blood and fury in Jared's nostrils made him want to gag.

Pulling his cuffs free from his belt, Jared was about to slap them on the wrists of his captive when a sound rang through the air that made the tiny hairs on the back of his neck stand to attention. A single word…

"*Silence*!" the voice boomed out, cutting through the noise and chaos until it was suddenly so quiet you could hear a pin drop.

When Jared looked up, Kelan Morgan was walking calmly into the fray. The dark glint in Kelan's eyes was the only indication of his anger, or was it disappointment Jared could see there? He couldn't be sure.

Kelan's younger brother Cody was walking alongside the alpha. Jared wasn't sure why Kelan had brought Cody with him—the younger wolf was a lot smaller and Jared doubted he'd be much use in a fight—but as Cody wound his way through the men, they seemed to calm down considerably.

Jared cuffed the young wolf beneath him but he needn't have bothered. His eyes were trained on Kelan and they were filled with fear and apprehension. It seemed none of the wolves present wanted to get on the wrong side of their alpha.

Kelan strode straight to the man who had been holding Jared's brother and knelt down beside him. The wolf's hand was pressed against the deep gash on his cheek and blood was seeping out from between his fingers.

"Nate, you okay?"

The man—Nate—nodded, but he didn't look at Kelan. His eyes were focused on Jared—wide and disbelieving.

"Mate," he whispered, almost reverently.

Chapter Three

Nate stared at the wolf in front of him, equal parts shocked and surprised at what he was seeing and what his body was feeling. He knew his face was bleeding—the warm, wet liquid was seeping through his fingers and trickling in a steady rivulet down his arm—but he couldn't feel any pain. He *could* however feel other things, things he should not be thinking about at a time like this. Things he didn't want to feel…not now, maybe not ever.

Nate was not the sort of person a man would want as his mate. He wasn't reliable—he let people down. If he couldn't even be there for his brother when he'd needed him, how the hell was he supposed to be there for a complete stranger? It was of little consolation but the wolf watching him—with a strong, masculine face and beautiful emerald green eyes—looked as devastated by the discovery as Nate himself.

This could *not* be happening.

Kelan patted Nate's shoulder and got up. "We'll talk later, okay?"

Nate had been so stunned to discover his mate that he'd forgotten Kelan was at his side, awaiting a reply to his question. "Sure, okay."

Kelan nodded, satisfied. He got up and crossed the lot to speak to some of the other wolves present.

"Jared, are you okay?" Tristan went to stand in front of the wolf who was still staring at him, mouth open wide with shock. Tristan's brother, Nate realised as soon as Tristan spoke the wolf's name. Nate's mate was Tristan's brother.

Jared nodded though he didn't look at Tristan. His gaze was still fixed on Nate. "I'm fine."

"Hey man, get off me."

The words seemed to yank Jared out of his daze. He shook his head as though to clear it and looked down at the wolf whose chest he was still draped over, pressing him to the ground.

"Don't move," he said to the young man.

Nate watched Jared get up and survey his surroundings. Kelan and Cody's presence had calmed the fighting wolves and even the humans that had got involved in the brawl were now somewhat subdued.

When he seemed certain the trouble had been contained, Jared strode to Nate's side and knelt in front of him. The proximity caused a rush of endorphins through Nate's body and when their gazes locked, Nate grew embarrassed at the way his body reacted. He cursed his stupid dick for hardening inside his pants, but it looked as though he wasn't the only one affected. Nate noticed a distinct bulge in the front of Jared's uniform pants.

"Your face is in a bad way." Jared took hold of Nate's hand, which was still covering his cheek, and moved it to inspect the damage. He curled his fingers around Nate's jaw.

Nate shrugged, his hand tingling from Jared's touch. He couldn't stop staring into Jared's bright green eyes. They were like beautiful gemstones.

"I've had worse. It'll heal," he said, surprising himself with his cool and indifferent tone.

When Jared frowned and removed his hand, Nate almost whimpered at the loss. He had an insane urge to reach out and grab it, to place it back in position under his chin.

"The wound is already starting to close. I think we'd better get you out of here before people notice."

Nate nodded but he couldn't seem to lift his body from the ground. He couldn't do much of anything, other than stare at the wolf in front of him. While he gazed at Jared's handsome face, Nate heard the sound of sirens approaching. *Typical. Why is the fucking cavalry always late?* Jared turned to watch the approaching cruisers and frowned.

"*Shit*. Sheriff Ferguson's here. You need a hand up?" Jared asked.

Nate snapped back to reality and shook his head. "No, I can manage. Only my face is hurt. Nothing wrong with my legs."

Jared stood up straight and stiffened his back. "Suit yourself."

Nate pulled himself up and watched Jared cross the lot to talk to the sheriff.

"Thanks for watching my back in there," Tristan said, stepping in front of Nate. "Appreciate that."

Nate jerked his shoulders in a pale imitation of a shrug. "Three against one wasn't a fair fight. And when I saw the humans itching to get in on the action, I had to step in."

Okay, so maybe that wasn't the entire reason Nate had helped Tristan, but it was all he was prepared to tell the young wolf for the time being. Tristan didn't need to know that Nate had felt a connection to him, an inexplicable need to protect him. Of course, he now knew where that desire stemmed from. He was currently standing not twenty feet away from the reason.

"How's your face?"

Nate shrugged. "It's only a scratch."

Tristan's eyes widened. "What are you? Some goddamn superhero?"

"Watch your mouth, kid."

Tristan lowered his gaze and his cheeks filled with colour. "Sorry," he whispered.

"So, that's your brother?"

Tristan's gaze shifted to the deputy talking to the sheriff. "Yeah, that's Jared. Man, he's gonna be pissed. Say, you wouldn't mind talking to him would you, explaining things to him, tell him it wasn't my fault back there? That I didn't start anything?"

Nate started to shake his head. He didn't want to have to spend any more time with Jared than was absolutely necessary, and he had a feeling the deputy felt the same way about him. But when he took in Tristan's pleading gaze, his determination crumbled. "Sure, kid, I'll talk to him. Can't guarantee he's gonna listen to me, though."

"He'll listen. Seems he listens to everyone but me these days." There was no anger in Tristan's voice when he spoke—only resignation. Nate wondered what the story was between the two brothers.

He sighed. "I'll see what I can do."

"Nate?"

When Nate turned, Kelan, Cody and Pete were standing beside him.

"How you holding up?" Pete asked.

Nate frowned. Why was everyone treating him like a damn invalid? It was only a scratch to his face. He raised his hand to inspect the damage. Okay, maybe it was more than a scratch. The gash on his face was deep and still bleeding, but not nearly as much as it had been. "Guess I'd better get this cleaned up."

"Come with me," Pete said. "I've got a first aid kit in the bar."

"I..." Nate swivelled in Jared's direction. The wolf was still talking to the sheriff but he was looking directly at Nate, a deep frown marring his handsome features. "Sure," Nate agreed reluctantly.

He followed Pete across the lot and through the door to the bar. He was halfway across the dance floor when Jared called out to him.

"Nate. You got a minute?"

Nate stopped in his tracks. The sound of Jared's voice sent chills through his body. He didn't turn around to look at him...he couldn't. Jared's voice was all business and although Nate didn't want any type of relationship with the wolf, it was only because he didn't want to hurt him. He knew he wasn't good enough for Jared. The man could do better than him. But from the tone of his voice, Nate could tell the wolf had his own reasons for not wanting anything to do with him and Nate was about to hear them. He wasn't sure he was ready for that, but he supposed there was no time like the present.

"Pete? Would you mind leaving us alone for a minute?"

Pete opened his mouth to object but he must have seen something in Nate's eyes that changed his mind because he closed his mouth quickly and gave a sharp nod of his head.

"Sure. The first aid kit is behind the bar. I'll be outside. Holler if you need anything."

Nate nodded his agreement and silently watched his friend walk out of the bar. He still couldn't meet Jared's gaze. He walked across the room, avoiding the smashed glass on the floor, and retrieved the first aid kit. Placing it on the counter, he clicked open the lock. While he was rooting around in the box, Jared crossed the room and stood in front of the bar.

"How are you doing?"

Nate curled his fingers around a bottle of antiseptic lotion and squeezed.

"I'm quite sure you didn't follow me in here to discuss my health."

He finally looked up and met Jared's gaze. His stomach lurched and his breath caught in his chest. Jared had to be the most handsome man he'd ever set eyes on, but the deep creases in his forehead and the tight set to his lips made Nate wince.

"You're right, I didn't. Look, nobody here in town knows about my preference and I'd like to keep it that way."

"Your *preference*?" Nate queried, although he thought he already had a good idea what Jared was talking about.

"For men," the deputy confirmed.

Nate scoffed. "You make it sound like a choice rather than something you're born as."

"I didn't mean... I..." Jared sighed and his shoulders slumped forward. He scrubbed a hand down his face. "It's just, I don't have time to start anything right now. I want to make sheriff and if people know I'm gay, I can forget about that, and then there's my brother, Tristan—he depends on me... I can't—"

Nate had heard enough. He raised a hand to silence Jared and at once the wolf stopped talking and waited to hear what he had to say.

"You don't have to say any more. I'm not in the market for a mate myself, as it happens."

Jared's mouth opened in surprise. "You're not?"

"No."

"Right, well, that's great then. Uh…yeah, great." Jared nodded his head and turned to leave.

"Jared?"

Jared paused then looked over his shoulder. "Yeah?"

"About the fight, it wasn't Tristan's fault. Thought you should know the kid wasn't the one to start the trouble."

Jared nodded. "Thanks, appreciate that."

Nate watched Jared's retreating form with regret. He was sure he'd done the right thing, so why did he feel like he'd just made the biggest fucking mistake of his life? It didn't matter anyway. Jared had made his stance perfectly clear. Seemed neither of them were in the right place to start a relationship, mates or not. It might hurt like fucking hell to ignore their bond but it wouldn't kill him…at least, he didn't think it would. Nate had never heard of a wolf rejecting their mate before. Why would they?

* * * *

Turning the key in the lock, Jared let himself into the room he shared with his younger brother. He took off his hat when he entered and threw it on the table near the door. Tristan was asleep on top of the sheets of his twin bed, still fully clothed, one arm curled under his pillow, the other resting beneath his cheek. He stirred as Jared crossed the room and took a seat on his own bed, but he didn't wake up.

It had been a long ass day. The paperwork Jared had to fill out about the fight at Jessie's had kept him busy until long after midnight and that was without dealing with the three fool wolves that had started the trouble in the first place. They were currently spending the night cooped up in a cosy little cell at the station. It was hell for a wolf to be locked up like that, but Jared hoped it would teach them a lesson. When he'd finished his work at the sheriff's office, Jared had made the dreaded call to the wolf council. It wasn't something he relished doing, but when he'd taken on the job the council had made it clear he had to report any and all incidents in the town involving shifters.

Of course, Jared had done his best not to think about the biggest event of the day, but as hard as he'd tried to banish all thoughts of the sexy wolf, Nate had never been far from his mind. As a result, Jared's work in the office had taken him twice as long as it should have. He just couldn't get Nate's face out of his mind, couldn't forget the things it had done to his body when their eyes had locked or the way his skin had prickled when they'd been close. Nate was a damn fine looking wolf. Tall and lean, with powerful shoulders and a wide chest housing what Jared could only assume were perfectly sculpted pecs. His face was rugged, rather than handsome…masculine. His jaw was strong and he had a slightly larger than average nose, which only added to his appeal.

Jared's stomach had lurched and his heart had soared when he'd curled his fingers around Nate's chin to check on his injuries, and for a brief moment as he stared into his mate's eyes, all had felt right with the world. Since then, Jared had been rock-hard all night at the station. At one point he'd had to excuse himself to the men's room to take care of the problem.

He waited outside the door to make sure he had privacy, then locked himself into one of the stalls. His cock was aching when he pulled it out of his pants and harder than he could remember it being. It felt hot and heavy in his hand. He'd never done anything like this at work before, but he couldn't help himself. His hard-on wasn't going away – he had to take care of it.

Jared started stroking, his bottom lip caught between his teeth. He closed his eyes when the pleasure got to be too much, and Nate's face was the only thing he could see in his mind's eye. He didn't want to think about Nate, it was pointless. They couldn't be together…but he couldn't get Nate's image out of his head. When his breathing came faster, his hand sped up to match. The pleasure was immeasurable, but as good as it felt, he wished it was Nate's hands on him – touching him and drawing out his release. He'd never wanted someone so much. He could barely breathe through his need for the strong and masculine cowboy.

His thumb circled the head, spreading around the pre-cum that had beaded there. He slid his other hand down to gently cup and squeeze his balls and a gasp escaped his lips. His hand moved faster, gripped tighter and he could feel his orgasm building – a slow burn that started in his groin and spread throughout his body until he thought he was going to fly apart. And then he did. But even as he came silently behind the stall door, he found no relief. The ache wasn't only in his cock, it was in his heart.

As difficult as it had been, Jared had made his decision and there could be no going back. Now all he had to do was live with it *and* himself. It was little consolation, but Jared doubted it would have made a difference if his life wasn't so complicated, and he'd actually wanted to forge a relationship with his mate.

The fact that he had to look out for his brother and wanted to make sheriff was irrelevant, because Nate hadn't wanted anything to do with him—that much had been obvious. Jared couldn't help but be a little bit cut up about that fact.

As he stared at Tristan's prone, sleeping form, Jared thought about leaving the talk with his brother until morning. He should wait until they were both rested, but as exhausted as he felt, he knew sleep would elude him until he'd said what he had to say to his brother. Even then, it was debatable if his mind would shut down enough to allow him the peace he needed to get some rest.

"Tristan."

Tristan groaned, his eyes opening slowly to meet Jared's gaze. He yawned. "What time is it?"

"Late. We need to talk."

Sitting up, his brother stretched his long, wiry frame. "It wasn't my fault."

"I know, that isn't what I want to talk to you about...well, not entirely anyhow."

"What is it then?"

"Our bid on the ranch was successful. We just need to wait for the paperwork to be sorted then we'll be able to move in."

Tristan's eyes widened. "Yeah? That's great!"

Jared couldn't help but smile. That was the first time he'd seen his younger brother excited about anything in months.

"Yeah. Couple o' weeks, I reckon, and we'll be in. I'll start making arrangements to get our stuff shipped down from Lubbock. I've got an appointment with the Realtor tomorrow to sign some paperwork, so I'll know more then."

Tristan nodded enthusiastically, but then his smile faded and he pulled his eyebrows together in a frown. "What has that got to do with what happened earlier?"

This was the difficult part. His brother always got defensive when he tried to talk to him about the way he was living his life, but they had to have it out. Tristan might not have instigated the fight in Jessie's, but he'd been right in the middle of it. If his brother didn't sort himself out, there were no two ways about it—Tristan was going to get himself killed.

"I know it hasn't been easy on you the last few months since Pop died, but I'm hoping you'll see this move as a new beginning for us both. We've got a real chance here to make a life for ourselves and a good'un if we play our cards right. When we move to the ranch, I'm hoping you'll stop drinking so much, maybe find yourself a job in town."

Tristan squared his shoulders defiantly. "I haven't got a drinking problem. I can quit any time I like."

Jared sighed. "I didn't say you had a problem with alcohol, Tristan, just that you've been overdoing it. Don't you think it's time you slowed down and started to think about your future? I know you are interested in mechanics—why don't you see if you can get yourself a start at Bob's place? I'll speak to him about it if you'd like."

Tristan pursed his lips. "You'd do that for me?"

"Of course I would. Well, what do you say?"

Tristan picked at a piece of fluff on the comforter and chewed on his bottom lip. "I've been thinking about that myself lately, but I'd rather wait until we get moved in first. Then I'll go to the garage and speak to the owner myself, okay?"

Jared let out the breath he'd been holding, relieved that Tristan hadn't fought him on this. "Yeah, that's more than okay."

Tristan nodded. "You know, before the fight started tonight I met a guy in Jessie's and...well...I liked him."

Jared tried to hide his surprise. He knew his brother was gay, of course, but Tristan had never spoken to him about boys before. "Yeah? Is he from town?"

Tristan nodded. "Yeah, he's from around here."

"What's his name?"

"Nate."

Jared's stomach lurched so violently he thought he was going to throw up. Was this the reason Nate didn't want anything to do with him? It would sure make sense.

"The cowboy that you were with when I got there?"

"Yeah." Tristan's smile was bright.

Jared could barely breathe through the pain in his chest. "Um, did you and he...?"

"Did we what?"

"Uh, you know..." *Fuck. Please let him say no, please God let him say no...* Because Jared didn't have a fucking clue what he would do if Tristan and Nate had been intimate in any way. And if Tristan were to find out that Jared was Nate's mate, the kid would be devastated, and he'd had enough shit to deal with already.

Tristan must have finally caught on to what Jared was asking because his eyes widened and he sucked in a sharp breath. "Urgh! That's *gross*. I didn't mean I 'like him' like that! Jesus, Jared, he's gotta be twice my age...that would be disgusting. I just meant I like him, you know...as a friend."

Jared closed his eyes and tried to get his breathing back under control. *Thank God.* Jared didn't mention Tristan's comment about Nate's age. The cowboy didn't even look as though he were in his mid-thirties, but then he supposed to someone who was twenty-one, anyone older was deemed ancient.

"I haven't made any friends since we got here and it was nice to have someone to talk to," Tristan continued.

Jared opened his eyes and met his brother's gaze. He sighed. "You know you can talk to me. I'm always here for you."

"I know, but it's not the same thing. Besides, we haven't been talking very much at all lately."

"I realise that, and maybe we're both to blame for it, but from here on out, let's make a promise that we'll try harder, okay?"

Tristan nodded. He was still picking at the comforter, but he held Jared's gaze. "I don't want to be a disappointment to you."

A lump rose in Jared's throat. He got up and crossed to his brother's bed and sat down. Pulling Tristan into a hug, he squeezed him tight and patted him gently on the back.

"You are *not* a disappointment to me, ya hear? I just know you can do more with your life, and it hurts me to see you throw it away like it doesn't mean anything."

When Jared pulled back and looked at his brother's face, tears were sliding in quick succession down his cheeks. He brushed them away with his thumb, but more appeared to take their place.

"I miss Pop," Tristan whispered.

Jared pulled his brother close again and stroked a soothing hand over his back. "I know, Tristan, I miss him too."

Jared wasn't sure how long he held his brother, but when they'd both cried the last of their tears and Tristan had finally fallen back to sleep, the early morning sun was peeking through the gap in the drapes, highlighting the coppery tones in Tristan's otherwise dark brown hair.

Chapter Four

Nate scrubbed a hand over his face as he stumbled down the hall to the kitchen. He'd polished off a fifth of Jack when he'd got back last night, hoping it would help him pass out, but no such luck. He hadn't slept worth a damn, and he felt like shit. His head pounded and his mouth was as dry as the Nevada Desert. Nate had spent a large part of the night thinking about Jared and an even larger part trying to forget him, but that had been an exercise in futility right from the get go.

The deputy was a fine looking man and the more Nate tried not to think of him, the more his frigging mind went there. It was those goddamn eyes that were the problem. Nate had never seen eyes that shade of green—they were intoxicating, and of course his stupid dick agreed. Nate was a man. He'd had erections before, but none that wouldn't go away no matter how much he stroked off. By morning, he wasn't sure what ached more—his hand or his dick.

When he entered the shared kitchen, Aaron was standing at the stove making eggs. The last thing Nate needed or wanted was to make small talk, but he still had to apologise to the young wolf and there was no time like the present.

"Aaron, you got a minute?"

Nate honestly hadn't thought he could feel any worse, but when Aaron spun around, eyes round and mouth open wide enough to catch flies, he felt like the biggest piece of crap imaginable. Aaron seemed genuinely surprised that Nate was addressing him. Had he treated the kid that badly that he was actually shocked Nate would have something to say to him? *Wow*. Nate had fucked up royally.

"Um, yeah, okay… I mean…whatever."

"Don't suppose you could spare a cup of that coffee, could you?" Nate asked, nodding to the still steaming pot on the counter top. He pulled out a chair from the kitchen table and sat down heavily in it.

"Uh…yeah, sure." Aaron poured out a cupful and handed it to Nate then stood in the middle of the room, coffee pot still in hand.

"Well, are you going to join me?"

Aaron's eyebrows rose so high they practically disappeared behind his hairline. "Okay…"

He stood for a moment looking at the pot in his hand then sprang into action. He discarded the pot then pulled the eggs off the heat before joining Nate at the table. "You look like shit by the way."

"Jeez, thanks, kid…just what a guy wants to hear first thing in the morning."

Aaron's face turned beet red. "Sorry, I just meant the cut on your face. What happened to you?"

Nate had forgotten about the gash on his cheek, which was a good thing—at least it had stopped hurting—but the skin there felt tight, wrong. He dismissed the question with a swish of his hand.

"Was nothing, got myself involved in a fight last night is all. It's already healed."

As Aaron stared at the cut, his eyes widened comically. Okay, maybe it hadn't healed as well as Nate had thought.

"What did you want to talk to me about?"

"Actually, I wanted to apologise."

"What for?"

"The way I've been treating you. Occurs to me I haven't been as friendly to you as I could have been. I'm sorry for that." Nate picked up his coffee and took a sip. The strong, bitter liquid tasted like a little piece of heaven. "Was never my intention to make you feel uncomfortable."

Aaron shrugged. "I thought it was because you were jealous, because you wanted Cary for yourself."

Nate nearly choked, spluttering as the coffee went down the wrong hole. "Jesus Christ, kid, warn a man before you go and make a stupid ass comment in future."

Aaron growled. His eyes darkened and his hand clenched into a fist on the table. "What's so stupid about that? Cary's gorgeous and sexy and smart and—"

"Whoa!" Nate said, raising a hand to silence Aaron. "Don't put words in my mouth. I never said there was anything *wrong* with Cary, but Jesus, he's nearly young enough to be my son. You surely couldn't have thought I'd be interested in him in *that* way. What sort of man do ya take me for?"

"Sorry, I just thought—"

"Well don't think—not if that's the sort of shit your mind comes up with."

"So what's the reason then?" Aaron asked defiantly, straightening his shoulders and meeting Nate's gaze head on. Nate had to give the kid props—he certainly knew how to posture, and he had an authoritative tone to his voice that exuded confidence and power and told Nate the kid would make a good alpha someday.

"You remind me of someone," Nate pursed his lips. "Well, not just someone…of my brother, Rick."

Nate took another sip of coffee but instead of sliding down his throat smoothly like the nectar of the gods he'd come to know and love, it felt thicker than tar and was as sour as month old milk. He was barely able to swallow it down.

Aaron's shoulders slumped and he stared at Nate apologetically. "I'm sorry."

Nate shook his head. "See, that's the thing. You have nothing to be sorry for. It's me that needs to apologise. It's my hang-up. When we were younger, my brother and I were close. Rick was funny, vivacious, so full of life he was a joy to be around. He was always so brave and idealistic and he stood up for what he believed in, too. More often than not, he got what he wanted because he was just that type of person. People warmed to him, see? They liked him and I see so many of those qualities in you that sometimes it's hard to look at you."

"Why didn't you say anything before?"

Nate smiled sadly. "When you can't even look at someone, how hard do you think it is to actually talk to them?"

Aaron nodded. "I can understand that I guess, but what made you tell me now?"

"Let's just say a certain someone showed me the error of my ways."

Aaron's face lit up like the fourth of July and his eyes sparkled. "Cary," he said around a happy sigh.

Nate grinned. "Yep, you've got a good 'un there. Treat him right, kid, and I suggest you tell him every day how special he is."

Aaron mirrored Nate's grin. "I do."

"Aaron? I thought you were making e— Oh! Hi, Nate!" Cary gasped and rushed to Nate's side. "What happened to your face?"

Jesus, was the gash on his cheek really that bad? He hadn't even bothered to check the mirror when he'd crawled out of bed. "I think that's my cue. Aaron will fill you in, I reckon. I'm gonna go grab five minutes before shift."

"Oh, okay." Cary walked around the table and planted himself easily in Aaron's lap. Nate could feel their eyes on him as he rose from the table and placed his coffee cup in the sink. He grabbed a bottle of water from the refrigerator on his way out the room.

"Remember what I told you, Aaron," Nate said, nodding at Cary.

Aaron wound his arms around Cary's waist and planted a kiss his mate's cheek. "Yeah…and Nate…?"

Nate paused on his way out the door. "Yeah, kid?"

"Thanks."

Nodding, Nate turned and left the lovebirds to their breakfast. He was halfway to his room to rest a while before he had to start his chores, when on a last minute whim he retraced his steps and headed outside to get some air.

Standing on the porch, he guzzled down half the water in his bottle while drinking in the golden rays of the early morning sun as it made its first appearance on the horizon.

Sun-up had always been his favourite time of day. The appeal was the new beginning with its endless possibilities, even though one day was usually pretty much the same as the last. But today, Nate couldn't find any comfort in it. The new day loomed over him—a gloomy, stark reminder of the fuck-up he'd made of his life, of the mess he'd made of his relationship with Rick and of the things he'd given up…

Of Jared.

Leaning back against the wall of the bunkhouse, Nate closed his eyes and tried to swallow down his anxiety. His only consolation in this whole fucking mess was that Jared would be better off without him. Jared had Tristan to take care of and something told Nate that was a full-time undertaking.

"Nate? You got a minute?"

When Nate opened his eyes, Kelan was striding purposefully towards him.

"Sure boss, what's up?"

Kelan climbed the porch steps and nodded to the bench seat that ran along part of the wall. "You mind if we sit?"

Nate shrugged and took a seat next to his alpha. Kelan's lips were pursed and he was silent for a moment while he looked out past the corral, then he turned to study Nate's face.

"The wound on your cheek is healing, but it would do better if you shifted."

"I know, but I had other things on my mind last night." Nate squirmed in his seat. What the hell had he gone and said that for?

"Yeah, and I'm betting it had a lot to do with a certain Deputy Ambrose."

Nate's head swivelled in Kelan's direction. "How did you…?"

Kelan met Nate's gaze and held it with ease. "I was there, remember? Right next to you when you realised. So, Jared's your mate?"

"Yep, but it doesn't matter. Neither one of us are in a position to do anything about that."

Kelan sighed. "Timing might not be right, but don't say it doesn't matter because it does. It matters."

What the hell was he supposed to say to that? This conversation was going down a road Nate didn't want to travel, so he decided to put an end to it. "I don't want to talk about this, Kelan. Is there something else you wanted me for?"

Kelan narrowed his eyes and Nate had a feeling he hadn't heard the last on this topic, but for now the alpha seemed content to let it drop.

"Yeah, but I don't think you're going to like what I have to ask any better."

"Try me."

"I'd like you to consider becoming my beta."

Nate shook his head. "I don't think that would be a good idea."

"Please, hear me out before you decide anything," Kelan said. "I've always had three betas. As you know, your brother Rick was my second in command. When Rick was killed, I was left with two. That would normally be enough to manage a pack this size, but Eric, who took over Rick's position, has mated with a girl from out of state. Turns out she won't even consider leaving her current pack so that means I'm losing Eric, too. And Pete...well, Pete does what he can, but he's got his own interests and I know he was never that keen on taking the position in the first place. I'm short, Nate. Need help."

"What about Stefan?" Nate enquired. "Wasn't he the alpha of his last pack?"

Kelan nodded. "He was. Stefan was never meant to be alpha—the position should have been his brother's, but he was killed in an accident when they were young. I do know Stefan would make a good beta and he's already agreed to step in, albeit reluctantly. Stefan was tired of the politics in his last pack, so I'm grateful to him for the help, but the problem is, two or three betas aren't enough anymore. In the last few years the number of shifters in town has all but doubled, and I hate to say it, but these past couple of months have been hell. There has been more trouble than ever before. I'm constantly being called on to break up fights and mediate when a couple o' hot heads can't see eye to eye, and now I've got the damn wolf council looking over my shoulder, too. They're just waiting for me to screw up. I need the extra help."

Nate sighed. He didn't want the position. He knew what an involved job a beta had—essentially being the enforcers of the pack—and he didn't feel up to the task. Hell, he didn't even know if he was going to stick around town. Now that he knew of Jared's existence, the best thing for both of them would be for Nate to disappear. It would be hard to have to keep running into the man, knowing he could never be with him.

Trouble was, Nate felt partly responsible for Kelan's predicament. If he'd been there for his brother when he'd needed him then maybe Rick wouldn't have done what he did and Kelan wouldn't have a beta position to fill at all. Now that he came to think of it, he was surprised Kelan was even asking him. How could Kelan trust him after everything his brother had done to his family?

"Why me?" Nate asked. "Why would you ask this of me?"

"What you really want to know is, why would I trust you after what your brother did, isn't it?"

Damn it, but Kelan was sharp. Nate gave a quick nod of his head. "Yeah, guess that's what I was asking."

Kelan let out a slow, deep breath and turned once again to study the corral. Nate thought the alpha wasn't going to answer the question but after several long moments Kelan started to speak.

"You know that Rick was my best friend."

"Sure. I remember the scrapes you used to get in when you were kids, too...drove Pop mad."

Kelan chuckled. "Yeah, Rick and I had a lot of history together. Did you know we were lovers?"

Nate stared at Kelan, unsure he'd heard the man right. "Say what?"

Kelan smiled sadly. "Oh, it was never anything serious, we both knew that. Just killing time, I guess, until we met our mates."

"I didn't know," Nate whispered.

"Don't suppose anyone did."

"Why are you telling me this now?"

Kelan turned and met Nate's gaze. "Because it's something you need to hear. Because I can see the same guilt in you that I had in me for the first few months after Rick was killed...but I had to let it go, and so do you."

Nate frowned. What would Kelan have to feel guilty about?

"I thought I knew everything about Rick," Kelan continued. "Thought we had no secrets from each other, but I guess I was wrong."

Nate wasn't sure he wanted to hear any more, but he couldn't stop the questions that came spilling from his lips. "What do you mean? What secrets?"

"You know, I had no idea you and Rick had fallen out. Not a damn clue. When I heard the ranch was in trouble, I felt bad for Rick, but I didn't have the money to help him out. All my money was tied up in this place and a few business interests in town. And through it all, Rick kept talking about how he couldn't lose the ranch, how he couldn't do that to his family…to you. All the while he wasn't even talking to you, and I should have known that, you see? He should have fucking told me that. Why didn't he tell me?

"I even asked him why he didn't ask you for the money because I knew you had it. He told me how much inheritance you both got when your mom died and I kept thinking, 'why don't you ask Nate for the money? He'd give it to you in a heartbeat.'"

Nate tried to wrap his head around what Kelan had just told him but it didn't make any sense. If they were so close, why wouldn't Rick have told Kelan about their argument? It had been two years since they'd spoken. *Two years…*

"If he'd told me he wasn't in contact with you, I would have helped. I would have sold something or gone to the bank myself… I would have done my damnedest to get him the money, but he never said a goddamn thing—just pretended like everything was fucking hunky dory, only it wasn't, was it?"

Nate felt like he was going to throw up. He took deep, calming breaths while he unscrewed the cap on his bottle then downed the contents in one go.

"I'm sorry to lay all this on you now but you needed to know. I see all of this guilt in you and you've got to let go of it or it's gonna eat you up inside. It wasn't my fault Rick didn't tell me how badly he needed that money, and it wasn't your fault either. Rick should have said something—to both of us—but he didn't. And then he went and made the worst goddamn decision of his life and I fucking hated him for doing that. I *hated* him."

Kelan spat out the last sentence then seemed to lose all the wind out of his sails and he slumped forward on the bench, scrubbing his hand roughly over his eyes.

"I hated him," Kelan whispered, "but I forgave him, and you need to forgive him, too."

Nate's throat felt raw when he asked the next question. "Why didn't he say anything to us?"

Kelan shrugged. "Pride? Shame? I don't think he wanted you to see him as a failure, and I think he didn't tell me you weren't speaking because he knew I'd interfere. He knew I'd find you and knock your goddamn heads together."

Kelan got up and crossed the length of the porch then stopped on the top of the steps.

"I trust you, Nate, and I want you to be my beta. Think about it." Kelan started down the steps then paused again and turned, pinning Nate in place with a look that was so intense he felt it right down to the core of his being. "Let it go. If there's one thing I know for sure it's that Rick wouldn't want you to live with all this guilt. He loved you, more than he loved anybody in this world, and he'd want you to get on with your life. He'd want you to be happy."

Nate couldn't get his throat to work, couldn't choke out a reply. Fortunately Kelan didn't require one. He walked down the steps and crossed the yard to the main house without looking back. Thoughts whirled around Nate's mind so quickly he couldn't concentrate on a single one, couldn't make sense of any of them. But Kelan had made him realise some things, at least—Nate wasn't the only one who was angry at his brother, he wasn't the only one felt guilty about his death, and he wasn't the only one who was hurting. And maybe, just as Kelan had done, it was time for Nate to let go of the guilt and get on with his life. But he'd been holding on to that guilt for so long now, it felt part of him, and he didn't have the first fucking clue how to relinquish it.

* * * *

The words on the screen of the temperamental old computer started to blur together. Leaning back in his chair, Jared massaged his temple and let out a long, frustrated sigh. If he had to fill out another Goddamn form today, he was going to throw the dark ages monitor out of the freaking window. He'd already had to fill out a couple of the forms twice after the computer had decided it had done enough work for the day and had shut itself down. Why the department couldn't cough up the few hundred bucks it would take to get a new machine, Jared had no idea.

If he were honest, his mind wasn't on his work today, anyway. He'd grabbed exactly ninety minutes of sleep, before he'd had to get up and go into the Realtor's office to sign off on the paperwork that made the purchase of the farm legal. In exactly two weeks, Jared and Tristan would be able to move into their new home. That had been exactly what they'd both wanted, but no matter how hard he tried, he couldn't bring himself to be excited about it. The mood he was in now, Jared wasn't sure that he'd ever feel excited about anything again.

A knock on the office door ripped him from his morose thoughts and brought him swiftly back to the present. He sat up straighter in his chair and ran a hand through his hair to tame his thick, unruly curls.

"Come in," he called out.

The door opened partially and Seth, the receptionist and database administrator, poked his head into the room. Seth was one of only three wolves, including Jared, who worked for the sheriff's department in Wolf Creek. His mother Molly ran the convenience store in town while his father stayed home. The word on the street was that Seth's father was a domineering and abusive jerk. Seth had often come into work with bruises, but he swore they were self-inflicted. Seth *was* a klutz, but Jared wasn't stupid—he knew what a punch to the eye looked like when he saw one. He'd tried to talk to Seth about his father once but the wolf had quickly changed the subject and then shut down completely. Today, thankfully, he was free of bruises.

"Sir? There are two men from the FBI here to see you."

Jared frowned. *What the hell are the feds doing here*? "Oh? Is Sheriff Ferguson here?"

"No, sir, not yet. He got called to Joe Walker's place on his way back. Joe's had another bull go missing."

Jared frowned and pursed his lips. *Another* bull? That made four in total. What the hell was going on? "Okay, thanks Seth, you can show them in."

"Yes, sir."

Seth ducked out of the room and a few moments later the door opened and two men strode inside. If his senses were correct, both men were shifters, but not wolves. *So, not your run of the mill feds then*. Jared suspected they were members of the council.

"Deputy Ambrose?" the larger of the two asked as he approached the desk.

Jared nodded. He got up from his seat and leaned across the desk to shake the man's hand. Now that he was closer Jared could tell he was some sort of cat, although he couldn't be certain of the species.

"Please, call me Jared."

The man nodded and showed Jared a badge. "I'm Gregory Hale and this is my partner, Ashton Monroe. We're from the supernatural council. We spoke on the phone once when you took on the position of deputy here in Wolf Creek."

"I remember," Jared replied, shaking Ashton's hand. His eyes widened when he took in Ashton's scent. He was some sort of bird shifter, if Jared was correct. Ashton must have noticed the surprise in his eyes because his face broke out in a knowing smile.

"Hawk," he clarified.

Jared whistled. "Wow, never met a hawk shifter before. I've heard you're pretty rare."

Ashton nodded. "Sadly we are. I know of only five other hawks in the entire state of Texas and two of those are my parents."

"Must make finding your mate extremely difficult," Jared commented. As soon as the words were out of his mouth, Jared regretted them. His thoughts instantly turned to Nate, and a deep sadness crept into the pit of his stomach. But it was the haunted look in Ashton's eyes that gave Jared pause for thought, making him wish he could take back what he'd said. Ashton didn't reply and, thankfully, Gregory got the conversation back on track.

"We've come to talk to you about the disturbances around town recently. In the last six months the council has been informed of more violent incidents involving wolves than there have been in the last six years."

Jared nodded. "Please, take a seat." He waited until both men were seated before responding to Gregory's statement. "I'm afraid to say there *have* been a lot of problems involving shifters recently."

"Why do you think that is?" Gregory asked.

Jared leant back in his chair and pursed his lips. "I suppose it comes down to numbers. A lot of wolves have moved into the area recently and I think it's inevitable that the more shifters there are, the more problems are likely to occur."

"Would you say that Alpha Morgan is doing his job correctly?"

"I don't know Kelan all that well, but from what I've seen he's a good leader. He handles the pack to the best of his ability. He's well respected around town, and feared just enough to keep most wolves on the straight and narrow."

"*Most* wolves?" Ashton asked.

"There are a few names that keep cropping up time and again—troublemakers from what I've seen. No respect for authority whatsoever."

Ashton pulled a small notepad out of his pocket and flipped it open. "Neil Rafferty, the wolf you called us about last night...is he one of the wolves you're referring to?"

"Yeah, he's one of them. Lives on the Jackson ranch a few miles out of town with a whole bunch of other wolves."

Gregory and Ashton turned to look at each other, and something passed between them. If Jared didn't know better, he would say they had been communicating silently.

"A whole bunch of wolves, you say?" Gregory asked, his gaze shifting back to Jared's.

"Yes, he lives there with his mother, a cousin, and I think there are a few teenagers on the property too. Might even be a couple of cubs."

"We were only informed of Neil and his mother Ellie. Does Kelan know they are all living there?"

"I don't know."

Gregory nodded to Ashton and the hawk pulled a cell from his pocket and went to stand in the corner of the room to make a call.

"Can you take us there?" Gregory asked. "I think we need to have a chat to Mrs Rafferty."

Jared nodded. "Of course, when would you like to go?"

Gregory grinned and raised one of his eyebrows. There was something about the glint in his eye that made him look every inch the crafty cat. "No time like the present."

Chapter Five

"Jesus, it's a hot one today." Kelan tipped his Stetson a little lower to shield his eyes from the glare of the midday sun.

"Sure is," Nate replied, pulling on the reins of his horse to veer left.

After spending the morning checking on the herd in the far pasture, Nate and Kelan were making their way back to the house to grab lunch before they went back out to mend a few holes they'd noticed in the fence along the way.

Kelan chuckled. "Not much of a talker, are you, Nate?"

Nate shrugged, even though Kelan wasn't currently looking at him and couldn't see the gesture. "Not much to say, I guess."

"You thought any more about becoming my beta?"

Nate frowned and chewed on his lip. He *hadn't* thought much about Kelan's request, if he were honest. The talk about Rick that morning had played on his mind and then, of course, there was Jared, who was never far from his thoughts. Even though Nate had tried to banish all notions of the sexy deputy from his mind, his mate pretty much consumed his every waking moment.

He opened his mouth to answer Kelan, even though he wasn't sure what that answer was going to be, when Kelan's cell starting ringing, interrupting him.

Kelan grinned. "Hold that thought a minute, will ya?"

While Kelan picked up the call, Nate turned to study the landscape. He loved this place—the vast open spaces were pure heaven for a wolf. Nate loved the town, too, even though Wolf Creek didn't feel like home anymore. But he supposed it wasn't the land that made somewhere home, or the building that stood on it—it was the people that filled that building. It was family.

"No, I most certainly did not!" Kelan fumed. "Okay, thirty minutes, I'll meet you there."

"Problems?" Nate asked when Kelan hung up the call and shoved it back into the pocket of his jeans.

Kelan turned and met Nate's gaze. "Yeah. Think this might be something I need help with, too."

"Anything I can do?"

Kelan pursed his lips. "I wouldn't ask, but Stefan and Cody have the day off and have gone out of town. Luke or Mark wouldn't be any good in this situation. This is something that will probably be difficult for you, though, Nate."

"What do you mean? Difficult how?"

"A couple of months ago I had a woman come pay me a visit—Ellie Rafferty. She petitioned for rights to stay in Wolf Creek with her son Neil."

"Neil Rafferty..." Nate said. "Where do I know that name from?"

"He was one of the troublemakers last night at Jessie's. Picked the fight with Tristan."

"Of course…Neil. He seemed like a nasty piece of work."

"Yeah, I didn't like him much when I met him—arrogant and bigoted young wolf. I couldn't find anything redeeming in him. But I allowed them to stay here because it was just the two of them. Didn't figure one young wolf like him could cause much trouble. But that was the council that just called, and apparently there are a lot more than two of them staying at the ranch now, so I need to go and have a chat to them."

"Doesn't sound like a problem," Nate said. "I'll come."

"That's not the whole of it," Kelan said, his tone grave. "There's something else you need to know."

"What is it?"

"The Rafferty's are living on a farm just the other side of the woods. It's the old Jackson place."

Nate sucked in a sharp breath, his stomach like lead. "But that's—"

"Yeah," Kelan nodded and averted is gaze. "It's the place Rick was killed."

Nate's heart thumped frantically in his chest. He hadn't been able to go by the Jackson place since he'd arrived back in Wolf Creek, even though he'd wanted to visit many times—wanted to see the place his brother had died with his own eyes, but he hadn't been able to face it. He wasn't sure he was ready to go now. But this was something he needed to do, so he found himself nodding his agreement.

"I'll come."

It took them twenty minutes to ride back to the ranch, feed and water the horses and lead them out to the corral. As soon as they were done, they jumped in Kelan's truck and headed out to the Jackson ranch.

"You sure you're okay with this?" Kelan asked just as they were pulling into the dirt drive that ran up to the property.

Nate sighed and turned to look out the passenger window—taking in the tall, bald cypress trees that led all the way down to the river. "As sure as I'll ever be, I guess. It's just a place, right?"

"What the *fuck* is going on?" Kelan screeched the car to a halt in the yard outside the old farmhouse.

As soon as they stopped, Kelan quickly got out of the car and sprinted across the yard. Nate got out and immediately saw what had caught Kelan's attention. Out front, to the left of the house, there were two young wolves, fully shifted and currently tearing lumps out of one another.

"Aww…fuck." Nate started running towards the wolves, too. He reached them seconds after Kelan and tried to get a hold on one while Kelan grabbed the other. It wasn't an easy task—even though the wolves were young, no older than twenty, they were fully grown and strong.

Both wolves were covered in gashes, their tawny fur matted with thick blood. The metallic odour of it hung heavy in the air. They snarled, their huge paws lashing out and scrabbling to find purchase, to tear at any piece of flesh they encountered. Nate's cowboy hat was knocked from his head in the scuffle as he tried to get a tighter grip on the wolf and pull him back.

"Enough!" Kelan roared. The sound boomed out, and the force behind it was enough to make even Nate whimper. But the wolves were senseless, like rabid dogs, crazed and unable to be reasoned with.

But there was one thing able to get through to them it seemed. While Nate struggled to keep hold of the smaller of the two wolves, a shot was fired. The larger wolf whined as a petite woman stepped forward, rifle raised and trained on Nate and Kelan.

"Let go of my boys!" she warned. The wolves quieted but they still fought against their restraints. "You won't get another warning, step away, now!"

Nate looked to his alpha for confirmation, when Kelan gave a quick nod of his head and let go of the wolf he was holding, Nate reluctantly complied.

"There's no need for the rifle, Mrs Rafferty," Kelan said. "We were only trying to stop them from tearing each other apart."

"Y'all needn't have bothered. It's nothing serious, just boys being boys."

Nate snorted. "'Boys being boys'? If we hadn't come along there'd be nothing left of your boys."

The two wolves had moved to flank Mrs Rafferty. Kelan looked at each of them in turn. His eyes glowed a deep amber colour, and Nate could feel the power he projected from where he stood as the alpha ordered, "Shift!"

The smaller of the two whined and immediately lowered his gaze. He lay down on the ground and rolled to his back, bearing his stomach and neck to the alpha but the older wolf stood his ground, eyeing Kelan defiantly. He curled his upper lip in what looked like a sneer before sitting down, his body contorting and shifting into its human form. The smaller wolf started his transformation, too. Mrs Rafferty still held the rifle high.

While the wolves were still shifting, Nate heard a car pulling up in the drive. He turned out of instinct and saw Jared exit his cruiser with Gregory and Ashton in tow. His stomach lurched and his breath caught in his chest as he stared at his beautiful mate. Jared's face was as white as snow and there was real fear in his eyes…panic.

"Drop the rifle!" Jared commanded. It was only then Nate noticed the deputy had his own gun drawn and pointed at Mrs Rafferty. "Now!"

Jared's hand shook as he held tight to his gun, his gaze fixed on Ellie Rafferty. "I said, drop your weapon!"

He edged closer to Nate and Kelan, keeping the woman in his sights. When Jared had seen the rifle pointed at Nate as they had pulled up to the house, he'd had to fight to keep his wolf contained and he didn't know if it was a battle he was going to win. His wolf was frenzied, snarling and struggling to be set free so that it could kill the person that was threatening his mate.

"This is your last warning."

"I ain't done nothing!" Ellie shouted, but to Jared's relief she lowered the rifle before letting it fall to the ground.

Gregory and Ashton walked over to Mrs Rafferty and Gregory kicked the rifle out of her reach. The two naked young wolves at her side scowled at the council members but remained quiet.

Finally Jared chanced a look at his mate. Nate's hands, arms, chest and stomach were covered in blood. Jared nearly threw up. Without warning, his eyes shifted to their wolf form and his incisors tore from his gums. Jared was dimly aware of a heated discussion between Kelan, Gregory, Ashton and Mrs Rafferty, but he had no idea what was being said. All he could see, all he could think about, was Nate... Nate who was completely covered in blood...

Barely managing to put one foot in front of the other, Jared crossed the yard to his mate, but when he reached Nate all he could do was stare. Nate reached out a hand and placed it on his shoulder.

"You okay?" he asked.

Jared shook his head, looking down at Nate's chest. "You're...you're...bleeding."

Nate looked down at his chest and frowned, then met Jared's gaze. "It's okay, it isn't my blood."

Closing his eyes, Jared tried to calm his racing heart and steady his breathing. *Not Nate's blood.* The relief that swept through him was so intense he felt a lump form in the back of his throat and the sting of unshed tears behind his eyes. *Not Nate's blood.*

"Hey," Nate said softly.

Jared opened his eyes and stared at Nate but he still couldn't force out any words, still couldn't get his eyes and teeth to shift back to their human form.

Nate smiled, his hand gently squeezing Jared's shoulder. "It's all right. I'm okay."

"What are you doing here?" Jared said at last.

Nate's gaze shifted to Kelan and the other wolves. He sighed and pulled his eyebrows together into a frown. "It's a long story."

"Jared?" Kelan called. "Can we talk to you for a minute?"

Jared felt a tinge of regret when Nate removed the hand from his shoulder. "Be right there!"

"You too, Nate," Kelan added.

Nate sighed. "I guess we'd better see what they want."

Jared nodded. "You sure you're okay?"

Nate's smile lit up his whole face and it made Jared's breath catch in his chest until he felt like he was suffocating. "I'm getting there."

Jared wanted to ask Nate what he meant by that, but now wasn't the time. He closed his eyes once more, centred himself, and felt his eyes shift back to their human form and his canines recede into his gums. When he opened his eyes for the second time, no trace of his wolf remained.

Nate bent down to retrieve his hat, dusted the top then placed it back on his head. As if by silent agreement they walked side by side to join the others. As they neared, Ashton led Mrs Rafferty and the two young wolves into the house.

"Nate, good to see you again," Gregory said. "How's that chest wound of yours?"

"Chest wound?" Jared's head swivelled in Nate's direction.

"Nate got shot a few weeks back, trying to save Cary's life," Kelan said.

"Shot?" Jared gasped. "Jesus."

Nate shrugged. "It's okay, it's healed now."

Jared nodded, working hard to keep his breathing steady. "What's going on here?"

Kelan let out a long breath. "It's a fucking mess. Ellie's running some sort of halfway house. There are six young shifters in total—all boys—and as you saw, she's not in control of a single one of them. Her husband left her several years ago. Neil, her son, is the oldest boy living here and he's hardly role model material. Ellie won't admit it, but she's way out of her depth."

"Where have the kids come from?" Jared asked. "Does she have legal guardianship of *all* of them?"

"That's the problem," Gregory replied. "Under normal circumstances she'd have to go through the courts, like anyone else—shifter or not—but she's insisting she has permission from the council to keep every one of them."

"And does she?" Nate asked.

Gregory shrugged. "It's the first I've heard about it. Ashton has gone with her to check the paperwork."

"But if the council sent you here to check on the disturbances in town, wouldn't they have told you about the situation here at the ranch?" Jared asked. "Especially seeing as Ellie's son has been involved in most of the trouble?"

Gregory pursed his lips and turned to look at Kelan. He opened his mouth to speak but stopped at the last minute and eyed Nate and Jared warily. "I don't..."

"You can speak openly in front of Nate," Kelan said. "I trust him with my life."

A look passed between Nate and Kelan that Jared couldn't identify. Jared watched Nate's throat bob as he swallowed and lowered his gaze. It had looked almost as though they shared a secret. He didn't like it.

What the hell is going on between them? Kelan is mated and so is Nate, Goddamn it!

As soon as the thought occurred to him, Jared felt a bite of pain in his chest. Nate was free to do whatever the hell he wanted. Jared had no hold on him. But the thought of him being with anyone else left him cold.

"And Jared?" Gregory asked.

Kelan sighed, his gaze shifting back and forth between Jared and Nate. "Jared's his mate."

Jared's head snapped up and he glared at Nate. How the hell was he ever going to make sheriff if Nate was running around shooting his mouth off, telling everyone he was mated to a man? More importantly, what was there between him and Kelan that made it so easy for Nate to confide in him? "You told him?" he accused.

Nate raised his hand. "I didn't need to tell him anything. Kelan was there when I found out, remember?"

"What's going on, Gregory?" Kelan asked, changing the subject. "What is it you have to tell us?"

Gregory looked to the house and sighed, nodding his head as though making up his mind. "This is to go no further than the three of us, understand?"

Kelan shook his head. "I don't keep anything from my mate but you can rest assured that Jake won't tell anyone and neither will I."

"Fair enough." Gregory looked to Jared and Nate for their confirmation.

"I won't say anything," Jared agreed.

Nate snorted. "I don't talk to anyone, but you have my word. It won't come from me."

"The council didn't send us here to find out about the disturbances around town," Gregory said. "Well, not exactly. They sent us to check up on Kelan, to find out if he's doing his job properly and to see if his position as alpha is safe."

There was a long, pregnant pause before anyone spoke. Jared was surprised by Gregory's statement. Kelan was a good alpha. Nearly all the wolves in town thought highly of him.

"That's fucking bullshit!" Nate roared, finally breaking the silence.

"It's okay," Kelan said. "I've been expecting this."

Gregory pulled his eyebrows together and lifted his right hand to scratch the top of his head. "How did you know?"

"I have a friend on the council," Kelan replied.

"I don't suppose you'd tell me who?"

"No, sorry…can't risk anyone finding out he's been speaking to me."

Gregory's lips thinned. "I'm trusting you here, Kelan. The least you could do is offer me the same courtesy."

"Don't take it personally, Gregory, but until I know you better and know I can trust you, it's not something I'm willing to disclose."

"Fair enough. If you have a friend on the council then you know about the…trouble that's been going on there."

"Yeah, I've heard about it."

"What trouble?" Jared asked.

Gregory met Kelan's gaze and gave a slight nod of his head. The action was barely perceptible, but it was enough for Jared to turn to Kelan to await an explanation.

"The Supernatural Council has been in existence far longer than the human government," Kelan said. "It was set up to keep an eye on the shifter population and to ensure that we don't expose our secrets to humans. But there have always been those in the council who think shifters should live their lives in the open."

Jared shook his head. "That would never work. Humans would be terrified if they learned of our existence. It would be out and out war."

Kelan nodded. "Yes, and those in favour of us 'coming out', as it were, have always been in the minority, but it looks as though their numbers are increasing and some of those people have risen to very influential positions within the council."

"What does that have to do with you?" Nate asked. "Why would the council send in members to check up on you?"

"I think I can answer that," Gregory replied. "Kelan runs a tight ship here in Wolf Creek. Any and all incidents involving shifters are dealt with quickly and there has never been any danger of the humans that live here finding out about us."

"Until recently," Kelan amended. "Until, it seems, those members in the council that are in favour of us living our lives in the open decided to send in more shifters—troublemakers—essentially making it more difficult for me to keep order here."

"And the more difficult it is for you to keep order, the more chance there is of humans here finding out about us," Nate said.

Jared turned to study Nate. He was practically vibrating with pent-up anger. The air was thick with it and the current zinged through Jared, making him shiver. Nate was a powerful wolf, that much was evident, and Jared couldn't help but be in awe of that power. It excited him—made him want things he couldn't have, however much he might wish otherwise.

"Exactly," Kelan replied.

Nate's strong jaw clenched and fury flashed in his eyes, making the tiny hairs on the back of Jared's neck stand to attention. The air around them crackled and almost as quickly as the ferocity had appeared, it vanished.

When Ashton came out of the farmhouse and made his way down the steps of the porch, Kelan and Gregory walked over to talk to him, leaving Jared alone again with Nate.

"So how's Tris—"

"What's going on between you and Kelan?" Jared interrupted before he could stop himself. *Jesus.* What the hell was wrong with him? Jared knew logically it was none of his business—he'd told Nate quite clearly how things stood between them—but it seemed he wasn't capable of rational thought, couldn't stop his mouth from saying the first damn thing that popped into his mind. Nate drew his eyebrows together and tilted his head.

"What do *you* care?"

What *did* he care? He shouldn't care at all. But the challenge in Nate's eyes made him square his shoulders and puff out his chest. Nate still hadn't given him a damn answer. He shrugged.

"Kelan is mated, didn't think he'd be the type to fool around, is all."

"So you're just looking out for your alpha's best interests?"

Jared frowned. "Will you answer the damn question?"

Nate's rich, brown eyes softened and he let out a gentle sigh. The emotion in those eyes had Jared rooted to the spot. He couldn't have looked away if his life depended on it. Nate's gaze held him in place and the electricity that arced between them was intense. A long moment passed as Jared stared into Nate's eyes...lost. He'd never felt so confused or so completely helpless, and he was sure his heart had stopped beating while he waited for an answer that had the capacity to shatter his whole world.

"There's nothing going on, Jared," Nate said. His voice was rough, thick and so full of emotion it caused a lump to form in the back of Jared's throat. "How could you think that?"

Jared tore his gaze away—had to. He cleared his throat and shifted his weight onto his other leg. "I—"

"Nate? We're all done here!" Kelan shouted across the yard.

Nate's shoulders slumped and he nodded his head. "Be right there!"

When he turned again to meet Jared's gaze, he lifted one eyebrow, his face full of something that looked like hope. "Jared?"

"Come on," Jared said, grateful for the interruption. Another minute alone with Nate and Jared was afraid of what he might have confessed…what he might have asked for or what he would have offered. It was certainly nothing he could afford to give. "Let's get back to the others."

Nate's features hardened and the emotion that had been present in his eyes a moment before disappeared. He gave a sharp nod of his head. "Right."

Without another word, Nate turned and strode across the yard. Jared waited a moment to calm his breathing and slow down his racing heart before following. When he reached the other men, he looked to Gregory, his eyebrows raised in question.

"The paperwork was in order," Gregory confirmed. "There's nothing more we can do here."

"There has to be something. If what you were saying about the faction in the council wanting to expose us is true, then we can't just let this go."

"We won't," Kelan said. "But we need to get together and discuss exactly what we *can* do."

Jared nodded. "Name the place, I'll be there."

Kelan pursed his lips. "Luke and Mark are having a party Sunday afternoon to celebrate their first year anniversary. Why don't you all come? I'm sure after the festivities have finished there'll be a chance for us all to get together and go over our options."

Gregory turned to Ashton, and they both nodded their heads in agreement. "We'll be there," he confirmed.

"I'm off work on Sunday, so yeah, sounds good." Jared wouldn't admit to it, of course, but part of him was excited about going—not because they'd be able to discuss what was going on with the council, but because it would give him a chance to see Nate again. Even though he knew that wouldn't be the best of ideas, he couldn't think of anything he wanted more.

"Good, then we'll see you all there. Nate, you ready?" Kelan asked as he turned to leave.

Nate met Jared's gaze and held it. Jared felt his pulse quicken as he stared back, every nerve ending in his body felt as though it were on edge—poised, waiting for something he knew couldn't happen.

Nate cleared his throat but when he spoke his voice was gravelly. "I'll see you Sunday." He tipped his cowboy hat then followed in Kelan's wake.

Jared watched his retreating form regretfully. They were halfway to their car when Kelan turned and called out, "Jared, why don't you bring your brother with you?"

Jared swallowed down the lump that had formed in his throat and nodded. "Will do!"

"I thought Kelan said you and Nate are mates?" Gregory commented, watching the two cowboys get into Kelan's pickup.

With much regret, Jared tore his gaze away from Nate. "I don't want to talk about it," he replied.

Chapter Six

"Do I *have* to go?" Tristan whined from his position in the passenger seat. "It's just some stupid party for a couple of old guys."

Jared rolled his eyes. "For your information, Luke is only a couple of years older than you, and his mate Mark is only in his mid-thirties. We've been invited by Alpha Morgan, and we're going—end of story. Besides, I thought you wanted to see the horses?"

Tristan sat up straighter in his seat and turned to face Jared. "Do you think I'll get to ride one?"

"I don't see why not, if you ask nicely and you don't cause any trouble while you're there."

Tristan made a tutting sound and Jared knew his brother well enough to know there had probably been an eye-roll, too. He tried to hide his grin, keeping his eyes on the signal in front of him.

"I wish you'd stop treating me like a kid, I'm twenty-one—an adult—and I don't appreciate it."

The light changed and Jared pulled away. "It was a joke, bro, get with the programme. 'Sides, it'll do you good to get out and meet people, you know. There are a couple of wolves working on the ranch—Aaron and Cary—about your age, I think, so you might make some new friends today."

Jared saw Tristan shrug his shoulders in his peripheral vision. "Maybe. What's got you so eager to go to this party, anyway?"

Jared gripped the steering wheel tighter, every nerve ending in his body suddenly on high alert. Just what had Tristan picked up on? "What do mean? I'm not *eager*."

"Please," Tristan sputtered. "You changed your shirt, like, three times this morning, and you're wearing cologne. You *never* wear cologne."

"There's nothing wrong with wanting to smell nice."

"You do know we're wolves, right?" Tristan rolled down the window, stuck his head outside, and very dramatically took in a large gulp of air before pulling it back inside. "I'm all for wanting to smell nice, but you didn't have to take a bath in the stuff."

"I'm sure other people will appreciate the way I smell even if you don't."

"Do you think Nate will be there? He told me he works for Kelan."

Jared's pulse went into overdrive at just the mention of the cowboy. How the hell had Tristan's mind jumped from Jared wanting to smell nice to Nate? He didn't like where this conversation was going, not one little bit. He didn't want to talk about Nate with Tristan. If he did, he might not be able to stop himself from blurting out that they were mates, and what would be the point of that? Neither he nor Nate wanted to do anything about their mating bond. Well...Jared might, but it was impossible anyway, wasn't it? He had no time in his life for a mate. He had Tristan to think about.

"How would I know?" he mumbled. "Possibly."

"I don't know what's got into you today, but you've been acting kinda funny."

Jared made a left and pulled into the country road that led to Kelan's ranch. As they travelled down the narrow lane, kicking up dust in their wake, Jared's breathing sped up to match his hammering heart. He hated lying to his brother. Jared *knew* Nate would be at the ranch, knew he'd be there to talk about the trouble in the council, but would he be happy to see Jared? Would he even care?

"You didn't hear a word I just said, did you?"

"Huh?"

"Exactly. *Weird.* I don't know what's wrong with you. You know it's full moon in a few days. Is that what's got your fur in a knot?"

Jared shrugged and gave a non-committal grunt and, mercifully, after that Tristan went quiet, leaving Jared to his thoughts.

The road out to Kelan's ranch was in need of repair and several times Jared had to swerve the car to avoid a pothole that would have been hell on his suspension. There was a wooded area to their right but to the left were open fields as far as the eye could see. Some held crops but most of the pastures contained cattle. Jared was no expert but they looked like Aberdeen Angus. That reminded him of Joe Walker's missing bulls, which in turn made him think about the fight at Jessie's, and inevitably his mind circled around to meeting Nate. *Everything* came back to Nate.

By the time the ranch house came into sight, Jared could barely breathe. He cleared his throat loudly and tried to take a calming breath to settle his nerves. "We're here."

"Well, duh."

Jared bit the inside of his cheek to stop himself from snapping at his brother while he unbuckled his seatbelt and waited for Tristan to get out of the SUV. He had to be careful not to take his mood out on Tristan. Things were starting to get better between them and he didn't want to do anything to interfere with that. When the passenger door slammed shut, he leaned his head back and closed his eyes, taking in a moment to collect himself. He could do this. There would probably be plenty of wolves at the party, so he might not even run into Nate. Matter of fact, chances were good that Nate wouldn't even show up. From what Jared had seen of the cowboy, he didn't seem like the socialising type.

"Are you going to sit in there all day, 'cause I thought you wanted to come to this thing? We can leave if you want."

When Jared opened his eyes, Tristan was glaring at him through the window. He sighed, killed the engine and got out of car.

"Not going to happen, bro. Come on."

Jared surveyed his surroundings as he nudged his brother to get moving towards the house. There was a large corral to their right, currently free of horses, a couple of outbuildings, and what looked like a bunkhouse just off to the side. He paused to stare at the building, wondering if it was where Nate slept, then shook himself and followed his brother to the steps of the main house. He had to stop thinking of the damn wolf. No good could come of it. But it didn't seem to matter how hard he tried, Nate was never far from his thoughts.

They climbed the steps to the porch, and Jared knocked on the large, wooden door. Tristan shoved his hands into the pockets of his jeans and slouched against the wall while they waited for someone to answer. He looked utterly miserable.

"Will you lighten up? We're going to a party, not a funeral."

Tristan rolled his eyes but he stood a little straighter and removed his hands when the door opened and they were greeted by an attractive, impeccably dressed man in his early to mid-thirties. Jared's wolf senses told him the man was human. He knew Kelan was mated to a human but he'd yet to meet him. He thrust out his hand for the man to shake.

"Hi, uh, I'm Jared Ambrose and this is my brother Tristan. Kelan invited us."

The man smiled warmly and took hold of Jared's hand. "Yes, of course. *Deputy* Ambrose, isn't it? We've been expecting you. I'm Jake, Kelan's mate. Come on in."

They followed Jake inside, waited for him to close the door and followed as he led the way through the house. Tristan tugged on Jared's shirt sleeve and leaned in near his ear.

"He's human." The words were barely more than a whisper and wouldn't have been audible to anyone but a wolf.

Jared rolled his eyes. "Jesus, Tristan. It's time you started taking an interest in the goings-on in the pack."

"What for?"

Jared shook his head. It wasn't the time to get involved in another argument with Tristan about his choices in life, but he made a mental note to take his brother to the next pack meeting. If Tristan made some friends in the area it might help him feel more at home in Wolf Creek. He needed people in his life that would be a good influence on him, not the hoodlums that frequented Jessie's. As much as Jared tried to involve him in things, he knew his brother needed friends his own age.

Jake led the way into a large kitchen then out through the back door. "We're all outside," he said, motioning for them to follow. "Kelan told me you moved here from Lubbock."

Jared nodded. "We did, moved down here so I could take the job in the sheriff's department."

"You like it here?"

"I do. Think we'll settle here. Just bought a house, actually. We'll be moving in in a couple of weeks."

"Oh, that's great news."

"Doesn't sound like you're from around here either," Jared commented.

"No. Boston originally, but I lived all of my adult life in New York."

"Wow. So how's small town life compared to the big city?"

Jake grinned. "Took some getting used to, I can tell you, but now I love it. Couldn't imagine living anywhere else, and of course, Kelan's here. That's what makes it home."

Jared felt a lump form in his throat but he quickly swallowed it down. Home was usually where your mate was, but Jared couldn't let himself think about that right now.

There was a lot of activity going on out back. Jared saw Luke standing behind a grill in the yard just a little ways away from the house, with his mate Mark at his side. It looked as though Mark was trying to tell his mate how to cook and Luke looked none too happy about it. Jared grinned when Luke grabbed a fish slice and whacked Mark on the back of the hand when he tried to steal something Luke had just set on a plate.

Jared recognised Cary, who was currently perched in Aaron's lap in a lawn chair, his mate's arms wrapped tightly around his waist. They looked sweet together, completely infatuated, with eyes for no one but each other. There were a few wolves present that Jared knew and more standing around chatting with each other that he hadn't met before.

A quick scan of the area told Jared that Nate wasn't present. He was equal parts relieved and disappointed by that fact, but he swallowed down his unease and plastered a smile on his face as Jake led them to Kelan's side.

"Hey, you made it!" Kelan exclaimed, switching his beer to his left hand and holding out his right.

Jared shook Kelan's hand and nodded. "We did."

"And you brought your brother. I'm glad. Good to see you again, Tristan."

Tristan's mouth curved up into a polite smile and he tilted his head slightly, bearing his neck. "Alpha."

"I think Tristan was worried what attending a party for a couple of *old guys* would do to his street cred," Jared teased. Right on cue his brother's cheeks turned a furious shade of scarlet and he glared at Jared.

Kelan threw his head back and laughed. "Old guys! Jesus, Luke's only twenty-three. If *he's* old then there's no hope for the rest of us. Say, y'all met my mate, Jake?"

"Y—"

"Is Nate here?" Tristan interrupted.

When Kelan's gaze flicked to his, Jared felt like a deer trapped in headlights. He couldn't get his mouth to work, but what would he say to Kelan, anyway, without revealing his secret to Tristan? Kelan must have seen the panicked look on his face because he didn't so much as miss a beat.

"He's tending to the horses right now, but he should be here any minute."

Jared finally allowed himself to take a breath. "I think Nate left quite the impression on Tristan when they met at Jessie's the other day."

Tristan shrugged. "He helped me."

"Oh, well, I'm sure Nate will be happy to learn he's gained a fan." Kelan chuckled.

It was only then that Jared noticed the confused look on Jake's face and panic engulfed him. He froze when Jake turned to Kelan, eyebrows raised.

"But I thought you said—"

"Oh look, here he is now," Kelan said, cutting Jake off before he could blurt the truth.

When Tristan turned to look, Jared mouthed *'Thank you'* to Kelan and before he turned, he saw Kelan bend down to whisper in his mate's ear.

Bracing himself, Jared turned around and his heart very nearly stopped beating when he saw Nate striding towards them, a grey, felt cowboy hat pulled low over his rich, dark brown eyes. Nate's face was still scarred from the fight at Jessie's but the wounds had lightened to a pale pink instead of the angry red they'd been just a few days before.

He was wearing faded denims that fit snugly to his legs and thighs and outlined what looked to be a very impressive package. A dark blue button-down shirt was tucked into his jeans and although it was a loose fit, it pulled tightly against his wide chest and broad shoulders with each and every step he took. Instantly, Jared's body reacted. His dick filled and he had to fight to stop his eyes and teeth from shifting. He took a few deep breaths and tried to slow down his heart rate.

"Hi Nate!" Tristan said when Nate stepped up next to them.

Jared hadn't heard such enthusiasm in his brother's voice for a very long time. The sound pleased him but he wasn't sure how he felt about Nate being the cause of his brother's change in mood. Why *Nate*?

"Hey, kid," Nate replied. "How's things? You been looking after that brother of yours?"

Jared didn't hear his brother's reply because halfway through Nate's question, the cowboy turned to meet his gaze and for the briefest of moments, they were the only two people who existed. He tried to look away, tried to stop the rapid hammering of his heart, which seemed suddenly so loud in his ears, blocking out anything and everything else. There was only Nate…Nate and the combined pounding of their hearts, beating together, almost as one…

Nate's mouth lifted at the corners but it was a cheerless smile, desolate. It caused a pain in Jared's chest unlike anything he'd experienced. Jared finally understood the term heartache.

"How are you, Jared?" Nate asked.

"I…uh…I'm…" *Jesus*. Jared couldn't get his mouth to work.

"Ignore him," Tristan said with a roll of his eyes. "He's been weird all day. Ever since this morning when he started getting ready to come here."

Nate was the first to break eye contact. He turned to Tristan and his smile grew wider, full of teeth and dimples and laughter lines, and it travelled all the way to his eyes, which sparkled with mirth.

"That a fact?"

Jared felt an irrational pang of jealousy towards his brother. He knew Tristan wasn't interested in Nate in that way, but what of Nate? How did *he* feel? Jared didn't want to admit to himself that *he* wanted to be the one to make Nate smile that big, bright and beautiful smile that made Jared's heart sing.

"Yep, I think he might be acting crazy because it's nearly full moon."

Nate's smile was still wide when he met Jared's gaze again, but as the seconds ticked on, it started to fade, the lights in his eyes dimming slightly, and that cut Jared to the core. They continued to stare at one another, neither man speaking, just looking their fill. Tristan seemed blissfully unaware of the silent exchange that passed between them and he ploughed on.

"I'm telling you, he literally showered in cologne before we left. You'd think he had a big date or something."

This time Nate's eyes did sparkle when he looked at Jared but it wasn't with mirth. There was a different emotion in those eyes but Jared couldn't quite work out what it was. For a moment Jared thought it was anger he was seeing there. But why would Nate be angry about a comment like that? Surely he didn't think…

"Tristan, why don't you come with me and Jake?" Kelan said. "I'll introduce you to Aaron and Cary."

Tristan shrugged. "Oh, okay, I guess so. See you later, Nate?"

Nate didn't take his eyes from Jared when he next spoke. "Yeah. See you later, kid."

They were barely out of hearing distance when Nate rounded on Jared, and a low growl tore from his throat. "A date? With who?"

Jared shook his head. He was about to deny the fact when a thought occurred to him. Was Nate *jealous*? He couldn't explain why that made him so angry. Sure, he might have felt the same way the other day when he'd witnessed Nate and Kelan's easy-going relationship, but so what? Nate didn't want him—he'd made that perfectly clear—so it was really none of his business who Jared dated.

"You wouldn't know him," Jared lied. No sooner were the words out of his mouth than Jared regretted them. What the hell had he gone and said that for? Was he *trying* to make Nate jealous? To what end? But the anger that had been on display in Nate's eyes fell away to be replaced by an unmistakable sadness. Nate dropped his gaze then and nodded.

"Right. Well, have fun," he said quietly. "I've got to go. See you around, Jared."

Jared opened his mouth to admit to the lie—to tell Nate that there wouldn't be anyone else for him, not now, not ever—but Nate had already turned and was storming through the yard towards the house.

"Hey, Jared."

Jared watched Nate disappear through the kitchen door before he looked to his right and saw that Gregory and Ashton stood beside him.

"Hey," he replied. He tried to smile at the two men but the action felt foreign to him and he dimly wondered if he would ever smile again.

"Glad you could make it," Gregory said. "Was that Nate we just saw leave?"

Jared nodded. "Yeah, that was Nate."

Ashton whistled. "Boy, he didn't look happy."

Jared's chest felt tight. No, Nate hadn't looked happy and as much as it pained him to admit, Jared had been the cause. He hadn't expected the look of utter devastation on Nate's face, but the wolf had seemed genuinely upset by what Jared had said. He looked...wounded—grief-stricken, even. Why would Nate feel that way if he didn't want anything to do with him?

Nate ran down the porch steps and hurried across the yard towards the bunkhouse, his heart breaking with every step he took. He'd never felt as alone and filled with despair as he did in that moment. Nate had believed the deputy when he'd told him he didn't want to get involved because of Tristan, and the fact that he wanted to make sheriff. Why wouldn't he? He genuinely hadn't imagined it was because Jared just didn't want him, which was quite obviously the case. They'd only found out they were mated a few days ago and already Jared was going out with another man? Nate had an insane urge to find the guy and rip his Goddamn throat out with his bare hands.

As the fury bubbled up inside him, a tear escaped the corner of his eye and slid slowly down his cheek. *What the fuck?* He was crying like some little girl now? He brushed it away roughly then balled his hands into fists at his sides, fury replacing the sorrow. He'd made it halfway across the yard to the bunkhouse when he stopped in his tracks and then changed direction, heading out towards the corral. It wouldn't do him any good to be inside. In his current mood, he'd probably end up tearing the place apart. He needed to displace some of the anger and pent-up energy that was driving his wolf to distraction. He needed to run, that would be sure to help, but it was the middle of the day and he couldn't take the risk of being seen.

The horses. They always calmed him down. He'd take Misty out to the north pasture to try to tame his mood.

"Hey Nate! Wait up!"

Nate closed his eyes and let out a long sigh. *Tristan*. He seemed like a good kid, and Nate liked him a lot, but Tristan was the last person Nate wanted to deal with in his current mood. The kid looked so much like Jared. They had the same beautiful green eyes. How could he look into those eyes and not be reminded of his mate?

"Nate?"

Nate turned slowly and tried to smile at the young wolf, but his lips didn't so much as twitch. "Hey Tristan."

"Where you going?"

"For a ride on one of the horses."

It looked as though Nate had said the magic word. Tristan's eyes lit up, and his mouth curved up into a broad grin, the likes of which he'd never seen on the kid's face before.

"Can I come?"

Nate was about to tell Tristan what a bad idea he thought that was, but when he saw the excited look on the young wolf's face, he knew he couldn't say no. He didn't want to let Tristan down. He had a feeling the kid had had enough to deal with lately.

"Sure, you know how to ride?"

Tristan nodded enthusiastically. "Yeah, I had lessons when I was a kid. Been a few years since I was on a horse, though."

Nate shrugged. "It's not something you forget. Come on, let's get the horses saddled."

They worked in relative silence while they got Misty and Lightning ready to be taken out. Nate watched

Tristan carefully line up the saddle pad and blanket before he threw on the saddle. He brought down the front and back cinch, checking to see if it was going to fit properly. When Nate was satisfied the kid knew what he was doing, he left him alone and concentrated on his own horse.

Ten minutes later they were riding out past the corral. Nate closed his eyes for a moment and took a deep breath through his nose, breathing in the sweet smell of the land, the pleasant familiar scent helped calm his nerves. It was only when they'd crossed through the first gate that Tristan spoke.

"What did my brother say to you earlier?" The query had been casual enough but it was a loaded question and Nate didn't have the first fucking clue how to answer it without revealing too much. What had Jared told Tristan about them? Did he know they were mates?

A few of the throwaway comments Tristan had made got Nate to thinking that he and Jared weren't as close as brothers should be. But it was the fact that Jared didn't want to recognise their bond that made his mind up. There was no way the wolf would have told anyone, even his brother. Tristan didn't know.

"Nothing important," he hedged. "Why do you ask?"

Out of the corner of his eye, Nate saw Tristan shrug his shoulders. "You only spoke for a minute, and when you left, you looked upset. That's why I came after you."

Well, hell. What was Nate supposed to say to that? He didn't want to lie to Tristan, but there wasn't a lot he could say without mentioning the mating bond, and that was out of the question. It wasn't his place.

Nate met Jared's speculative gaze. "Nothing you need to worry yourself about."

Tristan frowned but he let the subject drop, or at least Nate thought he had until a few moments later when Tristan spoke again. "I think Jared likes you."

Every muscle in Nate's body grew taut. How the hell had the kid got that idea? He couldn't be further from the truth. "What gives you that impression?"

Tristan shrugged again. "I can tell. Jared's my brother, I know him, and he acts…differently around you, kinda nervous and shy. And the way he looks at you… Well, I can see it in his eyes, ya know? Do you like *him*?"

Bringing Tristan along for this ride was the worst fucking idea Nate had ever had. He squirmed in his saddle and looked out at the cattle grazing in a nearby pasture, trying to bide his time. He had to swallow down a lump that had formed in his throat before he could choke out a reply, and the answer he gave didn't come close to the strength of his feelings for one Deputy Ambrose. "Sure, kid, I like him just fine."

When Nate turned back to Tristan, the kid tore his gaze away, but not before Nate saw what looked like a triumphant grin spread wide on his face. Nate sure hoped the kid wasn't getting any ideas about him and Jared getting together. However much Nate might want that, it wasn't going to happen.

They rode for a time in a companionable silence, and when Tristan did start speaking, it was mainly about Nate's duties on the ranch. The kid seemed eager to know all the fine details of a cowboy's job. He wanted to know what time Nate got up, what his chores were, how much time he got to spend with the horses… The questions went on and on, and Nate was grateful for them. The more Nate spoke about ranching, the less time he had to think about Jared. And the kid *did* lift Nate's spirits, no doubt. The more they spoke, the more Tristan seemed to come out of himself. He smiled more and his eyes sparkled. It was a good look for him.

Everything was going great until they brought the horses back in an hour later. The closer they got to the ranch, the more Nate's stomach churned, the faster his heart beat. Sweat broke out on his brow and he chewed on his bottom lip so much he tasted blood. His emotions—his anxiety—ramped higher and higher until Nate was more on edge than he'd been before they'd set out. His body felt like a rubber band that had been stretched almost to breaking point, and he wondered how long it would take before he snapped.

Conflicting thoughts ran through Nate's mind as they rode in past the corral. He knew Tristan must have been wrong about Jared liking him. If that were true, Jared wouldn't be going on a date with someone else, would he? Just the idea of Jared with another man made Nate feel sick to his stomach, and by the time they reached the barn, Nate thought he just might throw up for real. But what if Tristan *had* been right? Jared would have said something to him, surely…unless he thought Nate wasn't interested, of course. Nate sighed and jumped down from his horse before leading him to the barn. All this thinking and thinking and Goddamn thinking was giving him a headache.

Tristan de-mounted his horse and followed Nate to the barn. As they rounded the corner, Nate saw Jared in the yard talking to Pete. They were stood close together, Pete's hand on Jared's arm. Jared threw his head back and laughed at something Pete said and a fury like Nate had never known rose inside him. His wolf was snarling within. It had never been so close to the surface and so ready to attack in such a short space of time.

What the hell were they doing together looking so cosy? Was there something going on between them? Was Pete the man Jared was meeting for his date later? Each unwelcome thought made Nate's anger more pronounced until he was practically vibrating, and before he could stop himself, he let out a long, loud, warning growl that ripped from his throat, surprising himself and everyone around him.

He was dimly aware of Tristan's gasp, but his wolf was so prominent and focused on Jared and the damn cowboy he was talking to that he couldn't reassure Tristan everything was okay. Besides…it wasn't. Everything was *far* from 'okay'.

Jared and Pete had clearly heard Nate's growl because they both jerked their heads in his direction, with mirroring expressions of surprise, before quickly heading his way. Nate balled his hands into fists at his sides and closed his eyes, taking deep breaths to try to curtail his rage.

"Nate, you okay?" Jared asked.

Nate nodded, but he waited a moment before he opened his eyes. When he did, all three men were eyeing him warily, but it was Jared that took a step forward and put his hand on Nate's shoulder, and the simple touch calmed his nerves somewhat. How was Jared able to do that?

Jared didn't take his eyes from Nate when he next spoke. "Tristan, can you take the horses inside please?"

"But—"

"Come on, Tristan, I'll help," Pete said.

Nate couldn't look at either of them, couldn't shift his gaze from Jared's, and a moment later they were thankfully alone in the yard.

"You want to talk about it?" Jared asked. "What's got you so upset?"

Now that Nate had calmed down enough to feel relatively human again, he felt pretty damn foolish. He dropped his gaze and shrugged off Jared's hand. "I…uh…" *Jesus.* What the hell was he going to say? *I was jealous? I wanted to rip Pete's Goddamn head from his shoulders then tear him limb from limb?* What?

"It's nothing."

"The hell it is. Talk to me, Nate."

Nate sighed. "Is there something going on between you and Pete?" Nate felt even more stupid when Jared's eyes widened in surprise.

"What? You mind telling me how you got that idea?"

"You said you had a date, and when I saw you Pete together, I—"

"Put two and two together," Jared finished for him.

Nate nodded. "Yeah, pretty much. Sorry, I guess it's none of my—"

"I lied," Jared interrupted.

Nate jerked his head up and stared at Jared, unsure if he'd heard him right. "You did what?"

"I lied," Jared repeated quietly.

"What do you mean, you lied?"

Jared hung his head. "Just that. I lied about going on a date. I'm not."

If Nate hadn't been holding his breath before, he was now. But he wasn't sure he understood what Jared was trying to tell him.

"Why would you do that?"

"I don't know." Jared sighed. "You looked jealous before and it made me angry, I guess. I thought you had no right when you don't... Well, when you don't..."

"When I don't what?" Nate asked, taking a step closer to the deputy.

"When you don't want me." Jared's words left his mouth in a rush.

Nate saw the bob in Jared's throat as he swallowed, and then he tore his gaze away and stared at the ground, all the blood in his body seeming to pool in his cheeks. *Is that what Jared thinks*?

"That's not true," Nate choked out, his voice sounding rough to his own ears. "Matter o' fact, you couldn't be further from the truth. It's not that I don't want you, not at all. It was never about that."

When Jared lifted his head, something that looked like hope filled his eyes and Nate couldn't resist reaching his hand up and cupping the side of his mate's face. Their eyes locked and the magnetic force that thrummed between them seemed to deepen, to grow in magnitude and intensity. Nate slowly inched closer to Jared until their lips were a hair's-breadth apart. The warm air Jared breathed out fanned over Nate's lips, teasing and enticing. Nate's heart soared in his chest. It felt like a flock of damn hummingbirds had taken up residence there. It was as though his whole life had been leading up to this moment, to him and Jared alone, together. They closed the distance and...

"There you are!" Gregory's voice broke the spell that had been cast between them and Nate tore his hand away from Jared's cheek and stepped back. The disappointment evident on Jared's face made Nate's heart stutter.

"What is it, Gregory?" Nate practically growled.

"The party's winding down. I came to see if you're both ready for our meeting."

Nate nodded. "We'll be right in."

"Uh, Kelan wanted to know if it was okay to use the bunkhouse, as the main house is still full of people."

"Tell him that's fine."

Gregory nodded then headed on back to the house. Nate took a deep breath then once again met Jared's gaze. "Do you want to—?"

"Jared?"

This time it was Jared that sighed and slumped his shoulders when his brother interrupted.

"What's up, Tristan?"

Tristan stood next to Nate, a huge grin spread across his face. "Pete just said he'd help us with the move on Wednesday before he goes to work. That was good of him, wasn't it, Nate?"

No, it wasn't fucking good of him. He'd better stay the hell away from Jared or Nate wouldn't be responsible for his actions. *Wait a minute, what move*? What was the kid talking about? Nate frowned and watched Pete exit the barn and stand behind Tristan. Nate couldn't be certain but it looked as though the wolf was reluctant to meet his gaze. *What the hell is up with that?*

"Oh, well…that's great, thanks for the offer of help, Pete," Jared said.

Pete shrugged. "'S no trouble."

"You're moving?" Nate queried.

"Yeah," Tristan said. "Forgot to tell you earlier. We got ourselves a ranch, which means we'll finally be out of that damn guesthouse."

"Watch your mouth, kid," Nate chastised.

"Right, sorry."

"Tristan and I have been staying at Marnie's Guesthouse until we could buy a place in town," Jared said. "We were real lucky. Got an offer accepted on a place not far from here."

"That's great news," Nate said, genuinely pleased for them both. If Jared had bought a place nearby then that meant he intended to stick around, and Nate liked the idea of that a lot, maybe more than he should. "So where is this place you bought? Whose place was it?"

Jared shrugged. "Don't know the family, think their name was Stanford."

Nate drew in a deep breath, unable to find any words, as he stared at Jared, his mate…who was now the proud new owner of his family's farm. Pete was rubbing the back of his neck, his gaze shifting from side to side. No wonder he couldn't look Nate in the eye. He'd known where Jared and Tristan were moving to.

"Oh, um…well that's…uh…yeah, great," Nate stuttered.

"I know," Tristan enthused. "Jared and I are finally gonna have a proper home. Hey look, there's Kelan. Who is that guy he's with? He's *huge*!"

"I think it's a friend of Kelan's from the wolf council," Pete supplied. "Guess the meeting is about to start."

Nate looked over Tristan's shoulder and saw Kelan stride in their direction with a man he hadn't seen before. Tristan was right—the guy *was* huge, and not just tall. Even from twenty feet away Nate could see the muscles stretching out his shirt.

"Oh, okay," Tristan said. "Well I guess I'll go back in the house to talk to Aaron and Cary until the meeting is over. See you all later."

"Don't cause any trouble," Jared teased.

Pete chuckled when Tristan rolled his eyes and let out a heavy and much put upon sigh. Tristan started walking towards the house when a thought occurred to Nate, and before he had a chance to process it properly, he called out to the kid.

"Hey Tristan! You need any more help with your move?"

The kid's smile was so bright and so infectious, Nate couldn't help but return the expression. It didn't seem to matter how down he was feeling, Tristan always made him feel better.

"Yeah, we can use more help. Why? You offering?"

Nate nodded. "Count me in."

Nate supposed he should have cleared his offer with Jared first, but what if Jared had turned him down? And he definitely didn't like the idea of Pete spending too much time with Jared, even if there really was nothing going on between them. Pete might be his friend but he was a damn dog. He'd be all over Jared like a rash, given half the chance.

"Cool, well then, I guess we'll see you Wednesday," Tristan said before marching towards the house with a renewed spring in his step.

"I need to have a word with Kelan," Pete said. "I'll see you both inside."

"Sure, Pete," Jared said. "And thanks again."

"Yeah, see you, Pete."

Jared waited until they were alone again before he began to speak. "Thanks for the offer. You didn't have to, you know."

Nate shrugged. "Figured you could use the extra help."

"We can. So? Are you going to tell me what got your cage so rattled just then?"

"Huh?"

"When Tristan and I told you about our move, you got this weird look on your face…kinda sad. What is it? I heard the man that used to live there, Rick, was killed earlier this year. Did you know him?"

Nate pulled in a deep, calming breath and took a moment to gather his thoughts before answering. The wretched lump rose in his throat and he had to swallow it down before he spoke. He was getting damn used to that lump, but it never got any easier to swallow. "Rick was my brother. We grew up in that house. My family used to rent the spread…for a long time, actually."

Jared scrunched his eyebrows together. "What? You didn't want to live there anymore? Didn't you consider buying the place when the owners put it up for sale?"

Nate took off his hat and scratched the top of his head. The strange thing was that Nate wasn't even as upset as he would have expected him to be. He was glad that Jared and Tristan were moving into his old home. He couldn't think of two better people to live there, and he didn't want to upset Jared by telling him the truth, but neither could he lie.

"Yeah," he said at last, holding Jared's gaze. "I did—put several offers in, actually—but I was outbid."

Chapter Seven

"Okay before we start, for those of you who don't know him, this is a friend of mine, Dean White. Dean holds a position on the Supernatural Council," Kelan said, gesturing to the man in question.

Introductions were made and pleasantries exchanged. Jared took a seat at the kitchen table and rubbed at his palm, which still tingled from where Dean had squeezed it when they'd shaken hands. Describing it as a firm grip would be somewhat of an understatement—the man's hands were like shovels…large shovels. But they were by no means out of place on his enormous body. Jared was damn near six foot but he felt dwarfed by this giant of a wolf. It was impossible to guess his age, though. While he was certainly older than anyone in the room, his face had a timeless quality to it.

"You have some powerful friends," Gregory said, eyeing the man warily. "Mr White has an influential position in the council."

Dean shook his head. "Not so much anymore, I'm afraid. Since the numbers within the council increased to satisfy the needs of the shifter population boom in recent years, my responsibility has decreased. I've always been very outspoken about my views on keeping our identities secret, so whether or not that has hindered my standing in the council, I'm not sure. The jury is out, but one would assume my bluntness about the matter hasn't helped my cause."

Nate, who had taken the seat next to Jared, remained quiet, but he didn't need to speak for Jared to be aware of his presence. They were so close together that Jared could feel the heat radiating from the wolf's slightly larger body. His scent permeated Jared's senses, too, making it damn near impossible to concentrate on a single word that was being spoken in the meeting.

Jared still couldn't believe what Nate had told him earlier. Of all the houses he could have bought in Wolf Creek, he'd purchased Nate's home—his mate's. What were the odds? The worst part was that Nate had been fighting to keep his family home, and he'd lost it. He must have been heartbroken. Jared felt sick about that, and he didn't know what to do about it. Should he offer to sell the property back to Nate?

"You make it sound as though there is some sort of conspiracy against you," Nate said, tearing Jared from his thoughts.

"I believe there is," Dean replied. "As a matter of fact, I'm certain of it. I've been investigating a number of members within the council for months now who I believe to have been conspiring against me, and I'm quite sure there is some type of subversion afoot."

"You took a chance coming here today, didn't you?" Gregory asked. "You know Ashton and I work for the council. How do you know we are to be trusted?"

"You have a valid point, Mr Monroe." Dean grinned and for the first time since he'd arrived, his expression changed from one of friendly openness to something Jared couldn't quite place. Whatever it was, it gave him chills. "But I assure you everyone in this room has been *thoroughly* vetted before my arrival here today."

Jared frowned. He didn't like the idea that someone had been nosing around in his personal business. Not that he had anything to hide, but still.

"You said you've been investigating members of the council," Jared said. "What exactly did you find out?"

Dean pursed his lips. "Has anyone here heard of a wolf shifter named Michaels? Stan Michaels?"

When Jared gazed around the room, mostly everyone present was shaking their heads, including him. But Gregory and Ashton's faces had paled and they stared at one another for a long moment, their eyebrows pulled together in matching frowns.

"We know of him," Ashton said coolly. There seemed to be a trace of bitterness in his voice, hatred certainly.

"We've never met him personally," Gregory continued for his partner. "But his name was given to us recently when we investigated...*something*."

Gregory's gaze flickered to Ashton's and when Jared looked at the bird shifter he saw the same haunted look in his eyes that he'd seen in his office a few days earlier. Neither Gregory nor Ashton elaborated and Dean, it appeared, was watching them both closely through narrowed eyes, his lips pursed. Jared had no doubt the man knew what they were referring to. He seemed like the type who didn't let anything go under his radar.

"I'm not surprised that no one in the room but council members has heard of him," Dean continued.

"Although Stan has been a high ranking member of the Supernatural Council for years, he has always kept a fairly low profile. However I've recently learned that he is one of the key instigators in the bid to expose us all, and he has a lot of supporters. Too many. I'd go as far as to say he is the right at the top of the food chain, so to speak."

"But having an opinion as to how shifters should live their lives isn't a criminal offence," Jared argued. "Surely there's nothing that can be done to prevent the man from having his say, even if he is influencing a lot of people."

Dean nodded. "That's true, of course, but my investigations have led me to a few discoveries about Mr Michaels. Let's just say not all of his actions have been carried out within the scope of the law."

Jared noticed the silent exchange between Gregory and Ashton. "Do you have proof?" Gregory asked.

"No, that I don't, which is where all of you come in."

"What is it you think we can do?" Pete asked. "Other than Gregory and Ashton, none of us here have any connections in the council. We'd never get anywhere near council headquarters or this Stan Michaels."

"I have to agree with Pete," Nate said, "I don't see what any of us here would be able to do."

"You'd be surprised." Dean looked at each of them in turn. "You can all do more than you think. Some of my intel suggests Mr Michaels is doing business with someone here in Wolf Creek. Their activities are far from legal and this person has also joined the bid to expose us."

Kelan let out a low growl and his eyes darkened. Jared could practically feel the anger radiating from the alpha from where he sat.

"Someone in my pack? Who is it?" Kelan demanded.

"A Mr Joe Walker."

Gasps and murmurs spread throughout the room, getting louder and louder as each second ticked by.

"Son of a bitch!" Kelan raged.

Jared pursed his lips, his mind wandering to the day of the fight in Jessie's. "Would Mr Michaels happen to have a black sedan with tinted windows?"

Dean fixed his gaze on Jared's and the look he gave him made Jared shiver. "He does, how did you know?"

"I was at Joe's place, right before a fight broke out at Jessie's Dancehall the other day. As I was leaving, I passed the sedan. At the time I thought it was unusual—you don't see many cars like that around here—but then I got to Jessie's and had to deal with all the trouble and it went right out of my head. What exactly are they involved in?"

"A number of things, I believe, one being insurance scams, false claims…that sort of thing. But I also know that Joe has been giving Mr Michaels information about the town and its residents. I'm not entirely sure what Stan is doing with that information but I would assume he's identifying the troublemakers. I wouldn't be surprised if he's been getting someone to pay them a visit, to incite them."

"Goddamn it. I'm going to kill the old weasel," Kelan growled.

"I think it's best not to be hasty," Dean replied. "It would do us good to observe them together, see if we can catch them doing something illegal. If we can get them that way, it would stop this looking like a personal vendetta against Michaels because we don't like his views on shifter rights."

"Would any of these insurance scams have to do with missing livestock?" Jared asked, an idea forming.

"It very well might," Dean answered. "Why do you ask?"

"That's what I was doing at Joe's place that day. He said his bull had been stolen, said it cost him ten thousand dollars. And that wasn't the only one—he's reported three others missing in the last month. Actually, he pointed the finger at Kelan and his brothers. At the time, I thought it was sour grapes because of what happened with his son, but with everything I know now, I'm thinking this Michaels told him to accuse Kelan. It would cast aspersions on his character and doubt on his leadership abilities."

Kelan nodded. "I think you might be right."

"So what can we do about all of this?" Nate asked.

"The most important thing, for now, is to ensure the council has no cause for concern where Kelan's leadership is concerned. That will mean keeping a close eye on the main troublemakers here in town.

"As Mr Ambrose works for the sheriff's department, he'll have a better idea than most who to look out for, and of course Kelan's betas will need to be more involved should any situations arise."

Kelan sighed. "I'm down to two betas, Dean. It will be difficult for us to be everywhere at once."

Stefan was standing near the door and had thus far kept quiet, but after Kelan's statement, he loudly cleared his throat. "You know how I feel about pack politics, Kelan, but this is something important—something we all have to fight for if we want to keep hold of the lifestyle we've all grown accustomed to. You can count me in to help."

His mate Cody patted his back then slipped an arm around his waist, a proud smile stretched across his face.

Kelan nodded. "Thank you."

"I agree with Stefan," Pete said. "This is important. I'd be happy to be more involved."

"Thanks, Pete."

"And you have *three* betas, not two," Nate said. "I'll do what I can, too."

Kelan smiled warmly. "Appreciate that, Nate."

Jared sucked in a sharp breath. Did Nate just agree to be Kelan's beta? Jared turned to Nate and scowled. "You'll *what*? What if you get hurt?"

Nate's eyebrows skyrocketed and his mouth fell open in surprise. He stared at Jared for what felt like an eternity before his features softened and he chuckled, the corners of his eyes crinkling as he smiled. "In case you didn't notice Jared, I'm a big boy."

When the rest of the room chuckled along with Nate, Jared sank a little lower in his chair, feeling his face fill with heat. He just couldn't keep his fool mouth shut, could he?

It was Pete that chuckled loudest. "I can attest to that," he joked.

Jared's blood started to boil as his wolf quickly rose to the surface, ready to pounce. He turned on Pete and glared, a low growl erupting from somewhere inside. "He's *mine*!" he roared.

Pete recoiled, holding his hands up in front of him. "Sorry, Jared. I didn't mean anything by that, I... Wait, what?"

Oh God. Jared wanted the floor to open up and swallow him when he looked around the room and realised all eyes were on him. So much for keeping their mating a secret. It was of little consolation that Gregory, Ashton and Kelan already knew, but even they looked shocked by Jared's outburst.

But the one person Jared couldn't look at was the one person whose opinion mattered most—Nate.

"Uh, sorry," he mumbled to the room at large.

"Jared," Nate said quietly. "Look at me."

Nope. Jared shook his head. He was afraid to look at Nate. He'd made an idiot of himself and he felt wretched with both shame and embarrassment. And he knew everyone in the room was still watching him. He could feel their eyes on him, practically hear their confused thoughts. Nate sighed and placed his hand under Jared's chin, forcing his head up. Jared's face was on fire. He was tempted to close his eyes, anything to block out what he was afraid he might see on Nate's face, but when he caught Nate's expression, the wolf didn't look angry or upset. He was wearing the most beautiful smile Jared had ever laid eyes on. It lit up his entire face and his eyes all but danced. Nate looked positively triumphant.

Just when Jared thought he might pass out from lack of oxygen from holding his breath for so long, Nate leant forward and mashed their lips together, stealing what little breath Jared had left in his lungs. Just like that, in front of a room full of people, Nate kissed him, and it was no small kiss. It was hard, demanding and fervent, almost as though Nate were staking his claim. The groan that tore from Jared's chest when Nate's tongue slipped into his mouth and he tasted him for the first time surprised even him. Jared's wolf was howling within, elated. Eventually, Nate pulled back from the all-consuming kiss and turned to Jared's right.

"Pete," Nate said, the dorkiest smile covering his lips. "I'd like to introduce you to my mate."

The elation Nate felt from proclaiming Jared as his mate was short-lived. When his wolf calmed, Nate returned to his senses and turned to Jared, noting the expression on his mate's face. The room erupted into cheers and back pats and well wishes, but Nate was only dimly aware of them all as he stared at Jared, who looked as though he might throw up. He wasn't the only one. Nate's stomach was somewhere in his throat. What the hell had he just done?

It was obvious that Jared's retort to Pete had been a gut reaction, something instinctual brought on by their mating bond, and one he might have been able to explain away if Nate had kept his big mouth shut. But it was too late for that now. The proverbial cat was out of the bag and there would be no shoving it back inside.

"Why didn't you say something, old man?" Pete said, adding another slap to Nate's back.

"Uh..." *Shit.* Nate had no fucking clue how to answer.

"That was my fault," Jared said, saving him. "I asked Nate to keep our bond a secret. I'd like to make sheriff and I don't think that will happen if people around town know I'm gay."

"Well hell, you gotta know it wouldn't come from any of us," Pete said. "'Sides, I don't think many folks around here would have a problem with it. Look at Kelan—he's gay and he's about the best alpha this town has ever had. Folks know it, too."

"Yes, but the humans and..." Jared pleaded with his eyes for Nate to help.

"Look, everyone, thanks for the congratulations and all, but can we ask you to keep this among yourselves, please?" When Nate looked around the room there were a lot of confused faces and he couldn't say he blamed them.

Cody was the first to speak up about what they all must have been thinking.

"If that's what you both want, then of course we will," he said, "but a mating bond is something to be celebrated. I think you might regret keeping it a secret."

"Cody," Stefan chastised. "It's their choice. If they don't want anyone to know, well…that's up to them."

Cody's shoulders sagged and his expression became contrite. "Sorry," he mumbled. "You're right, of course. Just ignore me."

"On that note," Kelan said, "I think we can call an end to this meeting. I'll liaise with Dean to see what information we can discover on Joe and Stan and if we need help from anyone, we'll call on you. Oh, and Nate, Jared?"

When Nate turned, the alpha was smiling encouragingly at him.

"Congratulations," he said. "I'm happy for you both."

Nate returned the smile but he was too afraid to look at Jared to see what his expression might be.

The bunkhouse kitchen cleared out pretty quickly but Jared remained seated, so Nate stayed where he was, too. When the last wolf had exited, Nate finally lifted his head to look at his mate. Thankfully Jared didn't look upset or angry but there was definitely confusion clouding his features.

"I'm sorry," Nate said. "I don't know what came over me. I shouldn't have kissed you, I shouldn't have said that."

Jared lifted the corners of his mouth but the smile was devoid of humour. He shook his head. "It was my fault. When Pete made that comment about you, it made me angry and I guess my wolf reacted badly."

"Yeah, I realise that. Pete was just goofing off, so's you know. There's nothing going on between us, hasn't been for a lot of years now."

"Was that the real reason you were so upset when you saw Pete and I together in the yard earlier? Are you in love with him?"

"Jesus, *no* Jared." Nate grabbed hold of Jared's hand and squeezed it tightly in his own, his eyes pleading with his mate to understand. "When I saw you together and I thought there was something going on between you, my first reaction was that I wanted to kill *Pete*. It was about jealousy, sure, but not in the way you think, not *for* Pete. I swear to God."

Jared nodded and lowered his gaze. "Okay."

Where the hell did they go from here? Nate sighed heavily. Essentially nothing had changed. Sure a few more people knew of their mating, but if Jared was so set on making sheriff, then they could never be fully open about any relationship they might form. And Nate wasn't even sure it was a relationship *he* wanted, didn't even know if he was capable of one. Nate didn't know *what* the hell he wanted.

But he knew what he wanted for Jared. He wanted him to smile again, to be happy, and as he stared at his mate—who looked so deflated, so torn—Nate knew he'd do whatever the hell it took to accomplish that.

"Nate, about your house... When I put the bid in, I had no idea. If I'd known, I... I'd be happy to sell it back to you. I'm sure Tristan and I will be able to find something else."

Nate shook his head. He didn't even have to think about his reply. Yes he'd been sorry to lose out in the bidding, but Jared was his mate and he and Tristan needed a home, and that was all Nate needed to know.

"Thank you for asking, I can't tell you how much it means to me that you did, but no. I'm happy you and Tristan are going to be living there. It feels… right. I wouldn't want it any other way. Besides, it's a big old house, too big for me to rambling about in on my own. No, this is perfect."

"Thank you," Jared said simply. His mouth slowly curved up into a smile that was so warm and so bright it set Nate's heart alight. It made him forget everything. All his worries, cares, insecurities… They all vanished as though they'd never been there at all. Nate could gladly spend a lifetime looking at that smile. As soon as the thought flashed through Nate's mind, it made him both unbelievably joyful and inconsolable, all at the same time.

Nate knew without question that Jared could make him happy for the rest of his life, but could he do the same for Jared? If only it were that simple. Nate was a realist. Life wasn't always the bed of roses people wanted it to be. But the longer Nate looked at that smile—drank it in, basked in it—the more he wished for a happy ending for them both.

A low growl carried through the door, and then something that sounded like…purring? When Nate looked across, he saw Aaron was backing Cary into the room, their mouths fused together, while Aaron's hands disappeared into the back of Cary's pants. After a moment, Aaron broke the kiss.

"I've been wanting to get you alone all day," he rasped.

Nate cleared his throat. "Uh, I hate to tell you this but you're not alone."

Cary yelped and leapt out of Aaron's arms, dislodging the wolf's hands. Mouth agape, his gaze flitted back and forth between Nate and Jared and a furious blush spread across his cheeks. Nate felt for the kid.

"Crap," Cary squeaked.

"Uh, yeah, we thought—"

"You were alone?" Jared said around a chuckle. "Yeah, we got that part."

Aaron grinned, seemingly amused by the look of mortification on his mate's face. "Sorry," he said with a slight shrug of his shoulders. Being caught didn't appear to bother Aaron in the slightest. "Thought everyone had cleared out. Hey, Tristan's looking for you outside."

Jared got up from his seat and crossed to the door. "Thanks, I'll go find him." He turned back to Nate before he left the room, eyebrows raised. "See you Wednesday?"

Nate's answering was smile was so wide his face ached. "Wednesday," he replied.

Chapter Eight

Jared was halfway up the steps of the porch, large cardboard box in hand, when Nate's car pulled into the drive, next to the removal van. He was so nervous, he nearly dropped the box.

"Hey, watch it!" Tristan barrelled past him and down the stairs. "Mom's crystal is in that box."

Jared grunted and headed for the living room. He had no idea what they were going to do with four large boxes full of crystal ornaments but he hadn't had the heart to throw them out when he'd packed up the contents of their rented house in Lubbock. He set the box down carefully and took a look at the others, piled high around the room. The removal men had turned up an hour earlier than expected and they were making good progress but he had no clue where everything was going to go.

"Jared, look who's here." Tristan entered the room with Nate following in his wake, each of them lugging a large, white box.

"Uh, where does this go?" Nate asked, looking around at the already overcrowded room.

"Just dump it anywhere," Tristan replied.

Nate found a space near the window, put down the box, then turned to face Jared, his mouth curving into tentative smile. "Hi."

Jared tried to ignore the goosebumps that covered his arms and the shiver that ran down his spine. He met Nate's gaze and returned the smile, feeling absurdly shy all of a sudden. "Hey."

"How are you?" Nate enquired.

"I'm okay. Your face looks good."

When Nate raised a curious brow, Jared felt the onset of a blush creeping up his face and spreading across his cheeks. "Uh, I mean the scar, it's...uh, healed."

"Oh, right." Nate waved a hand in the general direction. "Yeah, I shifted."

Tristan's head was swivelling back and forth watching the exchange with piqued interest. "Wow, you two are like a couple of teenage girls," he remarked.

Jared was still glaring at his brother when they heard an almighty crash in the hall.

"I'm going to kill them!" Tristan growled, rushing from the room.

"Guess I'd better see what they broke," Jared said.

Nate grinned. "If it was anything expensive you should take it out of their fee."

Jared chuckled. "I will, believe me. Thanks for helping out today."

Nate shrugged and stuffed his hands into the pockets of his jeans. "It's no trouble. Actually it's nice to see the old place again."

"You sure you're good with this?"

"Yeah, more than. Pete not here yet?"

Jared shook his head. "Couldn't make it. He said Kelan asked him to do something last minute and he couldn't let him down."

"Oh?" Nate raised an eyebrow. "That's a shame."

"Yeah." Jared nodded his agreement, but he wasn't sorry Pete was busy—he was glad because it meant he got to spend more time with Nate. Whether that was a good thing or not, he hadn't decided. Judging by the look on Nate's face, *he* definitely wasn't disappointed, despite his words to the contrary.

As it turned out, the crash had been a box containing framed family photographs. The glass had broken in a few but the frames had made it unscathed. Three hours and a broken vase later, Jared was watching the van pull out of the drive.

With a weary sigh, he walked back into the living room and sat down heavily on the modular sofa, his muscles tired and sore. Tristan was perched in the middle and Nate sat the other end, his long, muscular-looking legs stretched out in front of him.

"Damn. Remind me not to move for at least another fifty years," Jared said, rolling his shoulders and cricking his neck.

"Why would you want to?" Tristan asked. "You've got everything you could want right here. Hasn't he, Nate?"

Jared frowned and stared at his brother. Just what was Tristan up to exactly? He'd been making strange comments for the past week but their frequency had increased since Nate shown up earlier.

Nate scratched the top of his head. "Uh, yeah kid, suppose he has."

"You mind if we leave the unpacking until tomorrow?" Tristan asked. "I've got plans tonight."

Jared narrowed his eyes. "What sort of plans? You're not going to Jessie's again, are you?"

"Have I been to Jessie's in the last few days?"

Now that Jared came to think on it, Tristan hadn't been back to the bar since the day before Luke and Mark's party. "Guess not, so where you going?"

"I'm meeting Aaron and Cary at the Crazy Horse. They said we can take the horses out to the river."

"Really?"

Tristan rolled his eyes. "Yeah, really. You mind?"

"No. Of course not. Uh…have fun."

Tristan grinned and got up from the sofa. "Thanks. I'm gonna go get ready."

When Tristan left the room Jared turned to Nate, eyebrows raised. "Well I'll be damned."

"What is it?"

"It's just good to see him get out and make friends, I guess. Tristan hasn't been interested in much of anything at all since our Pop died…well, other than getting trashed."

"Aaron and Cary are both good kids, looks like they made an impression on him."

"Yeah, guess they did. I'm glad he's cut down on the drinking at least. I was starting to worry about him. Jesus, speaking of alcohol, I could use a cold beer myself right about now."

Nate's eyes widened. "Crap, I forgot! Wait right here."

Jared looked on in confusion as Nate got up from the sofa and rushed out of the room, heading for the front door. A couple of minutes later he returned carrying a large cool box.

"Left this in the trunk." Nate opened the lid of the box and rooted around inside. "Nearly forgot about it until you mentioned beer." Pulling out a couple of cans, Nate handed one to Jared. "Figured you wouldn't have time to get anything in, with the move and all, so I brought supplies."

Jared scooted to the edge of the sofa and peered into the box. "Wow, thanks Nate, this is great."

Nate shrugged. "It's not much, just some coffee, sugar, sandwich fixings. Just to tide you over until you can get to the grocery store. And beer, of course—the most important item after a hard day's work."

Jared found himself grinning broadly, touched by Nate's gesture. "Thank you, really, I appreciate this."

Nate took a seat on the sofa, only this time he sat in the middle, closer to Jared, and stretched his legs out in front of him. Jared's gaze was immediately drawn to those strong, powerful legs. Muscular thighs led up to a lean torso, a broad chest, long neck and... Jared licked his lips. When he made it to Nate's face he realised the cowboy had been watching him salivate over his body, and he tore his gaze away, embarrassed.

"Sorry," he mumbled.

Nate chuckled and the sound was deep, husky. Jared's breath came faster.

"Can't say as I haven't been checking you out all day either."

When they next locked gazes, Nate's eyes were smiling, practically teasing, and it made Jared chuckle, too.

"What are we doing here, Nate?"

Nate sighed. "I wish I knew. I don't have any answers, don't even know what the questions are anymore. All I know is, I like being around you. Feels...*right*."

"Yeah, same here."

"I'm sorry for what I did the other day…you know, when I kissed you."

Jared felt a stabbing pain in his chest and suddenly there was no air left in his lungs. He might wish that things had happened differently between he and Nate, but there was no way he could regret that kiss. He'd thought about it every damn day since. It had kept him awake at nights. He swallowed, hard. "You're…sorry?"

Nate nodded. "Yeah. I mean, I'm not sorry we kissed, but it should never have happened like that, not in a room full of people. It should have been in private, when we were alone together…like now."

"Oh…" Jared drew a breath and stared at Nate. The tension in the room was palpable. Every nerve ending in Jared's body was on high alert, poised, waiting for something it seemed they both wanted. Nate snaked his tongue out and wet his lips. The action drew Jared's attention there and he found he couldn't look away.

Nate's eyes darkened as he leaned in closer, his gaze fixed on Jared's mouth. Jared's heart rate must have been off the charts. They were inches apart and…

"Hey, I'm heading out now. Can I have the keys to the truck?" Tristan asked, striding into the room.

Jared jumped back as though he'd been stung. "Uh, sure." He fished the keys out of his pocket and threw them to his brother. "What time you back?"

"Don't know, why? Am I on a curfew?"

"It was only a question, Tristan."

Tristan looked at the beers in their hands and grinned, sheepishly. "You sleeping over, Nate?"

"What?" Nate practically squeaked.

"You know you shouldn't drink and drive, right?"

"Uh, 'm just having the one," Nate mumbled.

"Right, well, see you both later. Thanks for the help, Nate."

"It was no trouble. See you, kid," Nate said.

Jared jumped up from the sofa and followed his brother to the front door. "Don't forget your promise," he said.

Tristan stopped halfway down the porch steps and turned. "What promise?"

"That you're gonna go by Joe's place as soon as we're settled to ask about a job."

"Oh, that promise, right. Haven't forgot, top of my to-do list. See you!"

"Yeah, bye."

Jared closed the front door and nearly jumped out of his skin when he turned and Nate was stood beside him. "Jeez, you scared the hell outta me."

"Sorry, guess I should get going," Nate said. "Got an early start tomorrow."

"Oh, of course." Jared tried to hide his disappointment but it was no easy task. "Well, thanks for helping out today, I'm grateful. Uh, we both are."

Nate nodded. "No problem."

The seconds ticked by as they stood in the hallway, neither man sure of what to say or do next. Tristan hadn't been far off the mark. Jared *did* feel like a damn teenage girl. Did he kiss Nate on the cheek as they said goodbye? Would they arrange to meet again? Did Nate even want that? Why did this have to be so Goddamn hard? They were mates for Christ's sake—talking, being together, should come as easily as breathing. Then Jared realised something. Actually all that stuff did come easy. *Being* with Nate was easy…it was being apart that was hard. With that thought in mind, Jared lifted his hands, threaded them through Nate's hair and pressed their lips together.

Jared wasn't sure who groaned the loudest when their lips made contact but he didn't care. Nothing mattered but the kiss, the combined beating of their hearts and the electric current that arced between them, joining them as though they were one life force in two bodies. When Nate deepened the kiss, slipping his tongue inside Jared's mouth, all rational thought fled. They both wanted this…hell, they needed it.

Seconds turned into minutes, minutes could have been days, so lost was Jared in the kiss that was setting his body alight and making his heart dance inside his chest. A low, needy growl ripped from Nate's throat and he lifted Jared, twisted him and pressed him up against the wall before taking his mouth again with a fierce possessiveness Jared felt all the way down to his toes.

Jared could barely breathe but he was terrified to pull back, terrified that it would all end and he wouldn't have this moment again. *What if this is it? What if this is all Nate's prepared to give?* Each thought made Jared's head spin and his heart ache and so he put everything into the kiss and more. It was only when he tasted blood that he realised his incisors had lengthened and he'd bitten into Nate's lip, but he still didn't stop…couldn't.

Their hard cocks ground together roughly. Jared was so turned on he was afraid he might come in his damn pants. Nate reached a hand down and palmed him through his jeans and Jared threw his head back and yelled out Nate's name. He was so close to the brink, but he wanted more, he needed…

"Hey Jared, I forgot my—"

Jared gasped when Nate pulled back from the kiss and they both turned to stare at the door. Tristan was standing there, eyebrows raised and a shit-eating grin spread across his face.

"Well it's about damn time," Tristan said, rushing forward and throwing his arms around Nate's torso, hugging him close.

Nate met Jared's eyes over the top of Tristan's head and looked as shocked and confused as he felt. *What the hell?*

"Watch your language, kid," Nate said automatically.

"Right, sorry." When Tristan pulled back he didn't look sorry at all. He was still grinning from ear to ear. "Welcome to the family," he said.

Jared couldn't process what was going on, and he couldn't get his damn teeth to shift back either. It was small consolation, but Nate's eyes and teeth had shifted, too.

"You knew?" Jared asked.

"Well duh." Tristan rolled his eyes. "I was standing next to Kelan when you guys found out."

Jared closed his eyes and scrubbed a hand down his face, trying to remember the events at Jessie's. It had been less than two weeks ago, but it might just as well have been a couple of years. "Why didn't you say anything?"

Tristan's grin got wider. "I could ask you the same damn question. Uh, sorry," he said, wincing at Nate. "I know how stubborn you can be and I figured Nate was just as bad, but I knew you guys would work it out eventually. I mean, you've got to, right? You're mates."

Right, mates. Why couldn't everything be as simple as it seemed to a twenty-one-year-old without cares or responsibilities?

"So now that you've finally come to your senses," Tristan ploughed on, "I guess we'll be seeing more of you, eh Nate?"

"Uh..."

"Why don't you come to dinner on Saturday?"

Nate closed his eyes and shook his head. Jared watched as he took a couple of deep breaths. When he opened his eyes again, they had shifted back to their human form and his teeth had shrunken back into his gums.

"Thanks for the invite, Tristan, but I'm busy Saturday, and I don't think I'll be up to doing anything in the evening."

"Oh, you're busy, huh." Tristan looked disappointed.

Nate nodded. "I'm going to visit my Pop. He's in a nursing home a couple of hours drive from here." Nate turned his gaze on Jared, his face hopeful. "Would you like to come with me?"

* * * *

Nate got out of his truck and crossed the yard to the steps that led up to his old home. He pulled off his cowboy hat as he climbed, patting down the top of his head, trying to tame his unruly locks. His heart beat furiously in his chest. He felt like a damn high school student about to collect their date for the prom. Well, Nate supposed this was what they felt like—he'd given his own prom a wide berth. He'd known he was gay by then, didn't even doubt it, so there was no way he was going to spend his evening slow dancing with girls.

He looked down at the clothes he'd chosen and chewed on his bottom lip, tucking the corner of his pale blue shirt into his jeans. Had he put on the right outfit? Shaking his head at his asinine behaviour, he lifted his hand to knock on the front door. It opened before he got the chance.

"Hi Nate!" Tristan whizzed past him and down the steps. "Bye Nate!"

Nate's mouth curved up into an amused smirk. "Where you off to in such a hurry?"

"I'm meeting Aaron and Cary," Tristan threw over his shoulder. "See you!"

Tristan climbed into Jared's SUV and screeched out of the yard without another word, tyres kicking up dust. Nate chuckled and turned to walk into the house but Jared was blocking his path. Just the sight of the deputy made Nate's breath come faster. He smiled.

"Hey, you ready?"

Jared nodded and stepped out onto the porch, closing the door behind him. "Yeah…uh, you sure about this? Bringing me along, I mean."

Nate frowned. "If you don't want to come, you—"

"No! I want to! I mean, are you sure you want me to meet your dad? Will he be okay with that?"

Nate lowered his gaze and twirled the Stetson in his hands. "I don't think it will be a problem. Pop has dementia, he barely recognises me when I visit. He has good days and bad but most often he's not…lucid."

Jared laid a comforting hand on Nate's arm. "Must be hard to see him like that."

Nate nodded. "Yeah. Gets harder every damn time."

They made it out of Wolf Creek and onto the freeway. Nate's nerves had calmed considerably but his arousal had kicked up ten notches. Jared's scent filled the space in his truck, making him practically light-headed. He had to use all his concentration to stop his eyes and teeth from shifting. That was the last thing he needed to happen when he was driving. His cock was like a damn lead pipe in his jeans. He was desperate to reach down and adjust himself, but he was too embarrassed.

Jared let out a small moan and when Nate turned to look at him, he was squirming in his seat, his hands covering his crotch. "Do you mind if we open the windows?"

"Uh, sure." Okay, so maybe they both had the same problem.

Nate gulped down the fresh air that rushed in. It helped somewhat but didn't alleviate the problem altogether. Jared was seated too damn close for comfort.

"How long has your dad been in the nursing home?"

"Three years." Nate honked his horn at a car that overtook and then slowed down in front of him, causing him to brake. Why the hell did people do that? *Idiots.*

"Are you the only person that visits him?"

"Naw, got a sister. She goes to see him couple times a week, but she lives closer than me."

"Do you see her often?"

"Never. We don't speak. My sister and her husband don't like the fact I'm gay."

"You don't think she'll come around?"

Normally Nate would be changing the subject right about now, but he didn't mind talking to Jared about his family, so he ploughed on.

"I'm sorry to say that's never gonna happen. They're both pretty stuck in their ways. When my brother Rick was killed, my sister didn't even contact me to let me know. I had to hear it from Kelan."

"Wow, that's harsh. Were you close to your brother?"

Nate sighed. "When we were younger, yeah, but we hadn't spoken in two years when he passed." Nate was about to let the subject drop but he found himself wanting to open up to Jared, to confide in him.

"We argued over our father. It was bad. Pop's dementia had started and it was becoming more and more difficult to look after him. I was down as his next of kin so I made the decision to put him in the nursing home. Rick didn't agree with me, said we could care for him ourselves, but there was no way.

"I came home from work one day to find the back door wide open and him gone. I shifted and tracked his scent all the way into town. I found him at the graveyard, near my mom's grave. He was naked and it was still light out. Must have shifted back when he got there. Humans could have seen him, you know? That was just one incident of many, so I put him in the nursing home. My brother and I fell out after that. We had a huge argument. He told me I was being selfish, that he hated me, never wanted to see me again, so I left."

Jared reached his hand across the small space and placed it on Nate's knee. "I'm so sorry, but I'm sure your brother didn't mean what he said. People say terrible things in the heat of the moment and it's hard to take them back. For what it's worth, you did the right thing. Wolves with dementia are unpredictable, dangerous. I'm sure it wasn't an easy decision to make."

When Nate next spoke his voice with thick with emotion. "One of the hardest things I've ever had to do. Only one thing tops it."

"What was that?" Jared asked.

Nate took his eyes off the road and met Jared's gaze. "Rejecting you the day we met."

Jared sighed heavily and squeezed Nate's knee. "For me too," he whispered. "For me too."

An hour later they were pulling up alongside the intercom box in front of the large, electronic gates that guarded the entrance of the nursing home. Nate gave his name and when the gates swung open with a loud creak, he made his way up the sweeping drive. Armed guards surrounded the grounds.

The parking lot at the back of the building housed only a few cars, so Nate pulled up near the door and killed the engine.

"You ready to go in?" Jared asked.

Nate nodded and unbuckled his seatbelt. "As ready as I'll ever be. Thanks for coming with me."

"I'm glad you asked. You shouldn't have to do this alone."

Nate led Jared through the building to the nurses' station where they both signed in before heading down the hallway to his father's room. Nate stopped outside and took a deep breath to calm his nerves before pushing open the door. His father sat in an armchair near the window.

"Hey Pop," Nate said, crossing the small space.

"Rick?"

Nate swallowed and shook his head. "No, Pop, it's Nate."

His father nodded and turned to look out the window. "My eyesight's not as good as it used to be. Where's Rick?"

Nate sighed. "Rick couldn't make it today, Pop…had to work."

Jared raised a curious brow, but he didn't comment.

"I brought someone to meet you, Pop. This is Jared, he's the deputy sheriff in Wolf Creek. Jared's my m—" Nate cut off what he was about to say. He didn't know if Jared would want him to introduce them as mates so he left it at that.

His father raked his eyes over Jared then turned to Nate and scowled. "You in trouble again?"

Jared chuckled, strode across the room and shook the old man's hand. "Good to meet you, sir. I'm Nate's mate, and no, he's not in any trouble."

The casual way Jared made the declaration made Nate's heart skip a beat, and a happy smile spread across his face.

"Oh, that's nice," his Pop said. "I'll have to get Lillian to invite you boys over for supper." He turned to stare once again out the window.

"Who's Lillian?" Jared mouthed to Nate.

"My mom," Nate mouthed back.

Jared's mouth curved sympathetically, but when he turned to Nate's father again, his smile was bright. "Thank you, sir, I'd love to come for supper."

"How you doing, Pop?" Nate asked, taking a seat on the small bed, next to his father's chair. Nate handed him a small paper bag and smiled when Jared sat down next to him.

His father shrugged. "Some damn lunatic down the hall keeps screaming all times of day and night. I'm telling you if he doesn't quit his antics, I'm going to go down there and rip him a new one." His father peeked into the bag. "Candy?"

"Yep, Werther's Butterscotch, your favourite."

He popped one into his mouth and grimaced. "Tastes like shit."

Nate caught Jared trying to stifle a grin and it made him smile, too.

"What do you say I bring you some peppermint next time? Maybe next week?" Jared asked, reaching into the bag to snag a piece of candy.

Nate's smile got even wider. So Jared planned on coming back with him? He wasn't sure what that meant for them both but the idea that there would be a next time, and soon, made him incredibly happy.

His father shook his head. "Gives me gas."

Jared laughed out loud, his eyes dancing. "Right, I'll keep that in mind."

This was the most lucid Nate had seen his father in a long time. Nate could almost make himself believe his father was back to his old self…almost. Everything was going great until his Pop turned to him again and asked, "Where's Rick?"

Jared put a hand on Nate's knee and answered for him. "Had to work, sir."

Nate gave a grateful nod of his head but he didn't trust his voice enough to speak.

An hour later, Nate rose from his position on the bed and bent to kiss his father on the forehead. "Gotta hit the road, Pop, but I'll come back and see you next week, okay?"

His father nodded. "I'll tell Lillian you came by."

Nate sighed. "Right, Pop."

"It was great to meet you, sir," Jared said. "Hope you don't mind if I come and visit you again."

"Naw, don't mind none."

Just before they left the room Nate's father called out, "Hey, Jared!"

"Sir?"

Nate was surprised his father had remembered Jared's name. The old man pinned Jared in place with a pointed stare, and it reminded Nate of when he was younger and his Pop would chastise him for something he'd done wrong—there had always been something. "You treat my son right, ya hear?"

Jared's gaze flickered to Nate's and he swallowed what must have been a lump in his throat before he answered, "You have my word, sir."

As soon as Nate closed the door to his father's room, Jared threw his arms around him and held him close. Nate revelled in the contact for a few moments before pulling back.

"You okay?" Jared asked.

"Yeah…yeah, I'm okay."

"Doesn't he know about your brother's death?"

Nate nodded. "Yeah, he knows. Doctor's said my sister told him when it first happened and I spoke to him once about it, too, but he forgets. The dementia, I guess."

"He thinks your mom is still alive too?"

"Yeah. Doctors said it would probably be best to play along with it, because every time you tell him the truth would be like the first time all over again. They said it would be best not to upset him, because when he gets upset, he shifts and turns nasty. A couple of times they've had to tranq him until he calms down and shifts back."

When Nate next looked into Jared's eyes, the emotion he could see there was raw. Jared reached down and squeezed Nate's hand. "Come on, let's go home."

Nate closed his eyes and let Jared's words permeate. He only wished Jared had meant home *together*. The thought paralysed him. Was that what he wanted? A home, with Jared? Is that where this was going? Nate shook the thought from his mind. Even if Jared wanted to forge some sort of relationship with him, it would a private one, behind closed doors. They would never be able to live together. Jared's dream of making sheriff was too important to him to commit on that level, so Nate needed to get any stupid notions of the two of them 'playing house' out of his mind.

As they made their way to the parking lot, a tall, slim woman with long dark hair strode past. Her gaze flicked to Nate but she kept on walking. Nate stopped. He turned to watch her go, his heart hurting. Jared stopped too.

"Hey, what's up?" He followed Nate's gaze. "Who's that? Wait, was that..."

"Yeah," Nate said quietly, hanging his head to stare at the ground. "My sister."

Jared growled and the intensity made Nate quickly lift his head. Jared's beautiful green eyes had become so dark they were practically black, he was shaking all over.

"To hell with that!" Jared said, and he marched off, leaving Nate standing in the corridor alone.

Chapter Nine

Jared raced down the corridor, his wolf furious and snarling within. Fury bubbled just below the surface but he tried to rein it in. What the hell gave her the right to treat Nate like he was some Goddamn stranger? Nate grabbed hold of his arm and pulled him back. "Jared, just leave it. It doesn't matter."

"That's your sister!" Jared snapped. "Don't say that it doesn't matter, it does."

When Nate met his gaze, there was real pain in his eyes and it stole Jared's breath. "You know, you're the second person to say that to me in just over a week?" He sighed. "Look, she might be blood, but she can't be forced into changing her mind about me and I doubt she can be reasoned with either."

Jared tore his arm out of Nate's grip. "She doesn't have to change her mind. But she's going to damn well listen, and she's going to get a piece of my mind whether she likes it or not. What's her name?"

Nate closed his eyes and scrubbed a hand over his face. "Lucy."

Jared hurried away before Nate could stop him again. He caught up with her in the corridor that led to Nate's father's room.

"Hey, Lucy!"

She turned. Now that Jared was able to get a good look at her face, he could see the resemblance. She had the same eyes as her brother, the same shaped mouth, which was currently turned down in a frown.

"Who are you?"

"I'm Jared, your brother's mate." Jared couldn't believe how easy it was to say aloud, and he realised the more times he said it, the easier it became.

She flinched then tore her gaze away from his. "I don't have a brother."

Jared growled. If she were a man he would have thrown a Goddamn punch. Instead he grabbed hold of her arm and forced her to look him in the eye. "Don't you dare say that! You had two brothers, two! One is dead, sure, but the other is alive and loves you. Don't you think about him? Don't you miss having him in your life?"

"He's sick," she said. "It ain't natural."

"Who the hell are you to say what's natural? Who are you to pass judgement on who a man loves?" Even as the words came out of his mouth, Jared wondered if they could one day be true. Could Nate come to love him?

"The Bible says…"

"Don't go preaching to me about what the Bible says. I know what it says as well as anyone. Doesn't the Bible tell us to love unconditionally?"

"It's wrong," she whispered.

"No. *You're* wrong. Nate is the only brother you have left. You won't get another, and if you throw away the chance to know him, to have him in your life, you'll live to regret it. I promise you that." Jared wasn't even sure who he was trying to convince anymore—Lucy or himself.

Lucy hung her head and Jared knew he'd said all there was to say, so he left her alone in the corridor. But as he was walking away, she spoke up.

"But my mate..." When Jared turned back, her eyes were pleading with him to understand.

"Your mate would want you to be happy, wouldn't he? Isn't that what we all want for our mates?" The confusion in her eyes was evident. "Think about it, that's all I ask."

As Jared walked along the corridor to find Nate, he became more resolute. It was time he took his own damn advice. He would never get another mate, and just as he'd told Lucy, if he let Nate walk away, he would regret it, of that he had no doubt. He knew he couldn't live with himself if he let that happen.

Jared was running out of reasons why he and Nate shouldn't be together. Yes, he still had his brother to think about, but Tristan knew about their bond, and he was happy for them. And Tristan wasn't drinking anymore, either. The dark cloud that had been hanging over his head for so many months finally appeared to be lifting. Jared still wanted to make sheriff but it was just a job, wasn't it? What was more important to him? When he rounded a corner and set eyes on Nate—leaning against the wall, waiting for him—he knew the answer to that question. It was standing not five feet away from him.

* * * *

Jared had been quiet on the drive back to Wolf Creek but Nate hadn't been in the most talkative mood himself. He was pretty sure Jared was upset the talk with his sister hadn't gone better than it had, but Nate wasn't surprised. Lucy hadn't spoken to him in nearly ten years. That was a long time to pretend he didn't exist. A two minute conversation with Jared wasn't likely to change her mind about him.

Even though Jared hadn't spoken much, Nate had felt his eyes on him the entire journey. He wondered what Jared had been thinking as he looked at him, but he'd been too afraid to ask. As he pulled up outside Jared's house and killed the engine on his truck, Nate couldn't stand it anymore. He had to know.

"Go on, spit it out."

"Huh?"

"I can practically hear the cogs turning in your head. What is it? What's on your mind?"

Jared averted his gaze and his cheeks turned bright pink. He was quiet for a whole minute before he answered. "Just been thinking about some stuff…well, about us, actually."

What the hell did that mean? Nate's mouth was suddenly as dry as a bone. "Oh? What sort of stuff about us?"

"Do you want to come inside and talk?"

Nate nodded even though Jared was no longer looking at him. When he at last found his voice, it sounded rough, hollow. "Okay, sure."

On the way to the house Nate noticed Jared's SUV was still missing from yard.

"Tristan must be having a good time," he commented.

"Uh huh."

Jared still wouldn't look at him and Nate found himself growing more and more anxious as the minutes ticked on. What exactly was Jared about to tell him? That he didn't want to see him anymore? When Jared had told his father he would visit again, Nate couldn't have been happier, but maybe he hadn't meant it. Maybe he was just placating an old man who wouldn't remember what he'd said the next minute, let alone the following week.

Nate took off his hat when they entered the house and followed Jared into the living room. He looked around for somewhere to put it, but decided to keep hold. If Jared was about to say what Nate thought he was then it was pointless making himself comfortable—he wouldn't be staying for very long.

Jared sat down on the sofa but immediately got back up. He paced around the room then stopped in front of Nate, keeping his eyes to the ground. *Oh God.* Nate's heart was hammering ninety to the dozen. Finally, right before Nate thought he would explode from the suspense, Jared looked up, his emerald eyes shining brightly.

"This is kind of hard to say."

"Then you best get it over with," Nate replied, more sharply than he would have liked. "No sense dragging it out."

Jared nodded and chewed on his bottom lip. "When I introduced myself as your mate, to your father and sister, I liked how it sounded."

Nate scratched the top of his head as he stared at Jared in confusion. That hadn't been what he'd expected at all. He cocked his head to the side and stared into Jared's eyes waiting for the '*but*'. It never came.

"I could get used to saying it."

"I don't understand."

"We're *mates,* Nate. I don't want to deny it anymore…I can't. Don't you feel how strong the bond is between us?"

All the air whooshed out of Nate's lungs. Was Jared saying what he thought he was?

"I think we should try, I think we should—"

Jared didn't get to finish the sentence. Nate slid a hand through the hair on the back of his head, pulled him close and kissed him hard, cutting off the rest of his words. Jared groaned into his open mouth, taking everything Nate gave with relish and returning it tenfold.

Without breaking the kiss, Nate threw down his hat, using his hand to grab hold of his mate's ass and pull him closer until their rigid erections were pressed together. Jared cried out and tilted his head back, grinding into Nate until they were both blissfully short of breath, their bodies begging for release. It was the sweetest torture Nate had ever experienced.

When Jared looked up, his eyes had shifted to their wolf form and there was a look of desperation on his face that was nearly Nate's undoing. Then, Jared whispered one word.

"Please."

That single, innocent little word sent Nate into a frenzy. His wolf was ecstatic. His eyes shifted to mirror Jared's and a low, gravelly growl tore from his throat. Nate lost all self-control. He reached down and tore at the button on Jared's jeans, fighting with the zipper before reaching inside and finally—*finally*—getting his hands on the prize. Jared's cock was like steel. When Nate slid back the foreskin, his hand becoming slick from the moisture that was leaking from within. Jared was trembling in his arms, gasping and panting and whispering words of encouragement in his ear. Nate didn't need any.

He sank to his knees and wrapped his mouth around Jared's cock, taking it right to the back of his throat, moaning in pleasure when he tasted Jared's essence for the first time. Jared grunted and grabbed a handful of Nate's hair, his hips jerking, forcing even more of his length into Nate's throat. Nate knew Jared wasn't going to last very long. His entire body was shaking as he thrust deeply into Nate's mouth over and over, each time harder and with more urgency.

"I'm home!" Tristan shouted from the front door.

Jared yelped and pulled out of Nate's mouth. He tucked his cock back inside his jeans and fumbled with the button. "*Shit.*"

Nate quickly got to his feet and swiped a hand over his mouth. Jared had just finished untucking his shirt and pulling it down to hide his erection when Jared's brother entered the room. Tristan took one look at them both then his mouth curved up into a smirk.

"I can go back out again if you guys—"

"No!" Jared squeaked, and then cleared his throat. "No, it's fine, really."

Tristan's grin got broader. "Uh huh."

"Did you, uh...did you have a good time?" Jared asked.

"Yeah, but it looks as though you were having an even better time."

Jared's face turned bright red. Nate, who had been watching the exchange between the two brothers with silent amusement, threw his head back and laughed. He reached out, slid an arm around Jared's waist and pulled him to his side, planting a kiss on his head.

"We were, as it happens," Nate said. "Hope that's okay."

"Hell yeah, it's okay," Tristan replied. "I'm gonna grab some water from the kitchen then I'll get out of your hair. Guess I'll see you both in the morning."

Nate couldn't keep the smile from his face. "Yeah, kid, see you in the morning."

"Uh, yeah, night," Jared said.

Tristan was almost out the door when he paused and turned. "Crap, I nearly forgot. I just saw Kelan before I left the Crazy Horse. He asked me to tell you to call him soon as you can. He said he'd tried to get hold of you both but your cells were switched off."

Shit. Nate pulled the cell phone out of his pocket at the same time Jared reached for his. It seems they'd both forgotten to switch them back on after they left the nursing home. When the phones blinked to life they beeped repeatedly. Nate looked at Jared and frowned.

"What the hell?" Nate pulled up three text messages that had been sent within the last half an hour and read them in turn. They all said pretty much the same thing. *'Urgent…Call me ASAP…Trouble.'*

Jared was wearing the same look of disappointment Nate was certain covered his own face. "Guess we'd better call Kelan," he said, hitting the button for speed dial.

* * * *

"I'm sorry for spoiling your night," Kelan said. "But thanks for coming so quickly. We only just got here ourselves."

Jared waved off Kelan's concern. "It's no problem, what happened?"

"There's been more trouble, it seems. Pete called. He didn't say much but I got the impression it's bad."

Nate and Jared strode across the parking lot towards Jessie's Dancehall alongside Kelan and Stefan. Jared couldn't believe there had been more trouble yet again, but he was relieved Tristan hadn't been involved this time.

"Has the sheriff been called?" Jared asked.

Kelan shook his head. "Pete said we should get down here first. I've already called Gregory at his request. He and Ashton are on their way."

"Must be bad if Pete wanted you to call the council," Nate said.

"My thoughts exactly," Kelan replied. "Pete sounded strange on the phone earlier... I don't know...*scared,* I guess."

"These occurrences are happening too frequently," Stefan said. "If something isn't done soon then there's a real danger of the humans finding out. I'm amazed we've been able to hide from them for as long as we have."

"You know, if Dean is right and this Stan is working with Joe Walker, then maybe we should be watching Joe round the clock," Jared said. "Stan has to show up sooner or later and when he does, we've got him."

Kelan nodded. "I'm inclined to agree. We'll talk to Gregory and Ashton about it when they get here. See what we can arrange."

Jared pushed open the door to Jessie's and the second he stepped inside, the smell of blood hit him. It was strong. His gums itched, his incisors threatening to elongate.

"Jesus, what the hell happened here?" Nate asked, stepping in behind him. Jared sensed the cowboy was having trouble containing his wolf, too.

Kelan and Stefan strode across the dance floor to the bar. The jukebox was loud and playing some country song about holding on to your man, but there was no sign of Pete or anyone else in the room.

There was smashed glass on the dance floor, tables and chairs had been upended and when Jared reached Kelan and Stefan at the bar, it seemed they'd located the source of the smell. Kelan's face was ashen and his entire body was shaking, anger radiating out of the alpha in waves. There was a man lying on the floor behind the bar—his blood soaked legs just visible, poking out into the room. When Jared leaned around Kelan to get a better look, he had to fight the urge to throw up.

"Who is it?" Nate asked, stepping up beside him.

"Don't know," Jared replied. "A human. He's dead."

"What?" Nate shouldered past Jared to take a look himself. He groaned loudly and quickly turned his head away from the body. "Jesus Christ, the guy's been torn apart."

The human's eyes were wide. There was a fixed look of terror on his face. But it was the state of his chest and the rest of his body that had Jared fighting his gag reflex. The man *had*, quite literally, been torn apart. His shirt was missing and the gaping wound that ran the length of his torso was so wide his rib cage was visible and his intestines were hanging out of his stomach. Deep claw marks covered his face, neck, arms and legs. And there was so much blood pooled around him, Jared would be surprised if the guy had any left in his body.

"Who did this?" Nate whispered. "What the hell went on here?"

The sound of a bolt sliding open on the store room door behind the bar caught their attention. A moment later the door swung open and Pete stepped out. Pete's body was covered in deep scratches and welts, his clothes were torn and the look on his face was grave.

"What happened?" Kelan asked.

"Neil Rafferty happened," Pete ground out. "That's what."

Neil Rafferty. Jared swallowed hard and turned to look at the mangled body. The fact that Tristan could have been here, could have been lying in the man's place, made his stomach heave. He clenched his hands into fists. "Was anyone else hurt?"

Pete shook his head. "I was getting ready to close up for the night when Neil came in with two of his friends looking for a fight, and, well, guess they found one. Neil was drunk—went crazy. Starting fighting with two other wolves that were at the bar, minding their own business, then Paul here stepped in…tried to calm them down, only he didn't know what he was getting himself into."

"They shifted?" Nate asked.

Pete took a deep breath then closed his eyes. "Neil shifted his hands into claws and cut Paul across the face. The two wolves that were here panicked and ran off, but Neil and his friends weren't going anywhere. I've heard of pack mentality before but I didn't think I'd ever see it up close and I swear to God I hope never see the likes of it again."

"Where are they now?" Jared asked.

Pete shrugged. "I tried to stop them. I did, but I couldn't fight them all. Then they started to shift fully so I locked myself in the storeroom and that's when I called Kelan. I had tried to get Paul in with me but it was already too late—Neil had ripped his stomach out right in front of me and I'm sorry to say I didn't stick around after that."

Kelan shook his head. "It's not your fault, Pete. I don't blame you for what happened. There was nothing you could have done."

Pete shrugged but he didn't look convinced.

"What are we going to do about Neil and the others?" Nate asked.

Kelan sighed and raked his fingers through his hair. "Normally I'd go to the wolf council with something like this, but I believe Gregory and Ashton can be trusted so we'll wait for them to get here. We'll go to Neil's house together."

Nate wrapped his arms around Jared from behind and Jared welcomed the embrace, sank into it.

"Pete, you have something here we can use to cover his body?" Jared asked.

Pete nodded. "Should be something out back. I'll go look."

Ten minutes later Gregory and Ashton arrived. Jared had found it difficult to look at the man's injuries but Ashton's reaction had been the most surprising. The bird shifter ran from the bar and lost the contents of his stomach in the parking lot. He was quiet and distant after that. Gregory pulled him aside to talk to him and that seemed to help but only marginally. He arranged for the man's body to be collected and while they waited, they took seats at the booths in the back of the room. Jared slid into the seat nearest the wall and the moment Nate sat beside him, he slipped his arm around his shoulder, pulling him close. Jared couldn't believe how easy it was to lean into Nate's body and let himself be held. It felt right.

"Who was the human, Pete? Did you know him?" Nate asked.

Pete nodded. "Yeah, name was Paul Bourne. The guy was in here a lot. A loner…don't think he had family around here, if he had any at all."

"Thank God for that," Gregory said.

Under normal circumstances Jared would have baulked at such an insensitive remark but he imagined they were all thinking pretty much the same thing. Paul's death would have to be covered up. They couldn't take the risk of any humans finding out about it. So the fewer people that would be left behind to miss Paul, the better.

They didn't have to wait long for a team from the Supernatural Council to show up. Two of the men took away Paul's body while a clean-up crew dealt with the mess that had been left behind. Gregory and Ashton took a few minutes to speak to a man who had stood back and watched the proceedings and looked to be in charge. When everyone else left, he stayed behind.

"Everyone, this is Riley Burnett," Gregory introduced. "He's my superior at the council. He's going to come with us to pick up Neil and the other two boys."

"You need us all to come?" Nate asked.

Riley shook his head. "That won't be necessary. I'll take Gregory and Ashton, and two others will be enough."

Kelan strode forward and shook Riley's hand. "I'm Kelan, I'm the alpha here in Wolf Creek. My brother-in-law Stefan and I will come with you."

Riley nodded. "Good enough."

"Pete, go home and get some rest," Kelan said. "Jared, Nate…thanks for coming tonight. I'll talk to you tomorrow about what we can do about Joe."

Jared and Nate said their goodbyes and waited for Pete to lock up before they made short drive back to Jared's house. Jared parked his SUV next to Nate's truck and switched off the engine. They were both quiet for a moment before Nate spoke up.

"Wow, it's been a hell of a day."

"Yeah, it has. Poor guy. What they did to him..." Jared shook his head. "I felt guilty, but when they were taking his body away all I could feel was relief. I mean, what happened to him was terrible, but I kept thinking, what if it were Tristan in that body bag? I don't know what I'd do if something were to happen to him."

Nate shook his head. "Nothing is going to happen to Tristan. He's a good kid. I think he was just lost for a little while, is all. But he's got a home now, he's making friends, and I'll be there for him as much as I can."

"You will?"

"Of course. You know, I never did answer the question you asked me earlier." Nate reached over and took hold of Jared's hand, running his thumb along the palm. The light touch was incredibly erotic, it sent shivers down Jared's spine and despite the exhaustion in his body, he couldn't help the way he responded to his mate's touch. His dick started to harden in his pants and his breath came faster.

Jared tried to remember what question he'd asked, but it was difficult to concentrate on anything when Nate was so close, the sweet, intoxicating scent of him filling the enclosed space around them, his fingers caressing Jared's palm.

"You asked me if I could feel how strong the bond is between us," Nate said with a small smile on his face. Was he aware how his touch was affecting Jared?

"I did?" As Nate continued to caress his palm, Jared could barely remember his own name.

Nate nodded. "You did."

"Okay..."

Nate abruptly pulled his hand away and Jared very nearly whimpered at the loss. But when he looked up at Nate's face, the wolf was suddenly serious and Jared had to swallow down his anxiety.

"I don't know what sort of mate I'd make, Jared," Nate said quietly. "But I can promise you one thing—I'll try my damnedest to make you happy if you'll let me. The bond between us? Strong doesn't even come close to describing it. I feel you in every part of my being. Sometimes I'm afraid I won't be able to breathe if I can't be near you. It's like I'm suffocating and the only way to get air in my lungs is to see you, or to touch you. My soul is incomplete without you."

When Nate peeked up at Jared there was uncertainty in his eyes. "Does that answer your question?"

Jared couldn't breathe. How the hell was he supposed to talk? He nodded dumbly and when he finally found his voice it shook with emotion. "That answers *every* question. I couldn't have asked for a more perfect response."

Nate's answering smile was brilliant, like a shining beacon lighting up the night sky around them. He leaned across the seat, and tenderly pressed his lips to Jared's before pulling back. "Can I stay with you tonight?"

Jared took Nate's face in both hands and looked him square in the eyes. "You can stay with me *every* night."

Inside the house, Jared grabbed a bottle of water from the refrigerator and then turned out all the lights. When they walked out into the hall, Nate was heading for the stairs, but Jared reached out and pulled him back. He shook his head.

"I know the bedrooms upstairs are bigger, but I took the room down here. I liked it better, I don't know why. It felt *right*."

Jared led the way down the hall and when they entered his room, Nate grabbed him from behind and pulled him back against his chest. His breath was hot against Jared's ear. "This used to be my room," he whispered.

Jared turned in Nate's arms and kissed him until they were both breathless. "Then it makes perfect sense why I chose it," he said against Nate's mouth.

The shower in the en-suite had only a small cubicle, barely big enough for one person, so they took turns using it. Jared was turning down the sheets on the bed when Nate emerged.

"God, I needed that," Nate commented around a yawn.

"Tell me about it." Jared turned and drew in a sharp breath when he caught sight of the large wolf strolling towards him. Nate was roughly towelling dry his hair. His torso was still damp from the shower, beads of moisture glistening in the light from the bedside lamp. A fluffy white towel was wrapped low on his hips, dangerously low.

Under Jared's awestruck stare, Nate's dick hardened beneath the material, tenting it. The sight made Jared moan. God he needed. His own cock was painfully hard inside his boxers, aching to be touched. Without a word, Nate threw aside the towel he'd been using to dry his hair, grabbed hold of Jared and kissed him, his tongue forcing its way into his mouth. Jared accepted it gratefully, opening his own mouth wider, deepening the kiss and sliding his tongue alongside his mate's. Jared couldn't believe how incredible Nate tasted, how light-headed the kiss made him. He had to grab hold of Nate's shoulders to stay upright.

"Oh God." Jared rested his forehead against Nate's while he tried to catch his breath.

"Jesus, that was—"

Jared silenced Nate with another kiss. It was so strong, so powerful, he could feel it everywhere. His lips, body, his heart and soul all responded to Nate in a way he never dreamed possible. The kiss was so hot, so intensely erotic that Jared lost himself in it until Nate broke away with a loud growl.

"This is your last chance to change your mind," Nate said breathlessly. "If we go any further I know I'm not going to be able to stop myself from taking you. My wolf..."

Jared didn't reply. Instead, he turned, pulled open the drawer in his nightstand and removed a bottle of lube, placing it on top. Nate growled, grabbed him from behind and thrust his hard cock against his ass, while he latched his mouth onto Jared's neck and sucked. Jared cried out. He tilted his head to the side, shivering when Nate ran his tongue up the length of his neck, tracing along the vein. When he reached Jared's earlobe, he bit down gently then snaked his tongue out to soothe the spot. Jared was right on the edge, and he knew it wouldn't be long before he went over.

Nate slid his hand around Jared's hip and over his aching cock. When he pressed his hand firmly against him, nimble fingers reaching for the head, Jared gasped then bit down on his lip to try to stop his impending release. Christ, he didn't want to come before they had even got started.

"Come if you want," Nate whispered against his ear. "I promise it won't be the only time tonight."

Jared shook his head. He pulled Nate's hand away then turned in his arms. "I want it to last."

Ignoring his throbbing dick, Jared took a step back and raked his eyes over the impressive muscles of Nate's torso. With shaking hands he reached down, grabbed hold of the towel that covered Nate's hips and pulled. Nate's impressive erection sprang free. It, like every other part of Nate's body, was simply perfect. Jared couldn't believe this man was his. As he watched, a bead of pre-cum leaked from the slit. Jared snaked his tongue out to wet his lips. He couldn't resist, he needed to taste. He knelt down and licked it away, groaning louder when Nate's flavour burst on his tongue.

Nate growled—the sound low and needy, igniting a fire in Jared's belly that he never wanted put out. Nate grabbed Jared under the arms, lifted him and threw him backwards on to the bed, coming down heavily on top of him and crushing their lips together, stealing what was left of his breath. Without breaking the kiss, Nate reached a hand down and tugged at Jared's boxers, pulling them down his legs. With some difficulty, Jared managed to kick them the rest of the way off. The instant their cocks met, Jared knew he was going to lose it. His orgasm was too close, his body too tightly wound. Nate ground against him once, twice and it was all over. Jared thrust up hard, pressed his head against the pillow and shouted out his release.

His orgasm seemed to last and last. His hot seed spurted out between them, coating both his stomach and Nate's. His eyes and teeth shifted when his wolf rose to the surface, howling within, elated. He was dimly aware of Nate reaching for something beside him but he couldn't focus on the action. He was still jerking, his hip muscles contracting wildly when he felt Nate's slick fingers rub against his ass. Without preamble, Nate pushed two fingers inside, intensifying Jared's orgasm and he instinctively opened his legs wider to allow Nate better access to his body as he continued to jerk and shudder.

Jared was so sated and boneless when Nate pushed another finger inside, he barely felt the sting. When he finally stopped shuddering, he looked down to watch Nate's fingers disappear inside him. He wasn't surprised that his dick was still hard.

"Oh God, you're gonna keep me up," he groaned.

Nate didn't reply and when Jared lifted his gaze to meet Nate's, he knew why. The wolf looked desperate. His incisors were visible through his open lips, he was breathing heavily and looked as though he were barely holding it together.

"Jared?" The low rumble to Nate's voice made him sound more animal than human and it sent a jolt of excitement through Jared's body.

Jared could only nod.

Getting to his knees, Nate grabbed the lube and squeezed a generous helping into his palm, using it to slick up his dick. Jared knelt in front of him until he was eye to eye with his mate.

"Take me from behind?" he begged.

Nate mashed their lips together and thrust his tongue inside. When he pulled back he already had his hands on Jared's hips trying to turn him.

"On your hands and knees," he ordered.

Jared complied. No sooner had his elbows touched the mattress than Nate's thick, slippery cock was at his entrance, pressing against him, asking to be let in.

"Do it," Jared breathed.

Nate's large body leaned over his as his cock slowly pushed inside. There was a sharp bite of pain at first and he hissed, trying to adjust to the sensation, but as he pushed back the pressure gave way to an immense sense of relief and pleasure…blinding, earth-shattering pleasure.

"Nate!" Jared's entire body was shaking, his dick leaking against his stomach. He gripped the pillow as Nate withdrew then thrust inside him over and over again, making his body sing.

The pleasure inside Jared increased to epic proportions as Nate fucked him, filled him, and he gave into it gladly. Jared was finally home. Their lovemaking only served to cement their relationship, and to seal their bond. Instantly Jared knew what he wanted. When Nate thrust again, Jared fell forward and Nate collapsed on top of him, the action driving Nate even deeper inside, hitting his sweet spot and making him moan. Nate was groaning and panting against his neck and when his tongue snaked out to lick his teeth scraping along the vein, Jared couldn't take it anymore.

"Do it, Nate! Do it!" he shouted.

Jared didn't need to elaborate. Without preamble, Nate's razor sharp teeth sank into his neck and the overload of emotions that rocketed through his body as Nate drew out his blood and claimed him sent Jared into orbit. He could feel their bond strengthening the more blood Nate took, could feel the invisible strands that held them together form an unbreakable knot. He could feel Nate, deep inside him, a part of his soul. And Jared knew without question this was what he had waited his entire life for, even though he hadn't even known he'd been waiting. Just as his second orgasm hit, Nate tore his teeth out and shouted out Jared's name as he filled his ass with the wet heat of his release. The sensations that rushed through his body went on and on until they reached a thrilling crescendo—the ultimate high.

"You're mine," Nate whispered in his ear when they finally stopped trembling, their sweat-soaked bodies sliding deliciously against one another. "Forever."

Jared was so happy he could have cried.

Chapter Ten

"Nate, Nate wake up."

Nate groaned and reached out to pull Jared back against his body but his hands came up empty. He cocked one eye open and was surprised to see Jared on the other side of the room, pulling on his pants.

"What's wrong?" Nate asked, sitting up. The deep frown lines etched into Jared's forehead woke him faster than a bucket of ice water would have. "What happened?"

"Kelan just called. We need to get over to Joe's place, quick as we can."

Throwing off the covers, Nate quickly got out of bed and retrieved his clothes. "Trouble?"

Jared nodded. "Looks like it. Kelan is driving back from council headquarters with Gregory and Dean. They've had news about Stan. He's on his way to meet Joe today, only it seems Ashton got wind of the news first and he's headed there right now. Kelan said he had a ten minute head start on them, at least."

"I don't understand. Why would Ashton go without them?"

Jared sighed and raked a hand through his thick, dark curls. "Apparently Ashton's mate Tania was killed six months ago, and in much the same way Paul was killed last night—torn apart. He and Gregory have been investigating her death since it happened. From what they've been able to find out, it looks as though Stan is responsible."

"Shit."

"It gets worse. Tania was eight months pregnant with their child when she was killed. Kelan said after Ashton saw what happened last night he lost it, said by the time they got back to headquarters after picking up Neil and the others, he was incensed—not thinking clearly. I guess it brought back painful memories.

"Kelan said they couldn't calm him down, couldn't reason with him, and then this morning when they got the news about Stan, they went to find him but he'd already left. Gregory called his cell and when he answered, he said he was on his way to make Stan pay for what he'd done. Looks as though Ashton is out for blood."

"Fuck, we'd better get there before he does something stupid."

"My thoughts exactly."

When they turned into the lane that led to Joe's property, Jared veered off-road and hid the car behind a dense line of trees. He killed the engine and unclicked his seatbelt.

"I think it would be better if we went rest of the way by foot. Ashton won't have made it here this quickly, and if Stan is already with Joe, we don't want them to see us, or we'll waste the opportunity to catch them together. If they know we're on to them, we might not get this chance again."

Nate got out of the car and walked around it until he was stood at Jared's side. "I've got a bad feeling about this," Nate said. "It doesn't add up. Why would Stan kill Ashton's mate? If his only goal is to expose shifters to humans, what would he have to gain from doing that?"

Jared's mouth was pressed together in a thin line. "I don't know."

"We don't know squat. And if Dean is the one who has been getting info on Stan then how did Ashton find out Stan was coming here today?"

Jared shrugged. "Guess we're about to find out."

Nate and Jared followed the tree line to Joe's ranch, keeping parallel with the road. When the house came into sight, Jared nudged Nate's shoulder and nodded his head towards a black sedan parked outside. They circled the yard until they reached the back of the ranch and two large outbuildings loomed before them. As they approached the nearest barn, Nate heard raised voices from within.

Quietly, they slid along the side of the building until they reached the door. Nate peered into the barn but he couldn't see anyone. The voices seemed to be coming from one of the stalls in the back of the building so he slipped inside, Jared following closely behind.

"You're being paranoid," Nate heard Joe say. "No one knows! We can't quit now, I've got another bull coming this afternoon and I need that damn insurance money to pay for it."

"Don't be greedy, Joe," a man replied. "How many times do you think you can get away with it before the insurance company becomes suspicious? Besides, we need to cool it. I'm certain someone at the council is on to me. I can't risk anyone finding out or I'll lose everything. We're committing fraud. Do you know how serious this is? We can both go to prison for it. I don't have to tell you what that's like for a wolf, do I? Isn't your son in prison?"

Nate turned to Jared and frowned. If that was Stan talking, then the whole situation made even less sense. Why would he be so concerned about something as small time as fraud if he was personally responsible for someone's death?

"Yes! " Joe snapped. "He is in prison, and it's all because of those fucking Morgan brothers! If you just did as I damn well said and planted one of my bulls in their fields, we could pin it on them and we'd be killing two birds with one stone. We'd take the suspicion off us and you'd get rid of Kelan Morgan in the process. Isn't that what you want?"

The man let out a weary sigh. "Yes, I've already got someone lined up to take over the position, but we need to tread carefully. We can't afford to have anyone find out what we're up to. I've worked tirelessly for years building a following of people that are loyal to me, that are sick of us hiding, living our lives in fear of humans finding out about us. I've got a lot invested in this and I'm not prepared to throw it all away for small amount of money."

Joe snorted. "This is hardly pocket change. We're set to make tens of thousands here, and that's only the beginning."

"I think I've heard enough," Jared whispered into Nate's ear. "We can get them for fraud if nothing else."

After what Nate had just heard, he wasn't convinced there *was* anything else but he kept quiet and nodded his head in agreement. They slipped out of the barn and waited outside for Joe and Stan to emerge.

A moment later both men stepped outside, squinting into the early morning sunshine.

"Stan Michaels?" Jared asked.

"Yes, who are you?" Confusion on the man's face turned into fear when Jared produced his badge.

"What the fuck is this?" Joe asked, his head swivelling back and forth between Nate and Jared.

"Stan Michaels, Joe Walker—I'm arresting you both on suspicion of f—"

Jared didn't finish his sentence. A shot rang out behind them and Stan shrieked and fell to his knees, his hand lifting to his shoulder as if by instinct. Blood started seeping out between his fingers and his face drained of colour almost instantly.

Jared pulled out his gun and spun around. Ashton was marching towards them with his own gun pointed at Stan. His eyes had shifted to their bird form and his face was filled with a deep hatred, the intensity of which made Nate shiver.

"Drop your weapon, Ashton!" Jared shouted.

Ashton ignored him and continued moving towards them.

"Ashton, I'm warning you! Drop your Goddamn weapon!"

"Stay out of this, Jared. This is between me and Stan," Ashton replied.

"He shot me, he fucking shot me," Stan said. "Don't just stand there, do something! Shoot him!"

"Shut up!" Ashton roared, waving his gun at Stan.

"You're making a mistake, Ashton," Nate said.

"You don't know anything about this, Nate. He *killed* my mate! Killed her! She was torn apart. Our *baby*..." Ashton's entire body was shaking and his hawk looked dangerously close to the surface.

"What? What the hell is he talking about?" Stan asked. "It wasn't me, I would never..."

"Don't *lie*! You ordered her death! I know it was you! Admit it!"

When Nate turned to look at Stan, the confusion on his face was unmistakable. He might have certain views on shifter politics and he might be committing fraud, but Nate was certain he wasn't a murderer. He wasn't responsible for Tania's death.

"I haven't killed anyone!" Stan shouted.

"You're lying! He told me it was you!" Ashton shouted.

"Who told you?" Nate asked.

"It was—"

"Drop your weapon, Ashton!" Nate turned to see Kelan, Gregory and Dean striding towards them. Dean had his gun drawn and pointed at the Hawk.

"Ashton, please," Gregory begged. "Don't do this."

"You know what he did—you saw what he did to her. He can't get away with this!"

"He won't," Gregory replied. "He won't get away with it, but just please, don't do this."

"You don't understand," Ashton said. "You've never been mated."

While Nate watched, a tear slid down Ashton's cheek. "I'm sorry," he whispered, and then he turned, pointed his gun at Stan's chest and pulled the trigger.

"Ashton, no!" Nate shouted.

The scene seemed to play out as if in slow motion. A second after Ashton shot Stan, Dean fired his own gun and Ashton fell face forwards on the ground. Gregory roared and rushed at Dean, punching him in the face, hard. Dean's head snapped back and Gregory was on him again, tackling the giant of a man to the ground.

"Jesus Christ, help me separate them!" Kelan shouted.

Nate ran forwards and grabbed Gregory's shoulders, dragging him backwards, while Kelan got a hold of Dean and pulled him in the opposite direction.

Nate wrapped his arms around Gregory's torso and whispered in his ear. "Shh, it's okay. It's going to be okay."

Gregory struggled at first, kicking and shouting, trying to free himself from Nate's grip, but after a few moments all the fight went out of him and his body became pliant and limp in Nate's arms.

Nate watched Jared check for a pulse in Stan's neck then cross to Ashton and check him, too. He shook his head, his face solemn. "*Both dead,*" he mouthed.

Epilogue

Nate put the plate holding his sandwich on the coffee table and took a seat on the sofa, stretching out his long legs. He sighed contentedly and unfolded the daily newspaper on his lap. He was just about to reach for his sandwich when the front door opened.

"I'm home!" Tristan breezed into the room, his entire body covered in grease. It was smeared over his hands and face and even looked to be in his hair. "Hi Nate!"

"Hey, kid," Nate replied, unable to keep the grin from his face. "How was work?"

Tristan groaned dramatically. "That place would go out of business if it wasn't for me, I'm telling you. I do *everything* there. I think I might ask Bob for a raise."

"Uh, you might want to wait until you've been working there longer than two weeks."

"You think? Hmm, maybe you're right. I guess I'll leave it until next week." Tristan made to sit down beside Nate.

"Don't you dare!" Nate shouted. "Your brother will kill you if you get grease on his new sofa and then he'll kill me for allowing it."

Tristan shrugged, grabbed Nate's sandwich and stuffed half of it into his mouth. "Mmm, good," he said. His mouth was so full the words were barely audible.

Nate looked down at his empty plate and growled. Tristan practically ran from the room, his laughter carrying all the way up the stairs.

"Was that Tristan?" Jared asked, walking in from the kitchen.

"Yeah, that was the little toad." Nate frowned.

Jared's face broke out into a wide grin. He sat down next to Nate and planted a big kiss on his lips. "What did he do this time?"

"He—"

"Hey! Did you eat that sandwich already? What did you do, swallow it whole?"

Nate rolled his eyes and grabbed the plate from the coffee table. "It went so quick I didn't even taste it."

Nate made it halfway to the kitchen when the phone started ringing. "You expecting a call?" he asked.

"Nope." Jared got up from the sofa, crossed the room and slid his arms around Nate's waist. He snaked his tongue out and licked a path up Nate's neck, making him shudder. "Probably just a sales call. Let the machine get it, if it's important they'll leave a message."

Nate would have replied but his mouth was busy. Jared kissed him hungrily, sliding his tongue into Nate's mouth. When he reached down and palmed Nate's suddenly very interested cock through his jeans, Nate gasped, breaking the kiss. The answer machine kicked on.

"Hello, Nate?"

Nate froze. The female voice on the machine was hesitant.

"This is…Lucy. Uh…I called Kelan and he told me you're living with Jared now, he gave me your number, I hope you don't mind, I…"

Nate tore himself from Jared's embrace and raced across the room to pick up the handset. "Hello?"

"Nate, is that you?"

Nate's heart was suddenly pounding furiously in his chest. He swallowed hard before he could choke out a reply, "Yeah, Lucy, it's me."

"Oh, um… I hope you don't mind me calling you at home."

"Of course not, it's good to hear your voice."

There was a long pause on the other end before Lucy replied. "It's good to hear yours too, Nate. Look, I did some thinking after I spoke to your gentleman friend and—"

"My mate," Nate corrected.

More silence. Nate had no idea what his sister was calling for, but Jared was Nate's mate, plain and simple. If she couldn't accept that fact then he had nothing more to say to her.

"Yes, your mate," Lucy said at last. "He seems like a nice man."

"He is," Nate replied. He turned to look at Jared and a warm smile spread across his face. Jared was grinning triumphantly. "He's one of the best."

Lucy let out a shaky sigh. "I did some thinking after I spoke with him at the nursing home. I know it's been a long time and I'll understand if you don't think it's a good idea, but I wondered if you'd like to meet up, talk. Maybe get to know each other again?"

"I'd like that, Lucy," Nate said sincerely. "I'd like that a lot."

Nate chatted to his sister for a few more moments then made a date to meet up with her before hanging up the call. He stared down at the empty plate in his hand, overcome with emotion.

"She's wants to meet up." Nate raised his head to meet his mate's eyes. "She wants to talk."

"I knew she'd come around." Jared crossed the room and gave Nate a small peck on the lips. "I'm so happy for you."

"It's your doing," Nate replied. "She said she got to thinking after she spoke with you and realised what she'd been missing out on all these years."

"Well, then I'm happy to have been of service." Jared grinned and checked his watch. "We've got an hour before Gregory gets here, what do you say we go and celebrate?"

Nate's breath came faster when he noticed the lustful glint in his mate's eyes. "I like the way you think. Let me just take this to the kitchen and—"

Jared shook his head. "Leave it, I can't wait."

Nate groaned when Jared grabbed his hand and placed it on the bulge in his jeans. He dumped the plate on the table that held the phone. "Lead the way."

Jared's mouth curved up and he lifted his eyebrows suggestively. He leant forward and pressed their lips together, slipping his tongue into Nate's mouth. Nate groaned when Jared pressed a hand against his cock squeezed. Christ, but he was hard and Jared's hand sliding up and down his length and gripping him through his jeans was only making the situation worse. He held the back of Jared's head and deepened the kiss, his fingers tangling in his hair, holding him in place while he devoured his mouth. He couldn't get enough of this man. He was the air Nate needed to breathe.

Their combined moans sounded loud to Nate's ears—almost loud enough to drown out the sound of his zipper sliding open...almost. Nate gasped when Jared reached into his briefs and made a tight fist around his cock. He broke the kiss and looked down just in time to catch the visual of Jared running his thumb over the head of his cock, spreading the pre-cum around. Nate threw his head back and moaned.

"Jared..."

Jared chuckled. Before Nate even realised what was happening, Jared had sunk to his knees and swallowed Nate's cock down to the base. Eyes closed, Jared moaned around him and the vibrations caused Nate's hips to jerk forward, shoving him deeper into his mate's mouth. Nate gave himself over to the sensations of his mate sucking him—the delicious slide, the tongue swirling around the head, the slight graze of teeth on every other pass. He watched in awe as his cock slid in and out his mate's hot, wet mouth. Then Jared opened his eyes and smiled around his cock. He winked then swallowed and Nate's cock slipped into his throat.

"Oh fuck!" Nate shouted desperately. Jared sucked harder.

Nate couldn't last. He was about to come into Jared's throat when it occurred to him that they were still in the living room, not in the privacy of their bedroom. Reluctantly, he pulled out of Jared's mouth and tried to calm his breathing while he tucked himself back into his jeans.

"We'd better finish this in our room," he rasped. "Tristan might come down."

Jared's eyes widened. He'd clearly forgotten about his brother, too. He quickly got to his feet.

"Shit."

Nate chuckled. "Come on, I'll repay the favour."

Jared's smile was bright. "I like the way you think."

They'd made it as far as the hall when there was a knock on the front door.

"Son of a bitch!" Jared fumed. "You've got to be kidding me."

Nate groaned. Why the hell had he made Jared stop? His dick was like a lead pipe in his jeans…he needed to come. He tried to will his erection away. "I told you we should consider moving to Alaska where nobody knows us."

"That idea is looking more and more promising." Jared crossed to the front door and swung it open. "Hey, Gregory, come on in."

"Jared, Nate." Gregory nodded, stepping into the hall. "I'm sorry I'm early but the council just called. I have to leave for Las Vegas right away to pick up a cat shifter."

"Trouble?" Nate asked, his cock deflating by the other man's presence.

Gregory shrugged. "Nah, don't think it's anything I can't handle. He's only twenty-one. Should be an in-and-out. The council is even letting me go alone." At that Gregory sighed and lowered his head.

Nate met Jared's gaze and frowned. "How you doing, Gregory?"

Gregory shrugged. "Ashton and I were partners for eight years. He was more than a work colleague—he was a friend…a close friend. I miss him."

"And there's not going to be an investigation into his death?" Jared asked. "I mean, Dean killed him for no good reason. Ashton wasn't a threat to any of us. How can he get away with that?"

Gregory snorted. "He already has. The council have closed the case, ruled his actions justifiable. But I swear to God I'm not going to let it drop."

"I think there's more to Dean than meets the eye," Nate said. "If he was the one that gave you the information about Stan's whereabouts, how did Ashton find out he was going to be at Joe's? It had to have come from Dean."

"I agree," Gregory said. "I think Dean has his own agenda. It stands to reason that if he wanted Stan out of the way, what better way to do it than to than to feed information about him to Ashton, knowing Ashton was grieving for his mate and wanted revenge for her death. I don't believe Stan was responsible for killing her."

"Neither do I," Nate said. "But there's something that's been bothering me. At the meeting at the Crazy Horse, Ashton said that you and he knew of Stan, that you'd been investigating something and his name came up. Was there someone else at the council giving you information about Stan?"

Gregory nodded. "There was. There's a wolf shifter named Deveraux working at the council that had been helping us. I thought he could be trusted at the time, so I believed the information he gave us was true. However I've recently found out that he and Dean are thick as thieves. Which means all the info he gave us could have been coming from Dean all along.

"I've got to say, the more I find out, the more it looks as though Dean could be the one responsible for having Tania killed. That's actually the reason I wanted to come by today, I've been doing some snooping around at the council. It seems Ashton was not the only one whose mate was killed recently."

"What? Council members' mates? Killed in the same way as Tania?" Jared asked.

Gregory sighed. "Yeah. All torn apart. I always knew the council discouraged mating but it looks as though someone there has taken that a step too far."

"Why would they discourage mating?" Nate couldn't see the logic in that.

"They don't want their representatives to have any ties. You both know how fiercely a shifter will fight to protect their mate. I imagine they see mates as a liability, someone that could be used as leverage against the council."

"And you think Dean is involved in the killing of these mates?" Jared asked.

Gregory shrugged. "I don't know if Dean is involved directly but after everything that happened with Ashton, I'm beginning to think he is. I just need to find proof. Which is what I wanted to talk to you both about today. With Ashton gone, I can't do it alone. Kelan said he'd help, too, but I wanted to know if I can count on you both for support if I need it."

"You don't even need to ask," Jared said. "We'll help you in any way we can."

"Of course," Nate agreed. "Call us right away if there is anything we can do."

"Thanks. I appreciate it. Well I guess I'd better go pick up that cat. Although I've got to say I'm nervous about handing him over to the council. It's getting to the point where I have no idea who to trust there anymore."

"Why don't you quit?" Nate asked.

"I had been thinking about it. But for now, I think I can do more good while I'm still working there. There are too many corrupt members, too many antiquated laws that need to be changed. And I can't leave until I find out who is responsible for killing council members' mates. I owe it to Ashton. I have to do that for him. He would have done the same thing for me. Anyway, I'd better get going. Thanks again."

Gregory was halfway done the porch steps when Nate remembered what he'd wanted to ask. "Hey, Gregory! Have you had any news on Joe Walker? What's happening to him?"

"Oh, I forgot to tell you. Joe got sentenced this morning. Looks as though he's going to be keeping his son company in prison."

"How long did he get?"

"Three years. Neil Rafferty and his friends are being sentenced later this week, but from what I heard, it doesn't look good for them. Neil was the one that killed Paul, so it's likely he'll be sentenced to life. His friends won't get off lightly, either. They're looking at ten years minimum apiece."

"It's nothing more than they deserve," Jared said.

"You got that right. See you both later."

"Yeah, see you."

They waited until Gregory got in his car and pulled out of the yard before closing the front door.

"Wow," Jared said. "It looks as though Gregory's got his work cut out."

"Yeah, I don't envy him one little bit. I'd rather be a rancher any day than have to deal with the things he does on a daily basis."

"You and me both. I thought I had it tough at the sheriff's department, but jeez."

"Isn't Sheriff Ferguson up for retirement soon?"

"Yeah, in another couple of months."

"You still gonna go for the position?"

Jared nodded. "Don't see why not. I might not get it, but at least I will have tried."

"I think you'd make a great sheriff," Nate said. "Kinda makes me want to get in trouble, just so's you can arrest me."

Jared chuckled. "You just want me to put you in handcuffs."

Nate growled, grabbed hold of Jared and kissed him hard. "You do that anyway," he rasped when he pulled back.

Gregory's eyes darkened with lust. "You done anything bad today I should know about, Nate? Anything you need to be punished for?"

Nate's heart started beating faster. "I'm sure I can think of something."

Jared grabbed Nate's hand and dragged him down the hall to their room.

"Hey Jared!" Tristan called. "Is dinner nearly ready?"

Jared's mouth opened and closed a few times before he groaned dramatically. It reminded Nate of Tristan. They were so much alike. Jared met Nate's gaze and raised an eyebrow in query.

"Alaska?" he asked hopefully.

Nate chuckled and gave Jared a quick kiss. "I'll start packing."

GREGORY'S REBELLION

Dedication

I'd like to say a huge thank you to all my friends and family who have supported me over the years. Your encouragement and praise have given me the strength to pursue my dreams and the belief that anything is possible if you work hard enough. You taught me to never give up, and for that I'll be eternally grateful.

Chapter One

"Well, go on." A brilliant smile spread across Mac's face as he nodded to the present in Hayden's hands. "Open it."

Hayden held on to the box as though it were made of glass. He stared at it longingly, allowing himself to get lost in the dream for just a moment, then shook his head and handed it back. "I can't accept this, I'm sorry."

"Now listen here, you'll offend an old man if you don't keep it. And you don't want to get on the wrong side of your boss now, do you?"

Hayden sighed. It had been a long time since anyone had given him a gift of any kind. He didn't mean to be ungrateful, but he didn't want Mac to think he was some sort of charity case.

"Uh, I don't know..." Hayden chewed on his lip while he tried to decide what to do.

"Look, it's your birthday and I'm giving you a gift. Get over it." Mac thrust the box back into Hayden's hands.

"Fine, I'll open it, but if it's expensive I swear to God—"

"Will you quit yakking and open it already? I'm growing old here."

Hayden rolled his eyes but the corners of his mouth tugged up into a smile. He had to admit he was curious to know what was inside. He picked delicately at the tape holding the package together.

"Christ, son, you're worse than my wife. You're not planning on keeping the paper, are you?"

Hayden felt his cheeks flood with heat. He would never admit it to Mac but that had been exactly what he had in mind. The paper was purple and sparkly and he could use it for…well, for *something*.

Mac tapped his fingers impatiently on the kitchen worktop. Hayden finally managed to get the gift unwrapped, revealing a white cardboard box.

"What is it?"

"Jesus, kid, give it to me. I'll open it myself."

"No, I can do it." Hayden lifted the lid on the box and peered inside.

He drew in a sharp breath, feeling a lump rise in the back of his throat, and tears began to form behind his eyes, threatening to shatter his resolve. It had been three years since he'd last cried and after the last time he'd sworn he never would again. But, as he stared from the gift in his hand to Mac's speculative gaze, he felt cracks begin to form in his carefully constructed dam.

"Well?" Mac asked. "Do you like it? If it's the wrong kind, I'm sure I can change it."

"No," Hayden said, "It's perfect. It's a, it's a…"

"I know. It's a Kindling." Mac sounded triumphant.

"A Kindle," Hayden corrected.

"Yeah, right. Well, I told my wife whenever you're on a break you've always got some scratty book in your hand so she said you might like one of these. Apparently all the kids have them."

Hayden bristled at the word kid. Today was his twenty-first birthday so he was now officially a man, but he let the comment slide. Mac was practically old enough to be his grandfather, so to him he probably did seem like a kid.

"I don't know what to say." Hayden swallowed down the lump in his throat, which had grown so big he felt as though he were choking on it.

Mac shrugged. "Just say thanks."

"Thank you," he whispered. He lifted his head to meet Mac's gaze. It was something he didn't do often, but, to his relief, Mac was looking him directly in the eye and his gaze didn't once drift lower.

"Welcome."

Hayden sniffed and a solitary tear escaped his eye and trickled down his cheek.

"Now, now...we'll have none of that." Mac cleared his throat and patted Hayden roughly on the back. "You'll start me off. It's nearly opening time and you don't want my damn customers to think I've gone soft, do you?"

Hayden chuckled and stared down at the gift in awe. He'd wanted an e-reader since they first came out but he couldn't afford one. Hell, he could barely afford his rent. When you added utilities and food on top, Hayden was flat broke for at least a week out of every month.

Now that he came to think about it, Hayden didn't even think he could afford the eBooks to read on the device. The books he usually read he got from yard sales or thrift stores—the same places he got all his belongings. And when he couldn't even afford that, he went to the library.

"Oh, I forgot to give you this." Mac placed an envelope on top of the box. "Mary said you'd need it to go with the Kindling."

Hayden put the box down and opened the envelope. Inside was an eBook voucher for a hundred dollars. Hayden practically choked on his surprise.

"This is too much, Mac." He shook his head firmly.

"Nonsense. You're worth it, kid. Best employee I got."

"But I just wash dishes here."

Mac raised an amused eyebrow. "Say what? You *used* to just wash dishes here. For the past ten months you've been helping out the cook *and* filling in when he's not around. I've had you cash up, do my banking… Hell, last week I had you lock up the joint, and do you know how many other people I trust to do that? None."

Hayden knew he worked hard but, while it was nice to be appreciated, he'd never been much good with compliments. Probably because he had no experience receiving them. He wasn't sure how to respond or if Mac required anything other than the thank you he'd already supplied. A loud banging on the diner door pulled Hayden from his thoughts.

"Mac! You in there?"

Mac grinned. "That's my cue, son. Enjoy your present."

"Thank you," Hayden said again. He didn't think he could manage anything more profound.

Mac nodded and walked into the diner to let in Dianne, one of the waitresses on the early shift. Hayden stared down at his gift again, shaking his head. He couldn't believe Mac had been so generous.

He would have to think of some way to repay his boss for the gesture.

* * * *

Ten long hours later Hayden put away the last of the pots and took off his apron. He wasn't sorry to be leaving—it had been a busy day, he was hot and tired and in desperate need of a shower, but he *was* sorry he had to go back to his crummy little apartment alone. Still, he was old enough to buy beer now. Maybe he'd stop off at the liquor store on the way home. He grabbed the gift on his way out the door and said goodbye to Pedro, Mac's one and only chef. Mac was busy fixing a drink behind the counter as he left.

"See you tomorrow, Mac."

"Yeah. Tomorrow, kid. Have a good night. Say, you meeting up with friends to celebrate your birthday?"

"Yeah, something like that," Hayden lied.

"Well, have a good'un."

"Thanks, Mac, and thanks again for the gift."

The heat barrelled into him as soon as he stepped out into the balmy night, making him feel even stickier than he'd been before he left. The diner wasn't fancy but it was doing okay by all accounts and Mac had just splashed out on an expensive new air-conditioning system for the place. It was essential for the hot, arid days and nights that were so commonplace in Las Vegas. But of course there was no cool air in the kitchens where Hayden worked—the last thing Mac needed was complaints about the temperature of the food.

Hayden had moved to 'Sin City' because it seemed like a place he could get lost in, a place he could hide. He'd been attracted to the bright lights and conveyor belt of new faces, but, since he'd arrived almost two years ago, he'd been on the main drag a grand total of twice. He may have been able to get lost in the sea of faces there, but he'd felt as though he were drowning in them. Every person he passed stared at him as though he were some sort of freak. Some days he really hated people.

Crossing the busy road outside the diner, Hayden kept his head to the ground, careful not to catch anyone's eye. It wasn't that he disliked people in general—he just couldn't stand to see the pity in their eyes when they looked at him.

Taking the familiar route, Hayden walked the few blocks home and stopped off at the liquor store across the street from his condo. He scanned the aisles, looking at the different types of beer on offer. Coors seemed to be a popular brand. He picked up four bottles then mentally added up the change in his pocket. He frowned, replacing two and taking the remaining two to the counter. The elderly clerk eyed him suspiciously when he placed the two bottles of beer in front of him.

"ID?"

Hayden pulled the card from his wallet and handed it to the man. The clerk looked from the picture in his hand to Hayden's face and the moments ticked on uncomfortably. Hayden squirmed under the scrutiny then lowered his gaze. He had to look away. He knew what the man was staring at—the same thing everyone stared at when they looked at him.

"Birthday today?" the clerk asked at last. He took Hayden's money and rang up the sale.

"Yeah."

"And you're only buying two beers?"

"Guess I'm not a big drinker," Hayden mumbled. He didn't want to tell the man two beers were all he could afford.

"Well, enjoy."

"Thanks."

The clerk picked up the newspaper he'd discarded, dismissing Hayden, but, just before he turned to leave, Hayden saw the man's eyes look over the top of the paper to stare at his face.

After he'd let himself into his tiny condo, Hayden threw his keys on the side table in the hall and stripped off his damp shirt. The place was like a furnace, but he couldn't afford the bill for the air conditioning so he had to suffer the heat.

He took a cold shower, threw on an old pair of cut-offs and stretched out on his threadbare sofa. The springs creaked loudly as he sat down and Hayden hoped the old thing would last because, as with everything else, he didn't have the money to replace it.

He was used to being broke, but sometimes—well, most of the time—he wished his life was different. Why couldn't he have had parents who loved him, no matter what? Hayden didn't often think about his life back home—he wouldn't allow himself. The memories of that time were too painful. But sometimes the thoughts crept into his head like weeds and took root. Once planted, there was no getting rid of them. Hayden might just be feeling nostalgic because it was his birthday, but he had a burning desire to call home.

It had been five years since his parents had kicked him out of the house for being gay. When his father had caught him making out with his friend Tommy, he'd got the worst beating of his life…and that was saying something. He'd spent the five years since struggling, feeling as though he were climbing a steep hill with no end in sight. He'd done things to get by that made his face burn with shame. Had his parents thought about him at all in the years since he'd left? What about his younger brother, Joey? Joey would be sixteen now, the age Hayden had been when he'd left. Did Joey ever ask about him? Did he have more siblings he didn't know about?

Hayden tried to shake the thoughts from his head. What would be the point in calling his parents? They'd made it perfectly clear they never wanted to see him again and that was just fine. He was doing great without them, wasn't he?

Hayden reached for the Kindle he'd left on his coffee table, a small smile playing over his lips. He might not have family in his life anymore, but he had Mac. The man had been good to him since he'd shown up at the diner, penniless and hungry. Hayden didn't want to think about where he would be now if Mac hadn't taken him in and given him a job. Would he still be giving hand jobs at truck stops for a ride to the next town and so he could eat that day? He shivered at the unwelcome thought. He might not have much, but he'd come a long way since then.

No, he couldn't call his parents. He was a man now—he didn't need them anymore. Mostly everything he owned, however cheap or old, he'd bought out of his own damn money, and that gave him an immense sense of pride. He'd proved to himself that he could make it on his own, without their help or love.

Sure, he might feel lonely once in a while but he always got over it. Hayden cracked open a bottle of beer and took a long drink. He grimaced. He didn't much like the taste of beer, but you didn't have to like it to drink it, did you?

Getting up from the sofa, he walked into his compact bathroom, leaned over the washbasin and took a good look at himself in the cracked plastic mirror on the wall. He rarely looked at his own reflection. Not because he was bad looking—he wasn't. He had pale blond hair, piercing light blue eyes and fleshy pink lips. His nose was narrow and turned up slightly at the end. It could almost be described as delicate. His features were very nearly feminine, but strong enough that he could never be confused for a girl. But it was the angry-looking scar that ran from the corner of his eye down his left cheek to his top lip that flawed his otherwise handsome face. It was an attribute most people couldn't see beyond, himself included.

Looking down at the half-empty bottle in his hand, Hayden curled his upper lip in distaste. He didn't feel like drinking anymore. Maybe the beer had been a bad idea. He knew alcohol was a depressant and that was something he most certainly didn't need. Even without alcohol Hayden sometimes got into a funk that was difficult to get out of. Emptying the remaining beer away, he brushed his teeth and got himself ready for bed.

Turning out the lights in his condo, he lay down, praying for sleep to take him quickly so he wouldn't have to be alone with his thoughts. And when he slept he would be free to dream of a better life than the one he was currently living.

* * * *

Gregory watched the young jaguar shifter cross the street from the liquor store and let himself into his condo. It was a run-down building in one of the seedier areas of the city, home to more street gangs and meth addicts than Gregory cared to think about. It was a dump.

The council had told him to bring Hayden in three days ago. Normally that wouldn't have been a problem. This was an easy job and Gregory had even been allowed to come alone. Actually he had *insisted* upon it. He'd refused to be paired up with another partner after Ashton had been killed a few weeks ago. Usually, on jobs like this one, he'd have got in, grabbed the kid and got out without breaking a sweat. Yet here he stood, three days later, still watching the young shifter like he had all the time in the world.

Gregory had to admit to being intrigued. *More* than intrigued, he was damn near infatuated. He reached a hand down to adjust his errant cock, cursing his damn stupid body for betraying him. He'd been painfully hard for the last three days just watching Hayden from a distance. God only knew how his body would respond when he came within touching distance of the young man.

It was Hayden's twenty-first birthday, but instead of celebrating, he had worked all day. And his night didn't look as though it would be any more exciting. The kid did the same thing every night. He went back to his condo alone. The only change in his routine had been two bottles of beer the kid had picked up at the store. Hayden didn't have any friends, of that Gregory was certain. He had spoken to no one but his co-workers and the store clerk in the past three days. Gregory suspected that was the reason the council wanted him brought in.

Unlike wolves, cat shifters did not live in packs. But they were still far from the solitary creatures people imagined them to be. They needed interaction with their own kind—thrived on it. When they didn't get it, they quite often became depressed. And that in turn led to them becoming feral. Feral cats were dangerous. Too dangerous to be allowed to remain in society where they could harm humans…or worse, kill them. And that was without mentioning the touchy subject of humans finding out about shifters.

With a drawn-out sigh, Gregory turned away from Hayden's condo. He knew he couldn't drag the job out much longer, but he couldn't grab the kid on his birthday. He'd give him the night at least. Let him drink his beers and celebrate his birthday, then in the morning Gregory would take him back to base. He didn't want to take the kid in at all, but he had no choice. If he waited any longer his superiors in the council would be pissed off and they'd send someone else to finish the job'.

The fact that Gregory hated Vegas made the job even more difficult. On the main drag the cacophony of noise and the abundance of tacky neon was murder on the eyes and ears. The place was a paradox. It offered hope and the prospect of a better life, but it rarely delivered—filled to bursting with people that wanted to lose themselves, that had ended up living there because they had no place else to go. People arrived with optimism and often left in despair. It sucked the soul right out of you.

If Gregory could just make his goddamn dick calm down long enough to get near the young jaguar and grab him, then he'd be out of this shit hole in no time. He needed to get back to Texas. He had work to do and a score to settle.

When Dean, a high ranking member of the supernatural council, had killed his partner Ashton for no good fucking reason, Gregory had made a promise to himself that Dean wouldn't get off scot-free. One way or another, Gregory would do what the council had failed to do. Dean didn't deserve impunity. He would pay for what he'd done. It wasn't that Gregory wanted revenge—he wanted justice and he wouldn't rest until he'd got it.

Gregory suspected Ashton wasn't the only person Dean had killed. He was sure Dean had been responsible for the death of Ashton's mate Tania, along with several other council members' mates who had been killed in recent months. He just needed to find the proof—he could do nothing without it. To do that he needed to be in Texas, but of course his job meant he had to be prepared to travel all over the country at a moment's notice. It was unavoidable, but sometimes he was his own worst enemy. He should have been home already, not skulking around Vegas watching a young man that intrigued him so much he'd all but forgotten about his responsibilities. His superiors would be furious if they found out...

He had enjoyed his work for the supernatural council when he was younger, had always loved the thrill of the chase. Back then, he'd thought he had been doing something good, something worthwhile. But the older he'd got, the more disillusioned with the council he had become. They didn't always play by the rules and they had too many corrupt members within their ranks, men that were only out for themselves. Everyone had an agenda it seemed. So much so, it had become impossible to know whom to trust.

Over the years, Gregory had witnessed first-hand how some of the council members treated shifters that didn't belong to a community or a pack. Many were treated little better than animals. As he walked back to his rented unit to attempt to get some sleep, Gregory tried not to think about what would happen to Hayden after he handed him over to his superiors.

He couldn't allow himself to think about that.

* * * *

When the early morning sun made its first appearance on the horizon, Gregory grabbed a quick shower and change of clothes and doubled back to the street outside Hayden's condo. Hiding behind a battered old Ford, he waited for the young jaguar to appear then watched him lock up and cross the street, heading in the direction of the diner.

The kid hunched forward as he walked, keeping his eyes to the ground. He looked as though he carried the weight of the world on his shoulders. Moving out of his hiding place, Gregory began to follow Hayden down the street. He felt for the kid…he really did. He wished there was something he could do to help him, but his hands were tied. He *had* to take Hayden in, because if the council sent in other operatives, Gregory would be in a shit load of trouble he didn't need.

Every few steps Hayden tugged at the waistband of his jeans to pull them back up his narrow hips. They were at least a size too big for him and dragged along the ground as he walked. The grey T-shirt he sported was threadbare and so washed out it had probably started its life as black.

Gregory wasn't an expert on fashion, but Hayden's clothes didn't look as though they'd been picked out to meet a current trend—they looked as though they were the only things he could find to fit him in a thrift store. Gregory couldn't help but wonder what sort of life the young shifter had led. What had happened with his family? And how in God's name had he ended up in this dump?

The report the council had given him to read on Hayden before he'd left for Vegas had been brief—the kid's age, address, the name of the diner he worked at. The report had said that Hayden's parents had kicked him out at sixteen, but it had held no information about the first three years he'd been on his own—nothing until he'd arrived in Vegas and started working at the diner. There was a picture of Hayden that had been captured from a distance, but the kid was barely distinguishable. In the photograph Hayden had his head to the ground, his shoulder-length hair and bangs covering his face.

Quickening his pace, Gregory all but caught up with the young cat shifter, walking no more than ten feet behind him. The closer he got, the harder his dick became. He cursed under his breath and kept on walking. What the hell did he find so appealing about the young jaguar? He was pretty, for sure—his body slim and lithe, just Gregory's type—but Gregory had never experienced this level of attraction before. And he'd never had this much trouble controlling his damn libido.

"Hayden!"

The jaguar stopped walking and turned to face him, pinning him in place with a narrow-eyed glare. "Who are you? How do you know my name?"

When Gregory caught his first glimpse of Hayden up close, his breath caught in his chest and the words he had planned to use on Hayden, to get him to come quietly, stuck in his throat. Hayden's icy blue gaze burned into his mind and imprinted on his soul. And his scent…

This couldn't be happening. "I, uh…"

"What do you want from me?" Hayden asked, eyeing him warily.

Gregory took a step closer to the jaguar and pulled in a deep breath to confirm his suspicions. He couldn't smell Hayden's cat at all, which was odd, but his body reacted to the shifter just as he'd thought it would. His hands broke out in a sweat and what felt like tiny currents of electricity zapped him everywhere at once. His heart raced and his eyes and teeth threatened to shift to their cat form. He had to work hard to contain his cat, to force it inside himself. Gregory had never felt anything like it before and knew he wouldn't again. The feelings, the sensations rolling around in his body, were unmistakable. He didn't need to have experienced them before to know exactly what they were *or* what they meant.

Hayden was his mate.

"Uh, my name is Gregory Hale." Gregory held out his hand for Hayden to shake. It trembled uncontrollably as it inched towards the young man.

Hayden's eyes widened and he looked at Gregory's hand as though it were something that could bite him. How the hell was Hayden so unaffected by their meeting? Gregory wanted to pounce on Hayden and rub himself all over the jaguar, to bathe him in his scent. But Hayden didn't seem to recognise their bond at all. If he did, he wasn't acknowledging it.

"How do you know who I am?" Hayden demanded.

Gregory knew he should tell Hayden he worked for the supernatural council. It was paramount that Hayden come with him. But his instinct to protect the shifter was so strong he couldn't bring himself to utter the words. And there was no goddamn way Gregory could tell the council Hayden was his mate. Council members were discouraged from mating, and after the spate of killings that had occurred recently, he couldn't take the chance. Not after what had happened to his partner Ashton's mate.

The *official* story was that Tania had disturbed some thugs that had broken in to burgle their house while Gregory and Ashton had been away on an assignment. But the fact that other council members' mates had died in much the same way had convinced Gregory that the council was behind her death, even though he hadn't been able to prove it yet. Ashton had thought he'd found the person responsible for her murder and he'd died getting revenge, but Gregory was certain Ashton had killed the wrong man. He was convinced Dean was behind the murders and when he found the proof he needed, he *would* make him pay.

No. Gregory would not willingly hand over Hayden to the council, no matter what it cost him. For once in his life, he didn't give a damn about the consequences. He'd fight every single member in the council if he had to…anything to keep Hayden safe.

"There will be men coming here to get you, Hayden." Gregory kept his voice as calm as he could so that he didn't spook the young shifter. "If you come with me now, I can protect you."

At first, Hayden looked at him as though he were crazy. But then a faint trace of fear reached Gregory's nose and Hayden began edging away. His eyes darted around as though searching for an escape route. *Crap.* Gregory couldn't have that. Maybe he needed to be firmer with his mate, more direct.

"Running won't do you any good. I know the diner you work at and I know where you live." Gregory didn't want to frighten the kid but how else was he going to get him to listen to him? *Whatever you do, Hayden, don't run.*

Hayden started running.

"*Fuck*!" Gregory took off at breakneck speed. Hayden was fast, but as they raced through the busy city streets, Gregory started to gain some ground.

"Hayden, wait!"

Hayden veered left, away from the direction of the diner and sprinted across a busy intersection, narrowly missing several passing cars. They honked their horns repeatedly, swerving to avoid him, but none of them stopped. Christ, if the kid wasn't careful he was going to get himself killed.

"Goddamn it, Hayden. Wait up!"

Gregory picked up his pace, pushing his legs to work harder and, to his relief, Hayden ran into a narrow alleyway. This could work to his advantage. He prayed the alley would lead to a dead end. He couldn't very well keep chasing Hayden around the city all day. The kid was fast, and Gregory had ten years on him.

Gregory thanked everything that was holy when the alley ended with a ten-foot brick wall. Unless Hayden had some major jumping ability, he wouldn't be going anywhere.

"Hayden, please!"

Hayden spun around when he reached the wall. His eyes were wide with fear and Gregory could see the small, prickling movements that rolled over the jaguar's skin. *Shit.* Hayden was about to shift. That often happened when a cat felt afraid or under threat.

"Stay back!" Hayden warned.

Hayden pinned his back to the wall and spread his arms wide. He closed his eyes and cried out as his face contorted with pain. His chest was rising and falling rapidly and his knuckles bulged as his sharp claws threatened to make an appearance. Gregory took a step closer. He might not have been mated before but he knew mates had a calming influence over each other if they were in close proximity.

Hayden's eyes flew open. "I said stay back. I don't want to hurt you."

"It's okay. You won't hurt me…you can't."

Hayden drew his eyebrows together then cried out again, from what must have been another burst of pain ripping through his body. He was fighting the onset of the shift, but Gregory didn't think it was a battle his mate would win. He'd never seen a shifter this close to shifting before that had been able to remain human. He knew Hayden couldn't fight it for much longer—the pain would be excruciating. Partial shifts were one thing but when the whole body began its transformation, a shifter could only go so far before there was no way back.

Hayden blinked and his eyes shifted to their cat form. A low hiss tore from his throat and, while Gregory watched, Hayden's limbs began to elongate, his bones lengthening and changing shape in front of his eyes. It was too late, but Hayden still fought. The strangest thing was that Gregory couldn't smell Hayden's cat. At all. Considering how close Hayden was to a full shift, his cat's scent should be prominent, but Hayden smelt damn near human.

"Hayden, listen to me." Gregory kept his voice quiet, soothing. "Don't fight it anymore, do you understand me? It's better if you shift. The pain will stop."

Hayden shook his head and continued to fight against the shift. Gregory took a step closer and pulled in a deep breath. There was still no trace of Hayden's cat and when he next met Gregory's gaze his eyes had shifted back to their human form.

"Ungh!" Hayden fell to his knees. His breathing was laboured and sweat poured down his face. His bones began to shorten and realign with sickening snaps and cricks. By the time Hayden glanced up at Gregory from beneath thick, dark lashes, every physical manifestation of 'his cat had disappeared. Gregory couldn't smell the jaguar inside him at all. If he hadn't been here to witness it, he would have never believed it possible.

Kneeling on the ground in front of his mate, he placed his hand on Hayden's shoulder and, to his relief, Hayden didn't shrug it off.

"How did you do that?" he asked in amazement. "You were so close to a full shift. How did you stop it?"

"Can't...shift," Hayden panted.

Now it was Gregory's turn to be confused. "I don't understand. What do you mean you can't shift?"

"Can't shift—too dangerous. Hurt...people."

Gregory watched in horror as Hayden's eyes rolled back in his head and he fell to the ground, unconscious. He didn't even have time to protect the jaguar's head before it slammed against the hard concrete with a loud crack.

Chapter Two

Pacing the floor of his rented unit, Gregory thought about his next move. He had managed to carry Hayden back without attracting too much attention but the young jaguar was still passed out on his bed. He made sure the door was locked and all the drapes were closed before walking into the bedroom and taking a seat in the small chair beside the bed. He studied his mate.

Only when he'd got Hayden back to the condo and resting on his bed had he been able to get a good look at him. Hayden was breathtaking. Truly spectacular. The only thing that marred the perfection of his face was a deep scar that ran from his left eye down to his lip. Gregory was surprised he hadn't noticed it before. He'd been watching Hayden for three days. How could he have missed something like that? In his defence, he'd been keeping a safe distance from Hayden and the jaguar always walked with his head down, eyes to the ground. Maybe his scar was the reason why.

The more he looked at it, the more the scar stood out. It appeared to have been there for some time, judging by the colour and texture. Gregory had never seen a shifter with a scar like that before. But then, shifters changed into their second form regularly, so any wounds normally had the chance to heal. But if what Hayden had said was true, and he hadn't shifted recently to his jaguar form, that would explain why the scar had never healed.

When the kid woke up, Gregory would have to talk to him about that. But it would be best to let him sleep, let his body recover. He had never heard of a shifter that fought the shift before. How had Hayden managed to do it? Cat shifters were different from wolves in that they weren't governed by the moon, but his body would still have been trying to shift at regular intervals. How long had he been fighting it, denying his cat? The near-shift would have been extremely painful and have used up a lot of Hayden's energy reserves. Gregory hoped he would feel better when he awoke. For the time being, he was content to sit and look his fill while he tried desperately to ignore the effect the young cat was having on his body.

Since he'd started working for the council, Gregory had met many mated couples and he'd heard often what it felt like when a shifter found their other half. But the descriptions had been wrong. Maybe not wrong exactly, but they had certainly been understated. Gregory didn't think he could put his feelings into words as he watched his mate sleep. Wonder, awe and an overwhelming sense of peace were some of the emotions that were the most potent. *Everything* about Hayden felt right.

And Gregory still couldn't smell Hayden's cat. It was as though the kid had pushed his jaguar so far inside himself when he'd fought the shift, buried it so deep, that only his human side remained. Gregory couldn't understand how Hayden had managed to do that. He suspected that to be the reason Hayden couldn't sense their mating bond. It was the animal side to a shifter that recognised their mate, but Hayden's jaguar had been kept too far at bay. It saddened him that Hayden didn't know who he was or what they were to each other. For Gregory, Hayden was the only light in a world of darkness.

A small smile played on his lips as he watched Hayden's eyes flicker and his body twitch. He was dreaming. Gregory would love nothing more than to glimpse into his mate's mind. As he watched Hayden in slumber, his cell began to vibrate. He fished the phone out of his pocket and checked the number. It was his superior at the council. Riley was the last person Gregory wanted to talk to, but he knew he couldn't put off the call.

He got up from the chair and took the cell into the bathroom in the hall. He closed the door quietly and pressed a button to answer the call. "Gregory."

* * * *

Hayden woke with a start and his eyes darted around the room while they tried to adjust to the low light conditions. How the hell had he got here? And what had happened to him? He felt exhausted—physically and emotionally. His head throbbed and every muscle in his body ached as though he'd run two marathons back to back. Slowly, the fog that clouded his mind began to clear and Hayden remembered running from the man—*Gregory*—on the street, being cornered and nearly shifting. He couldn't believe it had happened again. More and more frequently Hayden's body had been trying to shift, and each time it was increasingly difficult to resist. Hayden suspected he had passed out again. Had Gregory brought him here while he'd been unconscious?

Sitting up, Hayden looked around the small, sparsely decorated room. He swung his legs off the bed, fighting a wave of dizziness that threatened to topple him, when he heard a raised voice coming from what must have been the bathroom in the hall.

As quietly as he could manage, he slid off the bed and tiptoed across the room until he stood outside the door. He listened to the one-sided conversation.

"There was nothing I could do, Riley. He ran, got away from me. Yes, yes, I realise that. I don't know—I went back to his apartment but he didn't show up and he hasn't turned up for work, either."

At once Hayden thought about his job. *Shit*. Would Mac be pissed off at him for not turning up? Would he be worried? Hayden had never missed a day since he'd started working at the diner almost two years ago.

"I think he bailed," Gregory continued. "No. there's no need to bring anyone else in on this, I've got it covered. Fine, whatever. I'll call you if I find anything."

What the hell had that been about? He thought about making a run for it, but he didn't see the point. Gregory knew where he lived *and* worked and he had no place else to go. Besides, he wanted answers—needed them. Mostly he wanted to trust Gregory, which was a damn crazy idea considering he'd only just met the man and knew nothing about him. But, for some reason, he didn't think Gregory meant him any harm.

When he heard Gregory end the call, Hayden stood back from the door, leaned against the wall and folded his arms across his chest. Gregory pulled open the door and the second he set eyes on Hayden his face broke out into a wide, genuine smile that morphed his face into the most beautiful thing Hayden had ever set eyes on.

Bangs from Gregory's dark brown hair fell forward, slightly obscuring eyes that were the deepest shade of blue Hayden had ever seen. They were currently smiling at him. He tried to ignore Gregory's delicious smell and the things it was doing to his body. He needed answers—now was not the time to think about his dick, even though it felt harder than it had ever been. *Focus, Hayden.* He glared at the man.

"You're awake."

"Perceptive," Hayden scoffed. "I want to know what the hell is going on! Who are you and what do you want with me? Who is Riley? You said there were men coming for me—what did you mean by that?"

Hayden's questions came out in a rush. He was so angry he even forgot to turn his head so Gregory wouldn't have to look at his scar. He couldn't blame people for looking but he knew it made them uncomfortable so he tried to save them the embarrassment. As soon as he remembered he lowered his head, even though Gregory hadn't so much as glanced at it. He'd looked Hayden directly in the eye.

"Whoa, slow down a minute. I understand you have questions, lots of them, but please, come and sit down. I'll make you a coffee and explain everything, okay?"

Hayden only took a second to decide. He gave a sharp nod of his head and followed in Gregory's wake.

"How are you feeling?" Gregory asked over his shoulder.

"Okay." Hayden felt far from okay but he didn't want to give anything away until he knew who Gregory was and what he wanted from him.

Gregory sighed. "I know you're lying to me. You were seconds away from shifting. The way you fought it…well, that had to have been excruciating. It must have taken a lot out of you, physically and emotionally. I bet you're exhausted."

Hayden shrugged. "I'm used to it."

Gregory drew his eyebrows together. "That's what worries me. Take a seat."

Hayden shook his head and crossed his arms over his chest. "No, thanks, I'd rather stand."

Gregory shrugged but didn't say anything.

The small kitchen was attached to the living room, a breakfast bar separating the spaces. Gregory set about making coffee. He remained quiet while he worked and, after a few moments, Hayden couldn't stand the silence anymore.

"I want some answers," he demanded.

Gregory nodded. "I can understand that. What do you want to know first?"

"Who are you?"

"My name is Gregory Hale and I work for the supernatural council."

Oh, God. Hayden's blood froze in his veins and he couldn't catch a breath. They knew. They knew what'd he'd done and they'd come for him. How the hell had they found out? Hayden's hands began to tremble and his forehead broke out into a cold sweat.

Maybe he could make a run for it. His gaze shifted to the door. Could he make it in time or would Gregory catch him? What would he do if he got away? He couldn't go back to his apartment or to the diner, but where else could he go? There was nowhere *to* go, and he'd come too far to start hitching rides from truckers again and scavenging in restaurant bins for his next meal.

His hands started shaking uncontrollably and his knuckles stung, his claws feeling like razors, slicing him from the inside. A sharp pain tore down his spine. *Oh, God, not again.* His eyes shifted and his incisors lengthened, slowly and painfully tearing through his gums. Soon his entire body was shaking, his cat hissing and snarling within, desperate to be let loose. But he pushed it inside. He would not let it win.

"Hayden, look at me!" Gregory commanded.

When Hayden looked up, Gregory stood in front of him. His beautiful blue eyes were looking so deeply into his, it was as though they could see into his very soul. Slowly, Gregory reached out and placed his hands on Hayden's trembling shoulders.

"Calm down—it's okay. You're safe here, I promise you. Take some deep breaths. Try to relax."

Hayden couldn't be sure if it was the low, soothing tone to Gregory's voice that helped ease him, or the way the man's fingers caressed his shoulders and the back of his neck, sending pleasant tingles throughout his body. It could have been both. When Hayden closed his eyes and took a few deep breaths as instructed, he felt his cat settle within and he pushed it further inside himself until he couldn't feel its restlessness anymore.

"That's it, just breathe. Good."

When Hayden next opened his eyes, they had shifted back to their human form. His teeth had receded too. Jesus, that had been close…*again*. He had to try to relax. He couldn't afford to get upset, could not afford to shift. Because if he shifted…

"You want to tell me what that was all about?" Gregory asked, snatching him from his thoughts.

"I…"

"Have you had a bad experience with the supernatural council?" Gregory used the same gentle, comforting tone, lulling him into a warm sense of security.

Hayden shook his head, but he couldn't speak. Gregory still hadn't taken his hands off his shoulders and the man's touch was driving him insane. *Please don't look down.* Hayden grew upset at the way his body was responding to Gregory's touch, to his proximity. He was hard. Painfully so. He felt the heat of a blush creep up his neck and cheeks. Gregory continued to stare into his eyes and Hayden couldn't look away. He was drawn to Gregory in a way he'd never experienced. How did the man have such an effect on him? The most surprising thing was that Gregory still wasn't looking at his scar. It was as though he hadn't noticed it…or it didn't matter to him. Couldn't he see how ugly it made him?

Gregory cleared his throat and removed his hands from Hayden's shoulders. "I'll, uh… I'll get you that coffee."

Relief and disappointment battled for dominance inside him when Gregory stepped away and busied himself in the kitchen. For a moment it had felt as though Gregory had touched him for his own selfish reasons, because he needed the closeness as much as Hayden did, not merely because he'd wanted to calm

Hayden down. It had felt almost as though each had recognised something in the other—a sameness or some sort of bond. But Hayden must have been mistaken because Gregory couldn't even meet his eyes anymore.

Don't be stupid, Hayden. What would a man like Gregory ever see in someone like you?

Jesus, Hayden felt beyond embarrassed. Had Gregory seen the desire burning in his eyes? Had his lustful thoughts been obvious? Could Gregory smell his arousal? Hayden needed to be careful. He couldn't let Gregory see his attraction. He had been beaten up several times in the past for looking at a man the wrong way.

"I won't hurt you. You're safe with me, I promise." Gregory crossed the space and handed Hayden a cup of black coffee. "Here, drink this—there's lots of sugar. It will help you feel better."

Hayden nodded and took the drink. He felt stupid suddenly—standing in the middle of the room, nursing his coffee—so he took a seat on the edge of the small sofa.

Hayden took a deep breath. He had to know where he stood. "Are you here to take me in?"

Gregory nodded. "That's what I came here for, yes. Do you understand why?"

Of course he did, the council knew what he'd done, but he didn't say that. "Why don't you tell me?" he asked instead.

Gregory sat in the chair opposite and took a sip from his steaming mug before he spoke. "You've been away from your parents for several years now. You don't have any friends. You haven't been interacting with other cats. You—"

"How do you know all that?"

"The council keeps a close eye on all shifters. As I'm sure you know, we are all registered with the council at birth. I would imagine you've been on their radar since you applied for your social security card when you started working in the diner. I'm certain I'm not the only agent the council has sent here. They don't send in someone like me to make an extraction unless they have all the facts about a shifter. They need to know exactly what they're dealing with. You've probably been watched for some time to see if you made any relationships with other cats."

Hayden frowned. He didn't like the idea that people had been spying on him, but the reason for Gregory's presence calmed him significantly. The council didn't know what he'd done. *Thank God.*

"What's going to happen to me?"

Gregory lowered his gaze. He scrubbed a hand over his eyes and let out a long sigh. "I don't usually get involved after I've handed someone over to my superiors. Some shifters, those with...problems, are able to be rehabilitated. Wolves, for example, are encouraged to join packs. Younger shifters are placed with families. It depends on the individual and their circumstances. But others..." Gregory didn't finish the sentence—he didn't have to. Hayden had a fair idea what happened to others.

"Why can't I stay here? I have my apartment and a job. It's not like I'm a danger to anyone." Even as the words came out of his mouth, Hayden knew they were untrue. He *was* a danger, wasn't he?

"That's not going to be possible, Hayden, I'm sorry."

"But I don't want to leave," Hayden said quietly. "I've got Mac here—he's been like a father to me, more of a father than my own ever was."

"But he's human," Gregory argued. "You need to be with other shifters, with your own kind. And your cat needs to be able to run and to hunt. The more you fight the shift, the more difficult it will become to resist and then there's no telling what will happen. You could shift at any time, hurt someone. Cats that shut themselves away from others of their kind can become feral. You wouldn't want that to happen, would you?"

"No," Hayden whispered. He never wanted to hurt anyone again.

"When was the last time you shifted?"

"About three years ago." Hayden had made the statement casually as though he could barely remember, but he knew the exact date of when he'd last shifted. He could hardly forget. That day had changed him irrevocably. It had hardened him, stripped him of his trust and faith and hope. He couldn't forget that night even if he wanted to. The large angry scar that ran down the left side of his face from his eye to his lip had become a constant reminder.

Gregory pulled in a sharp breath. "Jesus Christ. Three years? But how? Why?"

"I don't want to talk about it." Hayden gripped his coffee cup tighter and pressed his lips together. He couldn't tell Gregory the reason he didn't shift without revealing what he'd done that day three years ago, so he kept quiet.

"When are you going to take me in?" Hayden asked in a small voice. "I need to collect my things from my apartment first and go in to the diner to say goodbye to Mac."

Gregory placed his mug on the coffee table beside him and got up from his chair. He crossed the space and sat next to Hayden. "We'll go right away to collect your belongings, but I'm afraid you won't be able to go back to the diner to say goodbye to Mac."

"What do you mean? Why not? I can't leave without saying goodbye to him." Panic started rising in Hayden's chest. Just what the hell was going on? Why did he have to leave without saying goodbye to the man that had become like a father to him?

Gregory reached out slowly and took hold of Hayden's hand. It was an incredibly intimate gesture for two men that didn't know each other. Hayden was tempted to snatch his hand back but he didn't. He liked Gregory touching him... He liked that Gregory *wanted* to touch him. It stirred feelings and desires that he hadn't realised he was capable of anymore. When Gregory threaded their fingers together, goosebumps rose on Hayden's arms and his breath came faster. He couldn't take his eyes off their clasped hands or stop the fast *thud, thud, thud* of his heart. Hayden had never been this turned on. His stomach was tight with anticipation.

"I need you to trust me," Gregory said. "Do you think you can do that?"

"I don't know, but I want to." Hayden replied honestly. "I'll try."

Gregory nodded. "There are some things going on in the council at the moment...bad things. I don't think it would be a good idea for me to take you back there. It wouldn't be safe for you. But if I were to leave you here, the council would only send in other men and they'd find you. I'm afraid they might already be suspicious. I was supposed to bring you in three days ago, but I couldn't. I..."

"You what?" Hayden leaned in closer, every nerve ending on edge, waiting for the rest of Gregory's sentence as though it held answers to questions he hadn't even dared to ask.

Gregory lowered his gaze. "Wow, this is difficult to explain."

Hayden gripped Gregory's hand tighter like it was the only thing keeping him grounded. "You can tell me."

He was surprised at how husky he sounded when he spoke. He'd never heard that tone to his voice before, never even knew it was a sound he had been capable of making.

"Hayden, when you look at me, when you touch me…do you feel anything?"

Oh crap. Hayden could feel a whole host of things, especially in the lower half of his body, but he'd be damned if he told Gregory what effect the man was having on his dick. Or how his proximity made Hayden's head spin, made his heart beat faster and made every nerve ending in his body thrum with anticipation. But why was Gregory even asking him that? Could he tell how turned on Hayden was?

"No," he lied. "I don't know what you mean."

Hayden noticed the bob in Gregory's throat as he nodded slowly. "Right."

"What does this have to do with me not being able to say goodbye to Mac?"

When Gregory next met Hayden's gaze, his mouth was turned down at the corners and he seemed to have lost the little spark that had lit up his pretty, pale blue eyes. Hayden wanted to do or say something to bring back Gregory's smile, to put the light back in his eyes, but he didn't know what.

"It has everything to do with it, but I don't think this is something I'm able to explain," Gregory said at last.

"I think it's something you need to experience to fully understand."

Hayden didn't know what the hell Gregory was talking about but he found himself nodding in agreement anyway. "Okay."

"You said you'd try to trust me, right?"

"Yes."

"And you believe me when I say I have your best interests at heart and I wouldn't do anything to harm you?"

That was an odd question, but even more curious was the fact that Hayden didn't have to think about his reply. He *did* trust Gregory, and, for reasons he couldn't explain, he knew the man wouldn't hurt him.

"I believe you," he breathed.

"Okay, good." Gregory scrubbed the hand that wasn't holding Hayden's on the leg of his jeans and, while Hayden watched, a bead of perspiration trickled down his forehead. He cleared his throat. "Hayden, I need you to do something for me. I need you to shift."

* * * *

Gregory watched Hayden hastily shove items of clothing into a beat-up, old backpack. When he stood, his usually lithe body looked stiff, his back ramrod straight, the tension in his shoulders obvious. The only time he chanced a look at Gregory, it was to glare at him.

"Hayden, please be reasonable," Gregory implored. If he hadn't asked Hayden five damn times, he hadn't asked him once.

"Reasonable!" Hayden spluttered "Don't be such a hypocrite! Do you even know what you're asking? How dare you tell *me* to be reasonable!" Hayden's entire body shook with anger. Wow, his mate had a temper.

Crossing the room quickly, Gregory stood in front of Hayden, halting his progress to the closet to grab more clothes. "What *am* I asking exactly? Why don't you tell me why it's so difficult for you to shift?"

Hayden glared some more. "Just drop it, Gregory. I already said I'd come with you. Can't you leave it at that?"

This was harder than Gregory had anticipated. "No, I can't."

"Urgh!" Hayden threw up his arms in exasperation. "You are unbelievable! You show up out of nowhere, and just expect me to leave everything behind and go with you to God only knows where. You expect me to leave my home, my job, my… my *family*!"

"Mac is your boss—he's not family," Gregory corrected. Jesus, he wanted to grab Hayden and shake him, to blurt out the truth.

I'm *your family, goddamn it! And if you'd just shift, you'd realise that!*

Hayden's eyes turned black with fury and his glare became more pronounced. "How *dare* you! You don't know a goddamn thing! Mac *is* my family! He's all I've got!" Despite his fury, Hayden's voice cracked on the last word.

Gregory wanted to pull Hayden into his arms and crush him in an embrace. He couldn't stand to see the pain in his mate's eyes. *He's not all you've got, Hayden.*

"And," Hayden continued, "how do I even know you're telling the truth, huh? How do I know you're from the supernatural council at all? You could be dragging me off to the desert to…to rape me, or murder me or something."

Gregory rolled his eyes. "I showed you my ID."

"ID can be faked!"

This was getting them nowhere. They'd been having this same damn argument for the past half an hour and Gregory couldn't see any end to it. He couldn't think of anything else to say to convince Hayden of his sincerity...well, short of telling him the truth. But he knew that wouldn't help matters—it would only make things worse. He'd been close to revealing everything to Hayden back in his condo but he'd changed his mind at the last second.

If Gregory admitted they were mates, Hayden would never believe him. How could he? A shifter knew when they met their mate. It was an instinctual thing, like a mighty revelation or the answer to every question they had ever asked. That was exactly how it had felt for Gregory. But Hayden's cat was buried so deep within himself, his human side so prevalent, that he couldn't see what was right in front of him. And if he didn't feel it, Gregory would be fucked. Hayden wouldn't go anywhere with him.

He pinched the bridge of his nose. He didn't even have the first fucking clue where he could take Hayden to keep him safe. He just knew he had to get him the hell away from Vegas. While he thought of another way to broach the topic of shifting, his cell started vibrating in his pocket. *Great.*

He pulled out the phone and checked the caller ID. *Kelan.*

"Hello."

"Gregory, Kelan. I've had some news I thought you might want to hear."

Gregory caught Hayden watching him out of the corner of his eye. "Is it about what we discussed?"

"Yeah, how much longer are you in Vegas?"

Pursing his lips, Gregory watched Hayden slip an e-reader into his backpack, then pause to look around the room at the rest of his meagre belongings, probably deciding what he should bring. Hayden appeared to be concentrating on the task at hand but Gregory had no doubt he was listening to every word.

For hours Gregory had been trying to decide on a place he could take Hayden where he would be safe from the council's clutches. A thought suddenly occurred to him. His answer was on the other end of the line, waiting for his reply.

"I'm leaving now, but I'm driving and it's a twenty hour run, so I'll stop halfway, spend the night in Albuquerque. I can be there by Friday. Can it wait until then?"

"Yeah, Friday's cool."

"Okay, good. I can't talk right now, but is it okay if I give you a ring from the road? I have a favour to ask." Gregory hoped Kelan would help him out. He trusted the alpha and he knew Hayden would be safe with him on the Crazy Horse ranch if he had to leave to deal with council business. And, of course, Cary was living at the ranch so Hayden would have the company of another cat.

But it was a lot to ask. Kelan could get into a shit load of trouble for helping him, and Gregory didn't even want to think about what the council would do to *him* if they found out what he'd done. And what would happen to Hayden?

Kelan groaned. "Why do I get the feeling I'm not going to like the sound of this?" Despite his words, there was a teasing tone to his voice and Gregory couldn't help but smile.

"Let's just say, if you can help me out with this, I'll owe you...big time."

Kelan chuckled. "I always collect."

When Gregory hung up, Hayden was sorting through a pile of clothes on his bed but his attention appeared to be elsewhere.

"Who was that?" he asked casually.

"Just a friend in Texas."

"A close friend?" Hayden's casual tone hadn't changed but he'd paused mid-sorting and his body had become as stiff as a starched cotton sheet.

Gregory crossed the room and sat on the bed beside his mate. He waited for Hayden to meet his gaze before he spoke. "*Just* a friend."

Hayden shrugged like it didn't make one damn lick of difference, but as he continued to sort through his clothes Gregory noticed a small smile tug at the corner of his lips. Gregory put his hands over his lap and tried to hide his pleasure at Hayden's reaction to him. Even without knowledge of their bond, Hayden was displaying the jealous tendencies a shifter often showed towards their mate. It delighted Gregory's cat.

Chapter Three

With a deep sadness, Hayden watched the '*Leaving Las Vegas*' sign whizz past the window as they headed out towards the desert. He might not have much to leave behind but what he did have he'd worked damn hard to get. His biggest regret was not being able to say goodbye to Mac. He wished there had been some way he could have explained his situation to his boss, or at the very least thanked him for everything he'd done, but that hadn't been possible.

He'd pleaded with Gregory to allow him to go to the diner, but Gregory's reply had always been the same. The supernatural council would send in more men to search for Hayden and they would undoubtedly question Mac. To see the man again, to talk to him, would only put him at risk.

Gregory had called his superior at the council to tell him he couldn't find Hayden and he suspected he'd left the city. After the call, Gregory had become quiet and he'd barely spoken two words to Hayden since. Hayden hadn't questioned him about the call but the further they drove from Vegas, the more it played on his mind.

Fear of the unknown had never been a problem for Hayden. He'd become used to moving from place to place. But he'd felt settled in Vegas—for the first time since he'd left home, he'd found a place where he felt needed. Leaving that behind was difficult, almost as hard as leaving his parents and brother had been. What would happen to him now? Would he be forever looking over his shoulder, wondering if the council was closing in on him? Where would he live? What would he do to survive? The questions weighed on his mind until he couldn't stand it anymore.

"What did your superior say when you told him you couldn't find me?"

Gregory sighed. "He said not to worry, they'd find you eventually. He told me to come back to base. He wasn't happy with me for losing you."

"What will they do to you if they find out you've helped me?"

"I don't know, Hayden, but I don't think it would be good."

"You're risking an awful lot for me," Hayden said. "Why is that?"

Gregory stiffened in his seat and Hayden noticed his hands grip the steering wheel tighter until his knuckles were white with the pressure.

"I've been doing this job for a long time," Gregory said. "The more I see, the harder it becomes. I used to think I was helping people, doing some good, but I'm not so sure anymore. I couldn't hand you over to the council not knowing if something bad could happen to you. I feel like it's my duty to protect you."

Gregory's words rang true, but Hayden suspected there was something Gregory wasn't telling him. After a moment, the cat let out a long breath, his body relaxing a little in his seat.

"What sort of cat are you?" Hayden asked.

Gregory took his eyes off the road and turned to stare at Hayden, mouth agape. "You can't tell?"

Hayden shrugged. "Guess my sense of smell is not what it used to be. I mean, I can tell you're a cat, I think, but I don't know what kind."

Gregory shook his head. "Your sense of smell is not what it used to be because you haven't shifted in so long. If you'd just listen to me, if you'd shift…"

"I'm not going over this again. I don't want to shift—now can you drop it, please?"

"Fine," Gregory replied through a clenched jaw.

"So what are you?"

"I'm a leopard."

"Oh, cool. Never met any leopards before."

Gregory nodded. "We're rare in this part of the country. There are a lot of snow leopards in the states that border Canada, but leopards are pretty much thin on the ground all over, especially in the southern states. Hardly any in Texas."

"Is that where you're taking me?"

"Yes. We're going to my friend's ranch. I haven't asked him yet but I think it will be okay. There's a young panther shifter living there called Cary—your age. I think you'll like him."

"Is your friend a panther, too?"

"No, Kelan is a wolf. He's the alpha of his pack."

Hayden gasped. "What? You're taking me to a pack of wolves?"

"Relax, Hayden." Gregory took his hand off the steering wheel and placed it on Hayden's knee. The touch had obviously been meant to soothe, but it had the opposite effect. Hayden's heart started beating faster and his dick hardened. He suppressed a moan.

"Kelan is a good man," Gregory continued. "You'll be safe with him. And I think you'll like the other wolves that work there, too. Cary has been there for a while now. He's the only cat and he's very happy living on the ranch."

Hayden looked down at the hand on his knee and sighed. He liked it there and didn't even think of removing it. He wished it meant more but he knew it didn't. Gregory was obviously a tactile person because he'd been touching Hayden constantly since they'd first met. It was always casual, though—a brush of fingers here, a hand on his shoulder there. When they'd first got into the car, Gregory had leant forward and brushed the bangs out of Hayden's eyes. Each touch was like a rush of adrenaline racing through his system. A constant high—and one he could become accustomed to. Hayden would be sorry to see it end when Gregory dropped him off in Texas.

"Isn't Kelan the person you spoke to on the phone earlier?"

"Yep."

Hayden frowned and turned to look at the stark and uninspiring view through the passenger window. He hadn't liked the way Gregory had smiled when he'd spoken to Kelan. It had made him feel…jealous—even though he had no reason to be. It was crazy because he and Gregory had only just met, but he hadn't liked it one bit.

"At the next rest stop I'll give Kelan a call," Gregory continued. "We'll see if he has some work for you on his ranch. You ever do anything like that before?"

Hayden shook his head. "I've never even been on a horse."

"Nothing to it—you'll be an expert in no time."

"I guess." Hayden wasn't so sure. He'd always been fearful of horses, but he didn't want Gregory to think he was weak so he kept quiet. "Can I ask you something?"

Gregory turned his head and flashed Hayden his thousand watt smile, his straight white teeth glistening in the midday sun that flooded the car. The smile caused Hayden's stomach to tighten. "Of course, you can ask me anything."

"When you drop me at the ranch, is that it? Will I ever see you again?"

A trace of emotion flashed in Gregory's eyes, but Hayden couldn't be certain what it had been. The hand on his knee squeezed tighter and the pressure caused warmth to spread through his body, making him tingle.

"You'll see me all the time, Hayden."

Hayden nodded. He let his head fall back against the rest and closed his eyes, relieved perhaps more than he should be by Gregory's response. He swallowed down a lump in his throat. This was so not good. He didn't want to form an attachment to Gregory, but after just a few short hours spent with him that was exactly what was happening. That was dangerous for a shifter. Stupid. But Hayden couldn't make himself care.

Hayden's last thought before he fell asleep surprised him. He realised that, for the entire time he'd been in the car, he hadn't once worried about how ugly his scar made him appear. It was a pleasing thought.

* * * *

"Hayden. Hayden...wake up, we're here."

Hayden opened his eyes and stretched out his stiff body. He rolled his head from side to side making it crick.

"Texas?" he asked around a yawn, peering out of the window into the darkness to try to get his bearings.

Gregory chuckled. The low, husky sound reverberated through Hayden's body and sent a zing of excitement racing up his spine. "You haven't been asleep *that* long, beautiful, although you have been out cold for a good eight hours. We're in Albuquerque."

Hayden's anger immediately rose to the surface. "Don't make fun of me!" he shouted.

Gregory jerked back as though Hayden had physically slapped him then drew his eyebrows together in confusion. "I didn't. What did I say?"

Turning his overheated face away, Hayden tried to take a few steadying breaths. When he finally got his anger under control, he spoke, but his voice shook with emotion. "I know I'm ugly. But I have feelings, you know. I expect that sort of thing from most people, but I never expected it from you. Guess I should have known."

Hayden tried to swallow down his hurt. He'd thought Gregory was different, but then he'd thought that about people in the past, hadn't he? Most of them turned out to be exactly the same—cruel…hurtful to those that were different from themselves.

"Hey!" Gregory's booming voice made Hayden jump. "Look at me!"

Hayden set his jaw and continued to stare out of the window.

"I said look at me, God damn it!" Gregory grabbed hold of Hayden's face and twisted it until they were eye to eye. Hayden thought Gregory might be about to apologise for what he'd said, but what happened next was the very last thing he could have anticipated. Gregory leant forward and crushed their mouths together, forcing his tongue into Hayden's mouth. The kiss was hard, fervent and incredibly hot. It felt almost like Gregory was claiming him. Hayden could do nothing but hold on for the ride and hope he didn't come in his pants.

When Gregory finally ended the kiss, he groaned and pressed their foreheads together. He was breathing heavily and when he pulled back Hayden saw that his eyes and teeth had shifted to their cat form.

"You are *not* ugly. You are the most beautiful goddamn man I ever saw and I'll tell you every damn day until you start to believe it, you got me?"

Haydon was so shocked he couldn't speak. He nodded dumbly, trying to avert his gaze, but it was no use. Gregory still held his head in a death grip between his hands.

"Do you understand me, Hayden?" Gregory pressed.

"But my scar..." Hayden whispered.

"Is just that—a scar. It doesn't take anything away from your looks, not for me. I don't even see it when I look at you, and it's not like you don't know how to get rid of it. You only need to shift."

Hayden closed his eyes. It was the only thing he could do to get away from the intensity in Gregory's stare. He couldn't hold that inquisitive gaze without blurting out his secrets and uncovering his skeletons. He wasn't ready for that.

"I can't," he whispered.

"One day soon you're going to tell me why," Gregory said. "Now, I'm going to get us a room for the night. Stay in the car until I get back, okay?"

Hayden nodded, but he didn't open his eyes. After a moment he heard Gregory sigh and his hands fell from Hayden's face. The car door opened and then closed again and Hayden was at last alone. His breath left him in a rush. Could it be possible that Gregory really thought he was beautiful and didn't notice his scar? Or had he just said that to make Hayden feel better about himself?

Gregory was the most incredible man he'd ever met. Handsome didn't even come close to describing him. His face had a rugged quality to it. Strong nose, strong jaw and the most alluring blue eyes Hayden had ever seen. Okay, so Hayden knew Gregory played for his team now, but someone like him could have any man he wanted. Could he really find Hayden attractive? Even with his scar? Hayden didn't dare believe.

Part of him realised the pointlessness of his thoughts, anyway. Most shifters didn't get involved in relationships because it would only complicate their lives if they found their mate. So would there be any point in the two of them starting anything? Hayden knew it would be easy to fall for Gregory and then, when the leopard met his mate, where would that leave Hayden? It was stupid of him to want things he had no business wanting. Reckless.

Maybe it would be better if he didn't see Gregory again after he'd been dropped off at the ranch in Texas. Better for them both. But the thought of never seeing Gregory again made his stomach ache. *Jesus.* What the hell was he getting himself into? He tried to get a handle on his anxiety while he waited for Gregory to return.

Gregory pressed his head against the cool glass of the door to the motel office and cursed under his breath. What the fuck had he just done? He couldn't believe he'd been so impulsive. He shouldn't have kissed Hayden, but he'd been angry when he'd heard his mate call himself ugly. His cat had been furious and had quickly risen to the surface. Gregory had wanted to show Hayden that he'd been telling the truth, that he *did* think he was beautiful, that he was genuinely the most beautiful man he had ever seen. But, whatever his reasons, that still didn't make it right. He should have had more damn sense. If he couldn't be more careful, he was in danger of scaring the jaguar off. If only Hayden would shift he'd understand everything… He'd *know*.

Gregory pushed open the door to the office and strode inside. The one-storey building was old and run-down, but it was the type of place that wouldn't ask any questions. Besides, he'd stayed in worse places. The elderly man behind the desk was watching a TV set on a bracket on the wall in the corner of the room. Gregory glanced at the set briefly before turning back to the man.

The man chuckled then turned to face Gregory, his smile wide. "Garfield," he drawled, shaking his head. "What a riot!"

Gregory's mouth twitched. "Hilarious. You got a room?"

The man pursed his lips and opened a register on the desk. He took his time looking through the pages to see what he had available, but Gregory had no idea why he'd bothered. He could see the room keys hanging on pegs on the wall. Every peg held a key, bar one.

"Yep, looks like I can sort you out. Hundred bucks," the man said, licking his lips.

A hundred bucks for this dump? Gregory shook his head, but reached for his wallet and handed over the money.

"We don't do breakfast," the man said, "but, if you want coffee, there's a machine just there." He nodded to the wall near the door. "Office is open all night. Name's Larry, by the way."

"Thanks, Larry. Is there a payphone around here?"

"Sure is, it's 'round near the pool, opposite the furthest unit."

Gregory nodded and took the key, which had a small block of wood hanging from it with the room number painted in thick red numerals.

"Thanks," Gregory nodded. "Have a good night."

Larry grunted a reply and before Gregory left the office the man had turned up the volume on his movie and was laughing along with it again.

After collecting Hayden from the car, Gregory led the way to their room, which was located at the end of a long row of identical units. Gregory unlocked the door, pushed it open and switched on the light. The decor was just as he'd expected…old. The furniture was tatty and in certain places the wallpaper was peeling away from the wall.

"One bed?" Hayden asked looking from it to Gregory, eyebrows raised.

Gregory groaned inwardly. It hadn't even occurred to him to ask for two beds, he'd just taken what Larry had given him. How the hell was he going to sleep next to Hayden all night and keep his hands to himself? His dick had been hard non-stop since he'd met Hayden and now he had to lie next to him in bed? *Christ.* This was going to be a true test of his willpower.

"I don't mind," Hayden said quietly, and as Gregory watched, his face coloured to a deep shade of pink. He could smell the arousal seeping out of Hayden's pores and it made his already hard cock ache with need. *Oh, God*. Gregory was done for.

He went to check out the bathroom to pull himself together. He was a grown man, but his body was reacting as though he were a damn horny teenager. It was embarrassing.

"How is it?" Hayden asked.

"It's basic, but at least it's clean. You can use it first. I need to find the payphone to make a call."

Hayden moved quickly to his side. "Are you going to call Kelan?"

Gregory had to hold his breath and shove his hands in his pocket as he slid past Hayden to stop himself from reaching out, grabbing the jaguar and sealing their lips together. That damn kiss in the car was to blame, he was sure of it. He couldn't get it out of his head. That kiss had made his already anxious cat whine in frustration and claw at him from the inside, begging him to take what was theirs.

"Uh, yeah. I need to ask if it's okay for you to stay there and I don't want to do it on my cell. I don't think the council are monitoring my calls, but I'd rather be safe than sorry."

"Okay," Hayden replied quietly. "Guess I'll see you in a while."

Gregory thought he heard a trace of jealousy in Hayden's voice but he didn't comment on it. He nodded. "Keep the door locked."

He went out into the motel forecourt and circled around to the back of the units until he found the small pool area. The phone was just where Larry had said it would be, opposite the last unit. He dug in his pocket for some quarters, fed them into the phone and dialled Kelan's cell.

"'Lo."

"Kelan, it's Gregory."

"Hey, what's up? How's the drive?"

"Good… Listen, I can't talk for long, I'm on a payphone, I didn't want to risk using my cell. It's about that favour."

"I'm listening," Kelan said.

Gregory pulled in a lungful of air before he spoke. "Kelan, I found my mate."

"Well, hell, congratulations. I'm happy for you."

"Thanks, but, uh… It's not quite as simple as that. He doesn't know."

"Huh?"

"He doesn't know he's my mate." Gregory could practically hear the cogs turning in Kelan's mind.

"Is he human?" he asked at last.

"No, he's a cat."

"Then how can't he tell?"

Gregory sighed. "It's a long story. The problem is he's the cat the council had me go to Vegas to collect. But there's no goddamn way I'm handing Hayden over to them, so I told them he got away from me, that I couldn't find him."

"Say no more," Kelan said. "He's welcome here."

Gregory finally let out the breath he'd been holding. "You sure?"

"Of course. I don't blame you for not wanting to tell the council about him. He can stay here for as long as he likes. I'm sure I can find work to keep him occupied. But we'll have to be careful. Dean has been here and he's been asking about you."

"Shit, what did he want to know?"

"If I'd heard from you. I didn't tell him you'd been in touch, but I'm not sure he believed me."

"Is that what you wanted to tell me earlier?"

Kelan hesitated before he spoke. "There's something else, but I'd rather tell you face to face."

"Sounds ominous."

"It's not good news, Gregory. Look, don't worry, just get yourself here and we'll figure out the rest."

"Thanks, I can't tell you how much I appreciate this."

"No need, 'sides, I know how you feel. I'd do anything to protect my mate."

Gregory looked across at the row of rooms to where his mate was showering somewhere inside. "Yeah, I think I'm finally beginning to understand that concept."

By the time Gregory got back to the room, Hayden had already taken his shower and climbed into bed. He had the sheets pulled up to his chest, his bare arms folded on top. *Christ, is he naked under there*? Gregory muffled a moan and crossed the room to the bathroom, trying to ignore his throbbing dick.

"What did Kelan say?" Hayden asked, stopping him in his tracks.

"He said you can stay on the ranch, but Dean has been sniffing around, asking questions, so we need be careful when we get you there. We can't risk him seeing you."

"Who's Dean?"

"He works for the supernatural council, and he's very influential." He sighed. "Let me grab a shower and I'll tell you the whole story, okay?"

While Gregory stood in the tub, letting the hot water ease his tired muscles, he debated how much he should tell Hayden about the trouble in the council and the things he suspected of Dean. In the end, he decided to be honest with his mate... Well, as honest as he could be without telling Hayden about their bond.

He dried off quickly and pulled on his briefs, padding into the bedroom barefoot. Hayden was laying on his side, propping up his head on one hand. Gregory sat on the edge of the bed and took a deep breath.

"You sure you want to hear this? Some parts of it are...disturbing." Something flashed in Hayden's eyes then, but Gregory couldn't be certain what it had been. Hayden nodded and sat up in bed, the sheets bunching around his waist.

"Please."

Gregory tried to keep his eyes off his mate's temptingly smooth chest when he spoke. "About six months ago my partner Ashton and I were sent on an assignment in Missouri. We had to bring in a wolf that had killed someone in his pack, gone crazy. The job wasn't any more complicated than dozens we'd been on before, but Ashton was uptight the whole time."

"Ashton was your partner at the council?"

"Yeah, we'd worked together going on ten years, had each other's back. I thought Ashton was so edgy because his mate Tania was eight months pregnant with their first child and he was worried something would go wrong, or that she'd go into labour early and he'd miss it."

"That wasn't the reason?"

Gregory scrubbed a hand over his face. "I don't think so. Ashton called Tania right before we picked up the wolf. He was upset after that phone call—seemed...distracted, I guess. I think maybe they'd had an argument. I know that Tania hated what Ashton did for a living. She worried he'd get hurt and had been constantly nagging him to quit. It had been causing a lot of tension between them. Anyway, we picked up the wolf and drove him back to council headquarters. When we got there, our superior Riley called Ashton into the office.

"I could tell it was bad news from the look on Riley's face. They'd only been inside a minute when I heard Ashton shouting… Well, screaming would be a better word to describe it, so I went in. Ashton was tearing the place apart, upending tables, throwing things—he was crazed. In the end Riley had to sedate him."

"Had something happened to his mate?"

Gregory nodded. "She'd been killed. Riley said it looked as though some burglars broke in, tried to rob the place and Tania got in the way. A neighbour heard her screaming and called the sheriff. By the time they got there it was too late. She was dead, the baby too, and there was no sign of the shifters that did it, no clues. A wolf in the sheriff's department called the council and they brought her body back to headquarters. The story sounded plausible until I got a look at her body. It was a mess. They tore her apart, Hayden. I've seen a lot of dead bodies during my time on the council, but hers was one of the worst. Her wounds weren't consistent with someone killed in a rush. Whoever did it took their time…got real pleasure out of it.

"Ashton was in pieces for months. I had to force him to eat, to shower… Hell, it was a struggle to make him get out of bed. Then one day he came into work as though nothing had happened, just another day at the office."

"Why the sudden turnaround?"

"I think his grief finally turned into anger and he needed to do something about it. Ashton pulled me aside that day and made me promise to help him find out who had killed Tania and their baby and make them pay for what they'd done. He said he wanted justice, but I know it was revenge he was craving. I couldn't blame him. I probably would have wanted the same thing if I was in his shoes. I agreed, of course. I would have done anything to help him and I was glad to have my friend back, but he wasn't the Ashton I'd known for all those years. He was different, changed in some fundamental way."

"Some people never recover from losing their mate," Hayden commented.

Gregory hung his head. He wanted to reach out and grab Hayden's hand, to tell him about their bond, but he forced his mouth shut and fisted the sheets beneath him to keep his hands busy.

"I found out recently that Ashton wasn't the only council member to lose his mate. There's a definite pattern beginning to emerge. The others' mates all died under similar circumstances."

Hayden gasped. "So you think someone at the council had her killed?"

"I'm sure of it."

"But why would they do that?"

"The council doesn't look favourably on its members mating. It's no secret that they discourage it, which in itself is ludicrous because what shifter is going to stay away from their mate once they've found them? Their reasoning is that because the bond is so strong, because a shifter will do anything to protect their mate, it creates a weakness and they become a liability. Weak shifters are of no use to the council."

Hayden nodded his head. "I guess I can understand their reasoning but it's hardly realistic. Did you ever find out who was responsible?"

A lump rose in Gregory's throat, but he tried to swallow it down. "At the time we thought we had. A wolf at the council called Blake Deveraux started to help us. I never really understood why. I thought it might be because he felt sorry for Ashton and didn't believe the council's story about his mate's death. He said he'd learned that the man responsible was someone called Stan Michaels, a high ranking member of the council, but he hadn't been able to find any concrete proof."

"Around the same time, there had been trouble in Wolf Creek, the town in which Kelan is alpha. We believed the council to be behind the trouble so Kelan called a meeting to discuss what we could do. He said he had a friend working on the council and, when Ashton and I went to the meeting, we met him. His name is Dean White and he holds a very powerful position. He's the man I told you about earlier, the one Kelan said has been asking questions about me."

"But I thought you said he was Kelan's friend?"

Gregory nodded. "Kelan thought he was someone that could be trusted, and at first so did I, but now we're not so sure. At the meeting Dean said he'd received information about Stan Michaels, that Stan had been involved in illegal activity with Joe Walker, one of Kelan's pack members. While we were dealing with some wolves at the council, Dean told us he'd had word that Stan was on his way to meet with Joe. I tried to find Ashton to tell him, but he'd already left.

"I called his cell and he told me he was on his way to make Stan pay for what he'd done. Kelan, Dean and I followed him to Joe's, but by the time we got there,

Ashton had already shot Stan, but he hadn't killed him yet. I pleaded with Ashton to think about what he was doing, but there was no reasoning with him. I know he wasn't in his right mind—he must have been thinking about what had happened to Tania. He shot Stan a second time, and then Dean shot Ashton, killed him."

"I'm sorry for what happened to your friend," Hayden said quietly. "But it sounds like Dean was doing his job. What makes you think he's behind the murders?"

Gregory sighed and lowered his gaze. "I did some checking into Dean's background and it turns out he's an excellent marksman. So he knew exactly what he was doing when he killed Ashton—it wasn't just an unlucky shot. He didn't have to kill him. Ashton wasn't a threat to any of us. I think it was Dean that had been feeding information to Ashton about Stan and he was worried that Ashton would say something that would point the finger at him, so he killed Ashton to silence him."

"What would Dean gain from making it look as though Stan were responsible for Tania's death? Do you think he did it just to throw suspicion off himself?"

"You know that there are members in the council that believe shifters should live openly, should come out to humans?"

Hayden snorted. "That's ridiculous. It would never work."

"I agree, and that's one thing Dean and I see eye to eye on. He's incredibly vocal about his views on shifter politics. Well, Stan belonged to a group that had been campaigning for shifters to come out, expose ourselves. He'd gained a large following by all accounts. From what I've been able to find out since, Stan had created a petition to take to the elders to propose they allow us to reveal ourselves to humans if we desired. The word at the council is that there are a lot of names on that list.

"Apparently, Stan had been working his way through each pack, trying to get the majority of members to sign. But he always went for the troublemakers in the pack first. He sought out the shifters that would love nothing more than to stir things up. I guess those pack members feel superior to humans and were happy to sign. Dean has been fighting to put a stop to the petition before it gets before the elders, but I think he's taken it a step too far. I think he used Ashton to get to Stan. That got one very large opponent out of his way. But I haven't been able to find a connection between Dean and the death of the mates at the council. I'm sure there's something there, but I'm missing it."

"Wow," Hayden said at last. "It's kind of a lot to take in."

"I know. And I debated whether or not I should tell you, but it's a volatile situation and I figured, if you're going to be staying at the Crazy Horse, you needed all the facts, needed to know what is going on around you." *And you're my mate,* Gregory added mentally. *If the council members find out about you, you're in great danger, too.*

"Is there anything I can do to help?" Hayden asked.

Gregory gave his mate a tired smile. "Yeah, stay away from any council members, especially Dean White."

Chapter Four

When Hayden opened his eyes he wasn't surprised to feel Gregory's arm wrapped around his waist, or a heavily muscled leg pushed between his own, the coarse hairs tickling where they touched. They'd started the night on opposite sides of the bed. Hayden hadn't been able to fall asleep for hours because he'd slept so much in the car. While he had lain awake, halfway through the night, Gregory had turned in his sleep and sought him out like a heat-seeking missile. He'd wrapped an arm around Hayden and pulled him closer until their bodies were touching from head to toe. The shelter of Gregory's arms had made him feel safe. It made him smile to think Gregory wanted to snuggle against him, even if he wasn't aware he was doing it.

If Hayden had found it difficult to sleep before, he found it damn near impossible wrapped in Gregory's embrace, especially with the man's hard cock pressed up against his ass. How the hell did he stay so hard while he slept? Hayden had been out of his mind with lust, his own cock begging for attention, but he'd ignored it…he had to. He needed to stop thinking of Gregory in an amorous way because no good could come of it.

"Hmm," Gregory moaned in his sleep and pressed himself closer to Hayden's back. Jesus, if the man wasn't still hard. Hayden groaned, allowing himself to enjoy the embrace for a solitary moment, to delight in the contact, and wallow in the fantasy. But right before he made to pull out of Gregory's arms, the man started to purr, the low rumble in his chest like music to Hayden's ears. He could gladly listen to it for the rest of his days on earth. Hayden couldn't remember the last time he'd been so contented that he'd purred. But Gregory made him want to, made him want a lot of things.

Lying in Gregory's arms was torture. Hayden had to do something. He turned around to face Gregory but it didn't rouse him from his slumber, so Hayden took a moment to study him. Jesus, he was beautiful. He looked so peaceful while he slept that Hayden very nearly left him that way, but they had to hit the road soon, and they had to get out of this damn bed before they did something Hayden was certain Gregory would regret.

"Gregory, wake up."

Very slowly, Gregory opened his eyes. The second he met Hayden's gaze, his mouth stretched into the widest smile Hayden had seen on the man yet. He waited for Gregory to awaken fully, to realise where he was and to push Hayden away, but of course he did the complete opposite of what Hayden expected. He was becoming used to Gregory doing the unexpected, which was ludicrous considering how long they'd known each other, but there it was.

Gregory tugged Hayden closer and pressed their lips together. The low rumble of a moan came from both their chests, as if in unison. Pushing his tongue inside, Gregory stole Hayden's breath, the wet heat of his mouth wringing an even louder moan from his throat.

Hayden knew he should stop the kiss, but Gregory's lips felt so perfect against his own, so…right, and when Gregory forced his mouth wider and pushed his tongue in further, deepening the kiss, Hayden let him. He couldn't have stopped now if he wanted to, and he didn't want to.

Firm hands slid down his back until they reached his ass and kneaded. Nimble fingers dug into his flesh and dragged him closer until their hard cocks came into contact. Gregory's purring became louder, drowning out the sounds of their whimpers and moans. With a low, throaty growl, Gregory flipped them until he was lying on top of Hayden, pinning him to the mattress beneath his firm body, their bare chests pressed together, igniting a fire in Hayden's stomach he never wanted put out. When Gregory started to rock, Hayden's own hips lifted to meet each gentle thrust.

Closing his eyes, Hayden pressed his head back into the pillow and let himself get lost in the feeling of Gregory's body grinding into his own. The closeness of their bodies made him happy. It filled his heart so full he thought it might burst clean out of his chest. He knew it was just lust. He was attracted to Gregory, but as their bodies moved together he dared to dream that it could be something more meaningful. Then Gregory ground harder against him and Hayden lost the ability to think at all. He needed to come so badly.

"Hayden, open your eyes."

Gregory's raspy voice pulled him from his reverie and he did as instructed. When he looked up, he saw that Gregory's eyes and teeth had shifted to their cat form. There was something so incredibly erotic about Gregory losing control like that...for him—for *Hayden*—someone that most people couldn't stand to look at. As their bodies continued the sensual dance Hayden felt his cat begin to stir. Even though he was so used to pushing it deep inside himself, he could sense its restlessness, was aware of it begging for the release denied to it for so long.

What could it hurt if he let him out to play for a while? He didn't think his cat could be a danger to Gregory, didn't think it possible any part of his being could hurt the man writhing above him...but then he *couldn't* be sure, could he? And so he did the only thing he knew how. He tried to push his cat even further inside, tried to banish him to the deepest recesses of his being. He might have been successful if Gregory hadn't leant down and mashed their lips together, stealing his breath along with his common sense, the slide of their wet tongues making him forget himself, making him forget what he had to do to keep his cat at bay.

If Hayden let himself go, if he gave himself over to Gregory and to the feelings that were becoming so powerful for the man above him, the inner battle that he'd fought for so long would be lost.

Gregory reached a hand between them, slid it into the front of Hayden's boxers and grabbed hold of his rigid cock. When he began to stroke, to slide back the foreskin, gently at first and then with more pressure, Hayden wasn't sure how much more he could take, how much longer he could hold out. He didn't want to hold out. He needed this. His cat needed this.

"Let go, Hayden," Gregory rasped. "Do it for me – give into it. Please."

The pleading tone to Gregory's request stripped away Hayden's defences layer by agonising layer.

Gregory bent down and nuzzled into his neck, inhaling him, drinking in his scent like an addict taking a fix, and the groan that tore from his throat was ragged, primal. His tongue scraped deliciously up Hayden's neck followed by a graze of teeth and the pressure of sucking lips and all the while Gregory kept stroking him, kept making his body want to fly apart. And then it did.

The pressure inside built and built until there was nothing left for it to do but erupt in a burst of light and feelings and emotions. He couldn't hold it back any longer. Hayden's cat burst through the walls he had constructed for himself. His cat rose to the surface, clawing desperately at his insides until it was finally free. Hayden's incisors ripped from his gums, his eyes shifted, his claws tore from his fingers and a low hiss burst from his throat. But, while all the physical changes were altering his body, it was the things going on inside that stole the breath from Hayden's lungs.

Gregory's face seemed to glow so brightly from within it nearly blinded Hayden. His entire body filled with the light from it until there was no space for anything else. Tiny currents of electricity zapped him everywhere at once, and, Jesus, but that smile… The smile on Gregory's face said everything, answered everything. It was a knowing smile, a triumphant smile. That smile was the last thing Hayden saw before a pleasure unlike any he'd experienced took over his body. And when he came he shouted out the only word it seemed he had left in his vocabulary.

"Mate!"

* * * *

Gregory had never been so happy. As he stared down at Hayden's face, contorted with pleasure, and heard him scream out the word he'd been longing to hear since the moment they met, a rush of pure adrenaline surged through his body. It was like a tidal wave of pleasure threatening to drown him. He was certain it would embarrass him later, but as he spent himself in his briefs—still gripping Hayden's overflowing cock and crying out his name—he didn't care. Nothing mattered but the man beneath him. His mate.

When he finally stopped trembling, he opened his eyes and looked down at Hayden's face. He wasn't sure what he had hoped to see there, surprise maybe or happiness, even a small amount of fear, but the one thing he prayed not to find was regret. Relief unlike any he'd known coursed through his veins when he took in Hayden's wide eyes and open mouth. There was definitely surprise etched on his face but beyond that was wonder, awe and a little incredulity.

"You're... You're..." Hayden couldn't finish the sentence.

Gregory placed a hand under his mate's chin and tilted it until their gazes locked. "I'm yours," he said with conviction.

Hayden choked out a sob. "You knew," he rasped. "All along you knew."

Even though it hadn't been a question, Gregory answered with a nod.

"Why didn't you tell me?"

Leaning down, he placed a gentle kiss on Hayden's lips. "Can you honestly say you would have believed something like that without feeling it, without experiencing it for yourself?"

"I don't know," Hayden said quietly. He seemed to think about it for a moment before continuing. "I guess not."

"I didn't think so. It was something you had to find out for yourself."

"I'm sorry, I'm so sorry." The words were spoken so quietly Gregory had to bend lower to hear them, and when he let them wash over him, he didn't like them.

His reply stuck in his throat but he choked it out. "What are you sorry for?"

Hayden rolled out from underneath Gregory and sat on the edge of the bed, covering his face with his hands. He scrubbed them roughly over his eyes then got up and headed to the bathroom. Gregory thought he wasn't going to get a reply but then Hayden stopped just inside the door and turned to look at him, his eyes full of sadness and pain.

"I'm sorry you got landed with me for a mate. Someone like you deserves better than someone like me."

Before Gregory could argue or refute or even shout at his mate for being so goddamn stupid, Hayden disappeared into the bathroom and locked the door, signalling the end of that particular topic.

The hell it was.

Gregory fell back on the bed and tried to gather his thoughts, to calm some of the anger building inside. Had Hayden's parents throwing him out made him feel that worthless, or had something else happened since? Was it because of his scar? Gregory knew there was a story behind the scar, but he couldn't force it out of Hayden. His mate had to *want* to tell him.

Whatever the cause, Gregory was determined to get to the bottom of it. If it took him the rest of his life, he would show Hayden how precious he was, how invaluable. He would make him realise he was someone that deserved to be cherished…to be loved.

* * * *

The ride back to Texas had been difficult for Gregory. A stony, uncomfortable silence had filled the car and every time he'd glanced at Hayden, his mate had been staring out of the passenger window, chewing on his bottom lip. Gregory had made a few feeble attempts to lighten the mood and to involve Hayden in a conversation about the Crazy Horse and some of the people that worked there, but for the most part Hayden had replied with one-word answers and offered nothing in return.

The mating bond was something that shifters revered, something they cherished, but Hayden was acting as though it was the worst thing that could ever happen to a person. His indifference to their bond made Gregory's heart ache. Didn't he realise how good they could be together? Didn't he care? Since Hayden had emerged from the bathroom that morning his cat been absent, shoved back into his hiding place, and now Gregory wasn't even sure if his mate could feel their bond anymore. He wasn't sure about a lot of things. Hayden was a mystery, and he wasn't forthcoming with any clues.

When the journey was nearly at an end, about five minutes from the Crazy Horse, Gregory decided to question Hayden because the not knowing was killing him. They probably wouldn't get the chance to talk when they arrived at the ranch and then he'd have to report to the council, so their talk had to happen now.

"Aren't you happy we found each other?" he asked, taking his eyes off the road for a moment to glance at his mate. Hayden shrugged.

"That's not an answer!" Gregory snapped. "Is it me? Are you sorry your bond is with me? Don't you like me?"

"I like you," Hayden said quietly. "I just don't get how you could like me. Let's be honest here—if it wasn't for our bond, you wouldn't have given me a second look."

Gregory lost it. "Don't fucking tell me what I would or wouldn't have done, Hayden! You don't even know me! For your information, I watched you for three goddamn days in Las Vegas when I should have picked you up because I was mesmerised by you, couldn't take my eyes off you, and that was *before* I got anywhere near you and knew anything about our damn bond!"

"Is that true?" Hayden whispered, eyes wide with surprise.

Gregory placed a hand on Hayden's knee and squeezed. "Yes, it's true. I wouldn't lie about something like that. You intrigued me, and, damn, but I thought you were beautiful. Still do. And before you say anything, I didn't even notice your damn scar. Are you ready to tell me how you got it?"

Gregory didn't need to be looking at Hayden to tell that his entire body had stiffened.

"I can't talk about it, I'm sorry."

Gregory sighed. He didn't want to have this conversation while he was driving, so he pulled over on a quiet road just before they reached the lane that led to Kelan's ranch. When he switched off the engine, he reached out and took hold of Hayden's hand. It felt small in his, but fit perfectly nonetheless.

"You know there's *nothing* you can't tell me, right? There is not a single thing you could say that could make me think any less of you, if that's what you're worried about."

Hayden snorted. "That's bullshit. I could tell you a ton of things that would not only make you think less of me—they would make you hate me."

"No, Hayden, you're wrong."

"Am I? Do you know what I did to survive when my parents kicked me out, huh? Shall I tell you, Gregory?" The anger radiating from Hayden crackled in the air between them. "Fine! If you want to know so goddamn much, I'll tell you exactly what I did. I—"

"Hayden—" Gregory interrupted.

"Sold m—"

"*Hayden*!" Gregory's voice boomed out in the enclosed space and Hayden snapped his mouth shut.

"I know," Gregory said, lowering his voice and staring into Hayden's eyes. "I know what you did."

"What? How do you know?"

"Your records at the council. I read them before I came to Vegas to pick you up. They said you'd been arrested twice for solicitation."

Hayden's gaze fell to his lap and his cheeks filled with colour. "And you still want me?"

Gregory sighed. "Hayden, you did what you had to do to survive. I don't blame you for that. But it's in the past. It's not who you are today."

A tear escaped Hayden's eye and trickled down the line of his scar. Gregory wiped it away with his thumb then leaned over and pressed his lips gently to the spot. Hayden gasped and tried to move his head but

Gregory wouldn't let him. He grabbed it firmly and trailed his lips from the top of the scar, just below his eye, to the bottom, above his lips.

A low moan tore from Hayden's chest and he turned his head so that their mouths pressed together lightly.

"I don't deserve you," Hayden said against his lips.

"You deserve far more than I can ever give you," Gregory replied. "But I promise I'll try to give you everything you could ever want."

Hayden started crying in earnest then, great heaving sobs that wouldn't seem to abate. Gregory wrapped Hayden in his arms and held him, rocking him gently until he'd cried the last of his tears and finally grew quiet. Gregory pulled back to take a look at his mate's face and the pain and guilt all present brought a lump to his throat. When Hayden next met his gaze he looked resigned.

"I need to tell you," he whispered. His voice, though quiet, was rough and raw with emotion. "I can't hide it any more. I have to tell you the truth. I'll understand if you never want anything to do with me again."

Gregory held the back of Hayden's head and looked him square in the eyes. "You can tell me—I promise I won't judge you. There's nothing you could say that would make me want to give you up."

Hayden opened his mouth several times before he finally found the courage to speak. "I'm a murderer," he said at last. "I've killed people."

Chapter Five

Taking in a steadying breath, Hayden kept his eyes on Gregory's face even though he was terrified of the reproach and rejection he might see there. He should have known better. Gregory didn't flinch. His hand stroked the back of Hayden's head gently, sending shivers down his spine. There was no accusation in Gregory's eyes, only curiosity.

"I might not have known you for very long, but I don't believe you would have done something like that except in self-defence. Is that what happened? Did someone try to hurt you?"

Hayden's voice sounded distant when he next spoke. "Yes."

Gregory sighed and kept up the soothing strokes to the back of his head. "Is that what you've been keeping inside for so long? The reason you won't shift. Is it out of guilt?"

Hayden's first instinct was to protest but he'd come this far and knew he had to go on. "Yes, in part."

"Tell me what happened?"

Hayden nodded. Gregory knew what he'd done now—all that remained were the details. Hayden had never told his secret to another living soul, and although it had been difficult to say the words, it was a relief to finally get them off his chest. He didn't want Gregory's pity, he didn't want absolution. He just needed to be able to share the burden of his secret, which had become too heavy for him to carry alone.

"About three years ago, I was drifting, moving around from place to place. I never spent longer than a week or so in each town or city back then. I always preferred cities because, with a larger amount of people, it was easier to get lost in the crowd.

"I'd spent some time out east, but I didn't like it there so I was making my way back to California when I got a lift to Des Moines with a trucker."

"What was his name?"

"Ramon," Hayden managed to say. "Ramon Lopez."

Gregory stroked Hayden's face with a whisper-light caress and, for the first time, Hayden didn't flinch when Gregory's fingers ghosted over his scar. He barely noticed, too lost in the painful memory.

Hayden drew in a shuddering breath and continued. "Ramon said he was picking up a load the next day and that he could take me as far as Denver. I'd travelled with him from Indianapolis, and I didn't like him. There was something...off about him, but I couldn't work out what it was. He was quiet for the most part but he had these black eyes and when he trained them on me, they left me feeling cold. I was pretty desperate to get back to Independence, though, so I said I'd go with him."

"Independence?" Gregory questioned.

Hayden attempted a wobbly smile. "I used to like to shift and hunt in Kings Canyon, but…I never made it there."

Hayden felt tears sliding down his face, but he didn't acknowledge them. Gregory leant forward and pressed a kiss over his scar and Hayden couldn't help flinching in response. It was an involuntary action that would take a long time for him to overcome. If Gregory had noticed, he didn't acknowledge it.

"If this is too difficult for you, you can tell me another time," he offered.

"It's okay," Hayden shook his head. "I'd rather get it over with."

Gregory nodded. "If you're sure."

"I left him that night so I could shift and hunt then met up with him the next morning. We headed south to Kansas City, which I thought was an odd direction to take but he said the I-70 was a better road to travel on than the I-80. I didn't know shit about roads so I went along with it. Not like there was much I could have said anyway—he was the one driving. Anyway, we got to Kansas City, and when we pulled up in the truck stop Ramon said he needed to call a friend and to wait for him outside the store.

"When he came back there was an even darker glint in his eyes and his mood had changed. He seemed…excited, I guess. He said he hadn't seen his friend in a while and that he was going to meet up with us so we could grab a drink together. He knew how old I was but he said he knew a bar where the owner wouldn't ask any questions and he'd buy me a couple of beers. I didn't like the idea all that much but I didn't have anything better to do so I agreed to go.

"His friend showed up and he seemed all right, at first. His name was Mario, but I didn't catch his last name. To be honest I didn't have any feelings about him one way or another. We went in his car. I thought we were going straight to the bar, but Mario said he needed to stop at his house because he'd come straight from work and he wanted to grab a shower and change his clothes."

Gregory raised his eyebrows and Hayden nodded. "I know. I can't believe I was so stupid, so naive. As soon as we got inside the house, I knew something was up. It was obvious they'd planned it all along. Mario started making comments about me to Ramon, saying things like he thought I was pretty and that he'd always liked twinks. The comments were harmless enough at first but they started to get more lewd. He said he hadn't been laid in ages and maybe I'd like to help him out."

"Why didn't you leave?" Gregory asked. "As soon as you became suspicious?"

Hayden hung his head. "By the time I realised what they had planned, it was too late. I started backing out of the room but Ramon was blocking the door and then Mario pulled a gun out of the drawer and pointed it at me. I guess I could have still run—I knew that if I got shot, chances were I'd heal from it—but it took me by surprise. The next thing I knew Ramon hit me over the head with something. It must have knocked me out cold because I don't remember anything after that except waking up in a chair with my hands tied behind my back."

"Oh, God," Gregory breathed. He took hold of Hayden's hand again and held it firmly in his own. Hayden could feel the suppressed rage inside Gregory. His hand was trembling violently, his jaw set tight.

Hayden wished there was something he could say to help Gregory's unease, but he didn't even know how to do that for himself so he ploughed on.

"Mario had a knife and he was waving it about while he and Ramon talked. It was all stuff like how they had a real pretty one this time, even if I was a lot older than they usually liked."

"You were, what, just turned eighteen?"

Hayden shook his head. "Seventeen. Hadn't had my birthday yet."

A low snarl tore from Gregory's throat and Hayden's hand was squeezed in an iron grip.

"Ramon started groping me through my jeans while Mario began rubbing his own cock. He was hard, they both were. He used his other hand to trail the knife down my face but he didn't cut me, not yet. I was out of mind scared, but the more I whimpered and pleaded with them to let me go, the more they seemed to get off on it. By then I knew what they had in mind. They made it pretty clear that they were going to rape me and then kill me afterwards. Said they'd done it before. They were real cocky about it, actually, about how easy it had been to get away with because they always chose kids that no one gave a shit about, that wouldn't be missed."

A single tear fell down Gregory's face but Hayden didn't have the energy to lift his hand to brush it away.

"I was so scared that my eyes and teeth shifted before I could stop them. It frightened them—they'd obviously never come into contact with a shifter before. They started shouting at me, calling me a freak. I guess I lost it after that, got pretty vicious. Ramon grabbed the knife from Mario and said 'Let's just kill the freak'. I fought against the ropes but I couldn't get loose in time and he stabbed me."

Gregory sucked in a sharp breath. "He what? Where?"

Hayden let go of Gregory's hand and lifted his shirt to reveal the small pink scar on his stomach. It had lightened over the years to a pale shade of pink but it hadn't disappeared. Gregory reached out with tentative fingers and stroked them over the raised skin. The light touch made it tingle.

"What did you do then?" Gregory asked.

Lowering his top, Hayden sighed and continued his story. "I shifted my hands into claws and managed to slice through the ropes they had tied around my wrists. Everything after that is blurry. We were all shouting, fighting. Mario had the gun again. I made a grab for it and wrestled it out of his hand but Ramon was coming for me with the knife. He tried to stick it in my chest but I managed to get out of the way and he stabbed Mario instead."

"Did he kill him?"

"I didn't know right then. Ramon and I started fighting and struggling and that's when he cut my face. The blade was so close to my eye I was sure I was going to lose it. I think that's what he was aiming for, but he missed. Well, as you can see, my face got cut pretty bad."

As he spoke, Hayden remembered the white-hot sting of the cut, remembered his blood creating an ever-expanding patch on the front of his shirt. Gregory's hand came up to cup his face and stroke him gently across his cheek.

"We were wrestling on the floor when the gun went off. Mario was still alive. I think the shot was meant as a warning to break us apart, because he was afraid he might hit his friend, but Ramon didn't stop fighting—he kept coming for me with the knife and I lashed out. I cut his throat with my claws, and I knew as soon as I did it that he wouldn't heal from it…there was no way.

"His wounds were deep. But I was practically crazy with rage by that point and I didn't even care. I was glad. I wanted him dead. I wanted them both dead. I pushed Ramon off me. Mario screamed and wailed and shouted when he saw what I'd done and he turned the gun on me again. I didn't stop to think. I lunged for him and slashed him across the face, just like Ramon had done to me with the knife.

"But that didn't stop him. He kept pushing and pushing, struggling for all he was worth as I tried to get the gun off him. And then it went off again and he fell backwards. While we'd struggled, I must have managed to turn the gun and it went off, got him in the chest. It killed him—*I* killed him. I sat there for a couple of minutes, in shock I guess. When I finally got up and went to check on Ramon, he was dead, too. He'd bled out from his injuries."

When he finished speaking, Hayden slumped forward in his seat. Reliving the painful memory he'd spent three years trying to forget made him feel weak, tired right through to his bones.

"No one could blame you for doing what you did, Hayden. Those men would have killed you. It was self-defence."

Hayden shook his head. "Don't you get it? I was glad. I was happy they were dead!"

A low hiss tore from Gregory's throat. "I'm happy they're dead. Because it means *you're* alive. They were rapists, murderers. God only knows how many other young boys you saved that day. They wouldn't have stopped, Hayden. Men like that never stop."

"I was so scared I was going to get caught, so I ran. My shirt was soaked through with blood, so I took one of Mario's and then I… I stole the money they had in their wallets so I could get out of the city and I ran. It was still light out and Mario lived in a busy neighbourhood so I couldn't change into my cat. I just ran, and ran, and kept on running until I'd made it out of Kansas City. I had to stop eventually, of course. I was tired, and still bleeding, even though the stab wound in my stomach and the gash on my face had begun to heal. I knew they wouldn't heal properly until I shifted, but I was so angry and upset and disgusted with myself for what I'd done, I was too scared to shift.

"I was afraid to set my cat free, afraid that he would be wild, infuriated. I was afraid of what might happen. What if he hurt someone else? So I didn't shift."

"What did you do when you got out of the city?"

"I caught a bus, but I didn't go to California as planned. I left Kansas, went south to Oklahoma, and then made my way across to New Mexico. I spent some time in Arizona then after a year of struggling to get by—begging, mainly, and…well, you know about the rest—the next obvious place was Las Vegas."

"And you still didn't shift?"

Hayden shook his head. "No. The knife wound in my stomach had closed up and the slash on my face had healed to the scar you see now. But by then, I'd left it so long I figured my cat would be angry at me for keeping him contained for so long. It was like a catch-twenty-two. The longer I left it, the harder it became.

"Besides, I didn't want the scar on my face to heal, not really, because it was a reminder of what happened. It was a reminder of the things I'm capable of. I never want to forget—I don't want to become complacent. I can't afford to forget, Gregory, because what if I do then something like that happens again? I know they were bad men and maybe they deserved punishment for what they'd done, but I killed them! I took away their lives! I don't ever want to forget that."

Gregory leant forward and wrapped his arms around Hayden, pulling him into his chest and holding him close.

"You don't have to forget," Gregory whispered against the side of his head. "But you do have to forgive yourself. It's time for you to let go, time for you to start living again."

"But I don't know how," Hayden said softly.

* * * *

Gregory pulled his car into the dirt drive of the Crazy Horse and killed the engine. He'd spent the last half hour holding his mate, trying to comfort him and reassure him. He understood how difficult it must have been for Hayden to disclose his secret, but he didn't blame him. It had been self-defence, pure and simple, and under the same circumstances Gregory would have done the same thing.

It made him angry to think about what had nearly happened to Hayden, but all the more determined to ensure his mate never be put in a dangerous situation like that again, even if it meant lying to the council and putting his own life in jeopardy.

"You ready to meet everyone?" he asked, reaching across the seat to take hold of Hayden's hand.

Hayden chewed on his bottom lip. "Are you sure they're okay with me staying here?"

"Yeah, I'm sure. Kelan wouldn't have agreed to it if he didn't want you here. You'll like him. He's a good alpha and a good man. You'll like everyone here, matter o' fact. They're good folks, all of them."

They got out of the car just as Kelan and Pete were coming down the porch steps to greet them. Kelan's lips were set in a tight line, but Pete merely looked amused.

"Hayden?" Kelan asked, reaching out and shaking Hayden's hand. "Howdy. I'm Kelan. I'm the alpha here in Wolf Creek and this is Pete, one of my betas."

"Pleased to meet you," Hayden said quietly. "Thanks for letting me stay here."

While he shook hands with Kelan and Pete, Hayden turned his face away, clearly trying to hide his scar. It troubled Gregory that his mate felt the need to hide, but he'd quickly learn that no one on the Crazy Horse would judge him.

Kelan smiled warmly. "Anything to help out a friend."

"Hayden knows about our bond now," Gregory clarified.

"Well then, I guess congratulations are in order."

"My regards to you both," Pete said brightly.

"Thank you." Hayden smiled back shyly.

Gregory was pleased that neither Kelan nor Pete had mentioned Hayden's scar, even though they must have noticed it.

"Come on, I'll show you where you can sleep," Kelan said.

Gregory nodded and placed a hand on Hayden's shoulder as they started to follow Kelan across the yard.

"Kelan!"

When Gregory turned, Kelan's mate Jake was running down the steps of the porch.

"What is it?" Kelan asked.

"I've got to go to the airport to pick up Tony. Just wanted to say goodbye. I'll see you later, okay? Hi, Gregory!"

Gregory thought he heard Kelan growl but when he looked at the alpha he was smiling, his eyes giving nothing away. Pete snorted.

"Hi, Jake," Gregory said. "I'd like to introduce you to my mate, Hayden. Hayden, this is Kelan's mate, Jake."

Hayden reached out and shook Jake's hand but he took a step closer to Gregory's side as he did. "You're human," he blurted out.

Jake chuckled. "Yep, last time I checked. Don't hold it against me, will you?"

Hayden's face turned bright pink. "Sorry," he mumbled.

"Who's Tony?" Gregory asked.

"Tony's my friend from New York. He's coming to visit for a while," Jake replied.

"Tony's his ex," Kelan said morosely.

Pete rolled his eyes. "Kelan's jealous."

"Am not." Kelan huffed, but the frown on his face contradicted his words.

Jake grinned and wrapped his arms around Kelan's waist. "I don't know why—he has no reason to be." He placed a kiss on Kelan's lips then pulled out of the embrace. "I've got to get going or I'll be late. It was good to meet you, Hayden."

"You too."

Gregory waited until Jake had got into Kelan's truck and pulled out of the yard before he questioned Kelan. "His ex?"

Kelan grunted.

"Apparently Tony's in love with Jake," Pete supplied.

"And you don't mind him coming to stay here?"

Kelan shrugged. "I trust Jake. But if that weasel so much as lays a finger on him, I swear to God…"

Gregory and Pete both chuckled, but when Gregory looked at his mate, Hayden's eyes were blinking rapidly and he was staring at Kelan with something bordering on fear. He leaned in close and whispered in his ear. "There's nothing to be afraid of. Kelan's just sounding off. He wouldn't hurt Tony."

When Kelan snorted, Gregory thought it best to let the subject drop.

"I've got to get going," Pete said. "I've got to open up Jessie's."

"Pete manages the bar in town," Kelan told Hayden.

"Has there been any more trouble there since I left?" Gregory asked.

Pete shook his head. "Nope, nothing to speak of. The place has been quiet since Neil and his friends were arrested."

"That's good to hear."

"Sure is. I'll catch you all later."

Gregory and Hayden followed Kelan to the bunkhouse and the door opened as they climbed the porch steps. Cary stepped out.

"Hi, Gregory!" he greeted enthusiastically.

Gregory nodded. "Cary. I'd like to introduce you to my mate, Hayden."

"Hello," Cary said, smiling shyly. "Kelan told me you're going to be staying here with us. It'll be nice to have another cat around. Not that's there's anything wrong with the wolves," he added quickly, glancing at Kelan.

Kelan merely chuckled.

"Where's Aaron?" Gregory asked.

"He's gone into town with his father. They shouldn't be long. Come on in."

They followed Cary into the bunkhouse and through to the kitchen.

"Feel free to use anything you find in here," Cary said. "Come on, I'll show you your bedroom. Where are your bags?"

"Oh, they're in the car," Gregory replied. "You go on ahead, I'll go back to get them."

Hayden looked over at Gregory with wide eyes.

"Don't worry," Gregory said, placing a kiss on his mate's cheek. "I'll be right back."

Hayden chewed nervously on his bottom lip. He looked hesitantly at Cary and Kelan and then nodded. "Okay."

"Through here, Hayden," Cary said.

Gregory walked back through the house and out into the yard. He doubled back to his car and retrieved Hayden's bags from the boot. He was about to make his way back to the bunkhouse when his cell started to vibrate in his pocket. He pulled it out and answered the call. "Gregory."

"Gregory, it's Dean. Where are you?"

Gregory looked across to the bunkhouse and pursed his lips before answering. "I'm in Wolf Creek," he said, cautiously. "What do you want?"

Dean chuckled. "Someone's been a bad agent. How is that little cat you kidnapped holding up?"

Gregory's stomach lurched. "I don't know what you're talking about."

"Come now," Dean said. "Let's cut through the bullshit. I know you have him. The store near Hayden's condo has CCTV."

Gregory swore under his breath. He hated hearing his mate's name on Dean's lips. How could he have been so stupid? He'd seen the camera when he'd carried Hayden back to his condo, but he'd been so intent on getting Hayden home to rest, he hadn't spared it a second thought. What the hell was he going to do now?

"I don't have to tell you how much trouble you'd be in if your superiors found out you're hiding the cat," Dean continued. "What's so special about him that you'd be willing to throw away your career in the council to hide him? Because that's exactly what you're doing, Gregory."

Gregory's stomach was in knots. "There's nothing special about him," he lied. "Just felt sorry for the kid. He's had a tough life and I wanted to help him out. I was afraid the council wouldn't have his best interests at heart. You know as well as I do how some stray shifters are treated." Gregory knew his story was paper thin, but it was the best he could come up with.

"That's very noble," Dean replied. "Stupid, but noble."

Gregory was losing his patience. "What do you want from me, Dean?"

"A favour," Dean answered. "If you help me out, I'll make sure your superiors don't see the tape of you with the jaguar." So, Dean was finally starting to show his true colours.

"Blackmail?" Gregory questioned. "I didn't think that was your style."

Dean made a tutting sound with his tongue. "That's a nasty word. I prefer to think of it as, if you rub my back, I'll rub yours."

Gregory rolled his eyes. Of course that's how Dean would see it. "What sort of favour?" he said through clenched teeth. He looked across the yard to the bunkhouse. Hayden was standing on the porch, waiting for him to return with the bags. As he watched his mate lean against the wall and cover his face with his hands, he knew in that moment he'd do anything to protect him. Whatever it took.

"I have a little problem," Dean said. "And I need you to make it go away."

Gregory didn't like the sound of that. "What sort of problem?"

"His name is Jared Ambrose," Dean answered. "I believe you're acquainted with him."

Chapter Six

Hayden leant back against the wall and sucked in a deep lungful of air. He'd forgotten how nice it was to be out in the country. No smog or the stench of exhaust fumes. No noise. It was refreshing. But he was so used to shutting himself off and avoiding strangers that he was having a hard time being around Kelan and Cary. He'd told them he needed to go out and get some air, but what he'd really needed was a moment alone. Cary seemed nice, but he was even quieter than Hayden—which was saying something—and he didn't think they had a lot in common. Hayden felt intimidated by Kelan and, although the alpha had been very welcoming, Hayden couldn't help but find the whole situation overwhelming.

It hadn't been that way with Gregory. Right from the beginning, Hayden had felt comfortable being around him. Hayden wondered if it was because of their bond. He hadn't known Gregory was his mate, but had he felt it subconsciously?

Walking to the edge of the porch, Hayden rested his hands on the top post of the hemlock baluster and took a look at his surroundings. Kelan had a nice spread. Not that Hayden had the first clue about what working ranches were supposed to look like, but the place had a good feeling to it. The bunkhouse was larger than anyplace Hayden had lived in before and far more appealing. The yard and fields were huge. *The perfect place to shift, run and hunt.* The thought surprised Hayden. Was he ready for that? Would it be safe for him to shift here and let his cat run free? He wasn't sure that was even what he wanted, but he did feel better than he had in a long time—more relaxed, even with the threat of the council discovering where he was looming over him.

Gregory was making his way over from the car with his two bags. He smiled as his mate approached. For the first time in years Hayden felt like he had the chance to make a proper life for himself, a real home. But could it be that simple? The council would always be looking for him, wouldn't they? It would be difficult to keep running from them forever.

"How do you like your room?" Gregory asked, as he climbed the porch steps.

"I like it a lot," Hayden replied. "It's nicer than anything I'm used to."

"I'm glad," Gregory replied succinctly. The wide smile that had been present on his face since they'd arrived on the ranch had disappeared. His mate looked preoccupied all of a sudden. Hayden wondered if it had anything to do with the call he'd seen Gregory take.

"Is everything okay?" Hayden took one of his bags and threw it over his shoulder.

Gregory wouldn't meet his eyes. He shrugged. "Why wouldn't it be?"

Hayden frowned. "I don't know, you just seem…distracted."

"Everything's fine," Gregory replied as he entered through the bunkhouse door. "Let's put your bags in your room."

Hayden followed and tried not to let Gregory's abruptness upset him. When they'd set the bags in his room, they rejoined Cary and Kelan in the living room.

"So what is it you had to tell me, Kelan?" Gregory asked, taking a seat on the empty sofa. "It sounded important."

Kelan nodded. "Yeah, and it's not good news, I'm afraid."

Hayden took a seat next to his mate and quietly watched the exchange.

"Jared has discovered something about Dean."

Gregory's entire body seemed to stiffen at the mention of the name.

"Who's Jared?" Hayden asked.

"Jared Ambrose is deputy sheriff here in Wolf Creek," Kelan replied. "His mate Nate is one of my betas and works for me here on the ranch."

Gregory grunted. "Has Jared been investigating Dean?"

Kelan nodded. "Yeah. I told him to be careful, but he won't listen. He's determined to find out what Dean is hiding."

"He needs to watch his back," Gregory said. "He shouldn't have got involved in this. It's too dangerous."

"That's hardly fair," said Kelan. "You asked him and Nate for their help. Did you honestly expect Jared to sit back and do nothing while you were gone?"

"Guess not," Gregory mumbled. "What did he find out?"

Kelan sighed and studied Gregory for a moment. He looked as though he was considering how to deliver bad news. "It's about Ashton, Gregory."

Hayden's head swivelled towards his mate to gauge his reaction. He reached out and put a comforting hand on Gregory's knee but Gregory didn't acknowledge it. He leant forward in his seat. "What about him?"

"Jared said you told him that a wolf named Blake Deveraux had been giving you information about Stan Michaels."

Gregory nodded. "Yeah, but after Ashton was killed I found out he and Dean are pretty tight, so I assumed all the information we got from Deveraux came from Dean."

Kelan pursed his lips. "That's partly true, but it's not the full story."

"So what is?"

"Jared went to talk to Deveraux."

"What the hell did he go and do a stupid thing like that for?"

"Don't worry—he didn't mention your name. He was careful about what he disclosed. He just said he was investigating some of the deaths of council members' mates. Jared said that Blake guarded himself carefully at first, but eventually he got him to admit a few things. It looks as though Dean is blackmailing Deveraux. Blake didn't admit that outright, but Jared said it was obvious from some of the things he said. He kept saying all he cared about was protecting his mate."

Gregory's shoulders tensed and met Hayden's gaze. Hayden thought he saw his mate frown before he turned back to Kelan, but the expression disappeared quickly.

"What does this have to do with Ashton?" Gregory asked.

Kelan sighed. "Blake indicated Ashton had been working for Dean in some capacity or other."

"No. No way," Gregory said resolutely. "Ashton wasn't dirty. We were friends and we worked together closely. I'd have known if he was doing something like that."

"Are you sure?" Kelan asked. "Maybe he wasn't doing it willingly. If Dean is blackmailing Deveraux, who's to say he didn't do the same thing to Ashton? If he threatened Tania then it's likely Ashton would have done what he wanted. I don't have to tell you what a shifter will do to protect their mate, do I?"

All of the fight seemed to go out of Gregory's body. He reached across and pulled Hayden to his side, kissing the top of his head. Hayden sank into the embrace. He felt safe in his mate's arms.

"No, you don't have to tell me that," Gregory replied.

* * * *

Gregory parked his car outside the sheriff's office and took a moment to gather his thoughts, which were flitting through his mind with such rapidity they were making him dizzy. Dean might not have asked him outright to kill Jared, but he had no doubt that was what the wolf wanted from him. There was no way he could kill anyone, let alone someone he considered a friend. And for no fucking good reason? That would make him no better than Dean. Gregory wondered if Dean had threatened Ashton in a similar way.

Had his partner done Dean's bidding? Had he killed someone for the wolf? Gregory didn't want to believe Ashton was capable of something like that, but he could understand the burning desire to protect his mate. The fact was, Ashton *had* killed someone. He'd killed Stan. He might not have done it under a direct order from Dean, but he'd done it just the same. It appeared Ashton had been the victim of manipulation all along and Gregory hadn't had a damn clue.

Hayden's safety might be of the utmost importance to Gregory, but he couldn't kill Jared to ensure that safety. There had to be another way. He just didn't know what it was. He covered his face with his hands as a sense of helplessness overwhelmed him. What would Dean do when he found out Gregory had dared to disobey him?

Gregory considered talking to Riley—his superior in the council—about Dean's threat, but he had no idea if Riley could be trusted any more than Dean. But, of course, if he confided in Riley that would involve telling the council about Hayden and by doing that Gregory could himself be putting his mate at an even greater risk than he was already in. Talk about a catch-twenty-two. The important thing was to tell Jared about Dean's threat. He had to know his life was in danger. When Dean realised Gregory had no intention of doing what he'd asked, he'd find someone else to do his dirty work for him. Jared needed to prepare for that. He couldn't fight an enemy he didn't know existed. Gregory was just stepping out of his car when Jared came rushing out of the door of the office like his tail end was on fire.

"What's going on?" Gregory asked.

"I just got a call about a disturbance. The address is Seth Armstrong's but the woman hung up before I could get any more information."

"Seth Armstrong?" Gregory questioned.

"Yeah, he's a young wolf that works here at the sheriff's office, administrative duties. He's a nice kid, but I think his father beats on him."

"Where is Sheriff Ferguson?"

"Already knocked off."

"You mind if I tag along?"

Jared shook his head. "Course not. I'd be grateful for the help."

Gregory followed the deputy to the cruiser and slid into the passenger seat.

"How was Vegas?" Jared asked. He put the car in drive and sped out of the lot.

Gregory shrugged. "Complicated."

"Sounds ominous. You talk to Kelan?"

"Yeah, just came from the Crazy Horse."

"So he told you about Deveraux?"

Gregory nodded. "Yeah, he told me. What were you thinking questioning him, Jared? You shouldn't get involved in this. It's too dangerous."

"I couldn't sit back and do nothing. People are dying."

Gregory bristled. "You don't need to tell *me* that. My own partner was killed, remember?"

Jared sighed. "Then why are you giving me shit about this? I thought you'd be happy I'm trying to do something to help."

Gregory bit his lip. He was reluctant to tell Jared his life was in danger before he went out on a call. It wouldn't be fair and would only serve to distract him. He'd tell him everything when they got back to the office.

"I don't want to see you get into trouble. Did you think about what would happen if Dean found out you spoke to Deveraux about him?"

"Of course I thought about it. But if Dean really is responsible for people's deaths then he needs to pay. He can't get away with it."

"What the hell does Nate think about you getting involved in all of this?"

Jared pursed his lips. He remained silent.

"Jesus, you haven't told him, have you?" Gregory groaned.

"Of course I haven't," Jared hissed. "He'd go ape shit."

"And rightly so."

There was little traffic on the roads as they drove through town, but enough that Jared still had to stop at all the lights to avoid a collision. After waiting at the fourth set of lights, he lost it.

"God damn it!" He switched on the siren and overtook a black Ford, narrowly missing an oncoming SUV. "If that son of a bitch has hurt Seth again, I swear to God I will press charges against him even if Seth doesn't want me to."

"Why hasn't he brought charges against him before?"

Jared made a sharp right. "Seth won't even talk about it. The guy might be a dick, but he's still his father, you know? How hard do you think it is for a kid to turn in their own flesh and blood?"

Gregory shrugged. "Don't know how anyone could treat their kid like that. Men like him don't deserve to be parents."

Jared turned into a quiet, tree-lined road and pulled up outside a large ranch-style house. As soon as he cut the engine, the neighbour's front door opened and an elderly woman trudged down the path in a blue floral dressing gown and slippers. Gregory and Jared got out of the cruiser and met her halfway. Gregory inhaled to catch the woman's scent. She was human. Her hair was light grey in colour with a sprinkling of pure white. Laugh lines surrounded her eyes, but there was no smile on her thin lips.

"Mrs Delaney," Jared greeted. "Thanks for putting in the call."

The old woman pursed her lips. "Are you going to do something about it this time? I swear the racket coming from that house—it sounded like someone was being murdered in there."

"What exactly did you hear?" Jared asked.

"Shouting mainly." The woman sniffed. "And plenty of it. I think it was Seth and his father. Then Mrs Armstrong was screaming and I'm sure they were throwing around furniture in there. I'm surprised the house is still standing."

Jared nodded. "Thank you. Now I need to ask you to go on back inside your house, Mrs Delaney. Don't want you to get caught up in anything."

The woman looked as though she were about to argue, so Gregory stepped in. "We appreciate your help, ma'am, but we've got it from here. Let us do our jobs."

With a last glance at them both, she nodded, turned on her heel and strode back to her house.

"How do you want to do this?" Gregory asked.

Jared sighed. "Let's just play it safe. If we go in there guns blazing, it will only upset everyone more. Let's just try to keep it calm, ask a few questions. Every time I've spoken to Seth's father in the past, he's been nothing but cooperative once someone of authority is there. I've no reason to believe he'll be any different tonight."

"Fair enough. I'll follow your lead."

Jared nodded and led the way to the house.

"What's his name?" Gregory asked.

"Duncan."

Gregory stood at Jared's side while they waited for an answer. After a moment, the door opened a fraction of an inch and a small woman with big blue eyes peered out. "Can I help you?" she asked.

Her voice was little more than a whisper and Gregory had to lean forward to hear what she said.

"Mrs Armstrong, sorry to bother you but we got a call about a disturbance here. You mind if we come in?"

"I don't think that's a good idea," she said, closing the door.

Gregory jammed his foot in the way. "Can we talk to Seth?" he asked.

Mrs Armstrong frowned. "What do you want with my son?"

Gregory chanced a look at Jared. "We'd just like to ask him a couple of questions."

"I—"

"It's okay, Mom," a young man said, shouldering Mrs Armstrong out of the way. "I'll deal with this."

"Seth, can we talk to you for a minute?" Jared asked.

The young man—Seth—slipped out of the front door and closed it behind him. He had a small cut on his lip and his left eye was nearly swollen shut.

Gregory whistled. "Wow, quite a shiner you have there. That's gotta hurt."

Seth shrugged and chewed on his lip. He winced when the action caused the cut there to reopen and he licked away the fresh blood with his tongue.

"How long is this going to go on before you let us do something about it?" Jared asked Seth.

He snapped, "You don't know what you're talking about."

"Then why don't you explain it to us?" Gregory asked.

Seth looked back at the house and sighed. He shoved his hands into his pockets then led the way to Jared's cruiser, stopping on the sidewalk in front of it. He kicked at the kerb with a sneaker.

"What's going on?" Jared questioned. "I can't help you if you don't talk to me."

"We don't need your help," Seth barked. "Why don't you just stay out of it?"

Jared shook his head. "That's not going to happen. If you don't start talking then I'm going to have to take your pop down to the station and get him to explain a few things."

Seth jerked his head up. "You can't do that!"

"Actually I can," Jared said.

Seth's wolf quickly rose to the surface. His entire body started shaking. Gregory reached out and put a soothing hand on his shoulder. "Relax, Seth. Help us out here. Why don't you tell us what happened? Has your dad been drinking? Did he lose his temper?"

"It's not like that," Seth said quietly. "It's not his fault."

"What's not his fault?" Gregory asked. "Talk to us. Tell us what's going on."

Seth sighed and his shoulders slumped forward. He looked at the ground when he spoke. "My pop is ill."

"Ill?" Jared questioned. "What do you mean ill? In what way?"

"I don't know," Seth whispered. "It started a while back. It was just little things at first. He was forgetful.

He kept going out, leaving the door unlocked. But he's been getting worse over the last few months. Twice I found him shifted in the back garden in the middle of the day and when he shifted back he couldn't remember what he'd been doing there."

"And the violence?" Gregory asked.

"He's not violent, really. He has...*episodes*."

Gregory met Jared's gaze and frowned. "Episodes?"

Seth nodded. "It's almost like a temper tantrum. He doesn't lash out at me or my mom, exactly. It's like he doesn't know what he's doing. Earlier, for example, he went out to the kitchen to make coffee and when I went to check on him he was just standing there in the middle of the room. When I asked him what he was doing, he got defensive and he started going crazy, throwing things around and breaking things.

"Then my mom came in and tried to calm him down, but it only made him worse. I tried to get hold of him and that's when he hit me in the face. But it wasn't intentional," Seth hastened to add. "He didn't mean to hurt me, I swear. I just got caught in the wrong place at the wrong time."

Jared sighed. "Has your pop seen a doctor?"

Seth shook his head. "He won't see one. He doesn't think there's anything wrong with him or he won't admit it. And my mom is worried that a doctor will tell the wolf council and they'll take him away from us so she doesn't push him to go either. The thing is, some days he's fine."

"How old is your pop?" Jared asked.

"Sixty-eight, why?"

"It sounds like your pop has the onset of dementia. I've had some experience with it lately. My mate's father is suffering from the same thing. When we went to visit him in the nursing home on the weekend, he'd been sedated for attacking one of the nurses."

"Nursing home?" Seth choked out.

Jared nodded. "It's really the only way to keep him and everyone around him safe. Wolves with dementia are very dangerous. What if your neighbour had seen him in the yard when he shifted, or some other human? What if he'd hurt them?"

Seth hung his head and stared at his feet. When he eventually looked up there were tears in his eyes. "What's going to happen to him?"

"He'll have to see a doctor. I'll arrange for someone from the pack to come and take a look at him, and I'll make sure I'm here, too, in case he becomes violent. If he has dementia then he'll have to go into the home, Seth. I'm sorry, but there really is no other way."

Seth sniffed and a tear escaped from the corner of his eye. Gregory was about to comfort him when his cell started vibrating in his pocket. He pulled out the phone and got Jared's attention.

"I'm sorry, I have to take this."

When Jared nodded, Gregory strode away from the cruiser, frowning at the number on his display.

"Gregory," he answered.

"What's your progress?" Dean asked. "Do I need to remind you what could happen to that little kitty Hayden if you don't do this favour for me?"

Gregory looked over his shoulder at Jared. The wolf had his arms around Seth and was patting him gently on the back, trying to reassure him. At the mention of Hayden's name, Gregory found a new resolve. He gripped the phone tighter and ground out, "Leave it to me. I'll take care of it."

Chapter Seven

"That's it, grab the reins and hold on tight. Perfect, Hayden, you're doing good."

Hayden wasn't so sure. His horse had looked at him kinda funny before he'd got on. "I don't think he likes me."

Nate chuckled. "It's a she, and she likes you just fine, trust me." Nate led the horse around the corral. The further they went, the more Hayden began to relax and enjoy himself. This wasn't so difficult after all!

"Okay, now we're going to go a little faster," Nate said. "How about we get the horse to trot?"

Hayden gulped. "Trot? I don't like the sound of that."

Nate threw his head back and laughed. "You will—just takes some getting used to is all. You ready?"

"Would it make a difference if I said no?"

Nate snorted. "Probably not, no."

"Then yeah, I'm ready," Hayden sighed. When the horse began to pick up speed, Hayden started to panic a little. He grabbed the reins tighter in his hands and pressed his thighs firmly to the horse's back.

"That's it, Hayden, you're a natural," Nate encouraged.

"Is it time to stop yet?"

Nate just chuckled and kept on running alongside the horse. When they turned and started their way back to the other side of the corral, Hayden saw Gregory watching them from beside the barn. He was leaning against the side of the building in that casual way of his that oozed charm and confidence and sex appeal. Hayden's dick started to harden at the sight. He couldn't help it. His body always reacted the same way when he was near his mate. But he wasn't complaining. It was a pleasant sensation and one he didn't want to end any time soon.

"Hey, there's Gregory," Nate said. "Why don't you go a little faster and show him how much you learnt today?"

Hayden liked the idea of letting Gregory see that he was good at something. He pulled on the horse's reins, turning him so that they headed in Gregory's direction.

"Is this right?" Hayden asked, pleased his horse offered little resistance as they headed back in towards the barn.

Nate chuckled. "Perfect. You'll be an expert at this in no time, you just wait and see."

Hayden felt himself blush at the compliment. He still wasn't used to receiving them and it was difficult to accept them from people he didn't know, but not one of the shifters that worked on the ranch had treated him like a stranger since he'd arrived two days ago. Everyone had done their utmost to make him feel at home, like he was part of a big, happy family. He was grateful for that, and he was starting to believe he could make a good life for himself here on the ranch.

Aside from his worries about the council finding out about him, his only other concern was about Mac. He missed his old boss and he still felt guilty he hadn't been able to say goodbye. He hoped that the situation in the council would change and that he'd be able to finally get in touch with Mac, but he didn't envisage that happening any time soon.

He pulled back on the reins just as Nate had taught him as they neared the fence and brought the horse to a stop. Gregory strode towards them. He had a huge smile on his face, but, despite the expression, Hayden couldn't help but think his mate had something on his mind that he was keeping from him.

He had hardly seen Gregory in the last couple of days despite his assurance before they' arrived that they'd see each other all the time. Hayden tried not to let it upset him, but he was sure Gregory was avoiding him for a reason. Had he changed his mind about wanting to be with Hayden? They might be mates, but that didn't mean they had anything in common.

Hayden still had his doubts that he wasn't good enough for Gregory, but he tried to hide them as best he could. The times they were together were good and Hayden didn't want to spoil that if he could help it.

"Hey, Gregory," Nate greeted. "How's it going?"

Gregory nodded to the wolf. "Nate. 'S going good. How's my man doing?" Hayden felt heat creep up his neck. He liked the almost possessive tone to Gregory's voice when he called him 'his man'.

"He's a natural," Nate said, looking up at Hayden. "He'll be running this place before long. We'd all better watch out if we want to keep hold of our jobs with this one around."

Gregory chuckled. "Well, it can't hurt to keep you all on your toes. How's Jared?"

Nate frowned. "You tell me. I haven't seen much of him in the last few days. I think you've seen more of him than I have."

"Just been helping him out with a few things is all."

Hayden looked back and forth between Nate and Gregory as he listened to the exchange. That was the first he'd heard about it. Seemed he was always the last to know what was going on around the place even if it involved his own mate. That made him frustrated. Did everyone think he was this fragile creature they had to hide things from? He was going to have to speak to Gregory about that when they were alone. He wouldn't do it in front of Nate.

"Thought I'd come by and see if you'd finished for the day," Gregory said. "You want to catch some dinner tonight?"

Hayden nodded brusquely. "Okay, sure. Let me see to Misty. I'll meet you in the bunkhouse."

Nate shook his head and took the reins from Hayden as he jumped down from the horse. "No need, I got it covered. Go and spend some time with your mate."

"Are you sure?" Hayden asked.

"Yeah. It's no trouble. You can repay the favour another day."

"Okay, thanks, Nate, I appreciate it."

Nate waved off his gratitude and began leading Misty towards the barn. "See you both later."

"Yeah, see you, and thanks for all your help today," Hayden said.

Gregory pulled Hayden to his side as they crossed the yard to the bunkhouse and planted a kiss on his lips. "You looked great out there. Nate's right, you're a natural."

"I like it here more than I thought I would," Hayden admitted. "The work, the people, feels…right. I hope I don't have to leave soon."

Gregory's brow creased. "What do you mean? Why would you have to leave?"

Hayden shrugged. "I can't stay here forever, can I? What if the council finds out about me?"

"They won't," Gregory replied tersely. "I'll see to it they don't. Come on, let's go and grab dinner. It's been a long day and I skipped lunch."

* * * *

"Damn, that was good." Gregory rubbed his stomach and leant back in his chair, a wide grin stretched across his lips.

Hayden chuckled. "You know, I never figured you for a pizza type of guy."

"Why not?"

Hayden shrugged. "Don't know—guess you just seem more refined than that. Thought it would be an à la carte menu and a bottle of red all the way for you."

"Looks can be deceiving," Gregory said. "I happen to love pizza. Matter of fact, I like all junk food, sloppy Joes, corn dogs, hamburgers…and I have the biggest sweet tooth. God, don't even get me started on chocolate or macadamia nut ice cream."

"I guess there are lots of things we don't know about each other," Hayden remarked.

Gregory nodded. "Well, sure, but we've got the rest of our lives together to discover them, haven't we?"

Hayden smiled. "Yeah, I guess we have."

Gregory leant forward in his chair and cupped the side of Hayden's face. "You have the most beautiful smile. It lights up your whole face."

Just as he expected, Hayden's smile became shy and colour flooded his cheeks.

"And your laugh? Man, when I saw you laughing with Nate earlier my stomach flipped. You know that was the first time I've ever seen you laugh? It looks good on you, Hayden, you should do it more."

Hayden shrugged. "Guess I haven't had much to laugh about in the last few years."

"It must be catching," Gregory said. "I saw Nate do a fair bit of laughing himself earlier, and, you know, I've never seen that man laugh before? Seems like you bring out the best in people."

"I like Nate," Hayden said quietly.

Gregory felt a stab of emotion in his gut that could only have been jealousy. He'd never experienced it before, but then he'd never been mated before either. "You like him?"

"Sure. I mean, Nate is quiet—hasn't got a lot to say—but yeah, I like him. He seems like a nice guy. He works hard and he's good at his job. What is his mate like?"

Gregory tried to take control of these new emotions before they overwhelmed him and he said something he'd regret. He knew he was being irrational and he wouldn't subject Hayden to his own insecurities.

"Jared is one of the good guys."

"Nate said you've been spending a lot of time with him in the past couple of days. What have you been doing?"

Gregory's stomach clenched. He did not want to talk about this with Hayden. "Nothing exciting. Just helping Jared with some things he's got going on in the sheriff's department."

Hayden's gaze dropped. "Is he handsome?"

Gregory shrugged. "I guess… Hey." Gregory leaned across the table and placed his finger under Hayden's chin. He lifted his head so that his mate met his gaze. It seemed Gregory wasn't the only one suffering at the hands of the green-eyed monster. "Not as handsome as you."

Hayden's cheeks coloured and he seemed content to let the subject drop, but when he next spoke, Gregory didn't like the new topic any better.

"You know, you still haven't told me what your superior said when you went in to work yesterday."

He squirmed in his seat. "Nothing to tell. Had some paperwork to catch up on. I didn't get out of the office all day."

"Didn't Riley ask about me?"

Gregory nodded. "Yeah. I didn't like lying to his face like that, but I had to stick to the story. Said I lost you in Vegas. I don't really want to talk about work right now, Hayden. Can we change the subject, please?"

Hayden shrugged. "If you want. What would you like to talk about?"

"How about what you've been doing around the ranch since I've been gone?"

Hayden got out of his seat and circled the table. He straddled Gregory's lap and leaned in close to his ear. His breath was hot against Gregory's neck and he got hard instantly.

"How about we don't talk at all?" Hayden rasped. He snaked his tongue out and trailed it lightly up Gregory's neck. It was blessed sweet torture. Gregory grabbed hold of Hayden's hips and ground their crotches together. Hayden's dick felt as hard as his.

Gregory groaned. "What do you want to do instead?"

Hayden leant back until he met Gregory's gaze. "This," he whispered and then he pressed his lips against Gregory's and slipped his tongue into his mouth.

Gregory wasn't sure who groaned the loudest when their tongues met and caressed. Hayden was writhing above him, grinding into Gregory roughly. Hayden's fingers bit into his shoulders as he devoured his mouth with a ferocious intensity.

"Let's go to my room," Hayden said when he pulled back to catch a breath.

Gregory couldn't think of anything he wanted more. He nodded his agreement, but he didn't trust his voice enough to reply.

Hayden got off his lap, grabbed hold of his hand and pulled him along. Once inside, he didn't give Gregory a moment before he pounced, pinning him to the wall and taking his mouth again. Gregory's brain shorted out. Hayden's kisses were exquisite and in that moment he forgot about everything else. All his troubles and cares might as well have not existed. His mate was all that mattered, all he could see or think about. Before Gregory realised they were moving, they were falling onto Hayden's bed, their legs tangled together.

"Well, this is one way to get to know each another," Gregory teased, running his hands up Hayden's thigh.

Hayden's laugh turned into a gasp when Gregory's fingers skimmed over his erection. The smell of Hayden's arousal assaulted Gregory's senses. Damn he needed. He'd been so busy the past couple of days he'd barely seen Hayden and they hadn't been intimate since the morning at the motel. It was only three days ago but it felt like a lifetime.

"What you thinking about?" Hayden asked, reaching down and running his fingers through Gregory's hair. The touch sent shivers surging down his spine.

Gregory met his mate's gaze sheepishly. "Would you think less of me if I told you I was thinking about sex?"

Hayden chuckled. "That depends."

"On what?"

"On what exactly you were thinking about it. If it was something along the lines of 'I want to ravish Hayden right now', then you just went up in my estimation."

Gregory grinned and crawled up his mate's body until their entire lengths were pressed together and they lay nose to nose, gazes locked.

"Do you want to be ravished?" Gregory asked, surprised by the deep, husky tone to his voice.

The primal look in Hayden's eyes spoke volumes. The rawness of it made Gregory's breath catch in his throat, made his dick ache.

"By you? Always."

Gregory couldn't contain the groan that tore from his throat when he leant down and tasted Hayden's lips. He couldn't think of anything more perfect than their warm breath mingling together while their tongues sought each other out. Tasted each other. Gregory was in heaven.

"I want you to take me," Hayden said against his mouth. "I want you to claim me."

Gregory pressed their foreheads together. "You sure that's what you want? You know it can't be undone. We'll belong to each other forever."

Hayden chewed on his bottom lip and lowered his gaze. "If it's not what you want, I'll understand. I mean, I know I'm not—"

"Don't even think about finishing that sentence," Gregory chastised. "I want it more than I can say. I want *you* more than I can say, but I want you to be sure."

"I am," Hayden whispered.

Their mouths met hungrily and their bodies pressed together. Gregory couldn't get enough of the taste of his mate. They undressed each other slowly between kisses. Gregory took his time, mapping out every inch of Hayden's body. His fingers traced every line and muscle, every vein and freckle. Hayden was breathtaking in his beauty. Gregory followed the pale blond treasure trail of hair to Hayden's erection with the tip of his finger, delighting in the moan it elicited from his mate's lips. The gasps and whimpers only spurred him on, gave him confidence to touch Hayden with more fervour and know that his mate loved every second of his caresses.

When they were both naked, Gregory sat up and just looked. How did he get this lucky? His awe turned to amusement when Hayden's chest coloured to a deep shade of pink and the blush worked its way up his neck and face.

"There's no need to be embarrassed with me, Hayden," Gregory soothed, trailing his hand over his mate's chest. Hayden's breath caught when Gregory's finger ghosted over a nipple.

"Guess I'm not used to people looking at me that way."

"Well, you'd better get used to it because I'll never stop looking at you this way, you got that?"

Hayden nodded. "Please?" he begged.

Gregory groaned and looked around the room. "We need..."

"Oh." Hayden rolled to the side and opened a drawer in his nightstand. "Here you go."

Gregory looked down at the bottle of lube in his hand. "Where did you get this? You bring it with you?"

Hayden shook his head. He wouldn't meet Gregory's eye and, while he watched, Hayden's cheeks coloured. "Cary gave it to me," he whispered.

Jesus. Now that was a conversation Gregory would have loved to have been a fly on the wall for. How the hell had they managed it? They were both as shy as the other.

Whatever... Gregory didn't question Hayden, he couldn't. He was desperate for relief. He prepared Hayden quickly. He tried to go as slow as he could but he wasn't entirely successful and it seemed Hayden wasn't in the mood for a go-slow either. Gregory was under no illusions, they *both* needed this. Hayden writhed on his fingers, canting his hips, begging with his body for more. Gregory gave him everything he had to give and more. Soon they were both sweating, panting, wanting—the need in their bodies too strong to ignore.

"Please," Hayden said again.

Gregory chewed on his bottom lip. His hand shook from the pressure of keeping it propped up near Hayden's head while he used the other to lift Hayden's hips, push back his knees and position his dick at Hayden's entrance. He looked up and met Hayden's gaze. When his mate gave a slight nod of his head, it was all the permission Gregory needed. He pushed in, crying out when he felt Hayden's channel pull him deeper. Hayden was hot and tight and, Jesus, but he felt good. Sex had never been like this for Gregory, but then he'd never had Hayden.

He took his time, pushing deeper inch by agonising inch until he was all the way inside and then took a moment—both to get his breathing under control and to allow Hayden time to adjust to the sensation of being stretched and filled. Hayden was shaking in earnest beneath him, his hands fisting the sheets, knuckles white from the pressure.

"Gregory, please move," Hayden pleaded.

Gregory moved. He went slowly to begin with, building up speed gradually until he was pounding into Hayden, the sweat dripping from his forehead evidence of their exertion. Hayden was lifting his hips to meet every thrust, spurring Gregory on with his low, untamed cries and moans. It was too much. Gregory felt the pressure building, his balls drawing up ready to release. He tried to think of anything but the need to come, about how good Hayden felt wrapped around him drawing out his orgasm. But the sensations in his body were nothing compared to the surge of emotion that zapped him when he met Hayden's gaze, saw the wonderment etched into every line on his face.

A low, rumbling purr erupted from Hayden's chest and he tilted his head to the side, offering his neck. Gregory lost it. Instantly, his incisors tore from his gums and he leant down and plunged them into his mate's neck, claiming him. Gregory was dimly aware of the purr in his own chest as he drew Hayden's sweet blood into his mouth. Hayden gasped and his ass felt like a vice around Gregory's dick, pulsating and drawing out his orgasm as his mate shuddered through his release, the wet heat coating both their stomachs. Gregory couldn't hold back any longer. He didn't want to. He threw his head back and shouted out Hayden's name as his dick released burst after burst of seed into Hayden's ass.

When they'd both finally stopped shaking, Gregory fell forward, his hands just managing to brace himself above Hayden and support most of his weight. He'd never felt so alive or so at peace. The realisation that they had bonded together for life filled him with the utmost joy. Gregory would allow nothing or no one to come between them—whatever it took, he would keep Hayden safe. He had to. If anything were to happen to Hayden, Gregory knew he wouldn't survive it.

Chapter Eight

Hayden finished brushing Misty's coat and carried the brushes back to the tack room. He'd been afraid of the horses when he'd first come to live on the ranch, but they'd grown on him in the past week and now he loved spending time with them. He'd usually worked with Nate, Aaron or Cary while he'd learned the ropes, but today was Nate's day off and Aaron and Cary were out riding fence in the north pasture. Hayden didn't usually mind being alone—he'd become used to it over the years—but he hadn't had a moment alone since he'd come to the ranch and he had to admit he'd grown used to always having someone around. He hadn't once felt lonely since he'd arrived. And then at night Gregory was with him, and that's when the place started to feel like a real home.

Hayden had come to care for Gregory a great deal in the couple of weeks they had known each another, but sometimes he wondered if his mate reciprocated his feelings. Gregory hadn't said anything particular that had led Hayden to believe he was indifferent about their mating, but he had grown more and more distant over the past week and he wouldn't admit that anything was wrong. But Hayden wasn't stupid—he could tell Gregory had been distracted. He just wished he knew what was bothering him.

When Hayden checked his watch, he realised it was nearly lunchtime and decided to leave the mucking out until after he'd taken his break. He left the barn and strode across the yard to the bunkhouse. As he approached he could see a tall, muscular man climbing the steps to the porch. Hayden stopped his advance, unsure of what to do. He hadn't spoken to anyone except the people that worked on the ranch and Pete since he'd arrived. He knew he had to keep a low profile in case someone from the council showed up, so he started edging backwards, about to head back to the barn, when the man turned and spotted him.

"Hello? Hayden, isn't it?" the man called.

Crap. How did he know who Hayden was? Hayden didn't know what to do. But the man was smiling broadly and he seemed friendly enough so he took a few cautious steps forward.

He nodded. "Who are you?"

"No need to be afraid," the man said. "I'm Gregory's friend from the council. He told me all about you."

Hayden's eyebrows skyrocketed. "He did?"

The man chuckled. "Yes. Don't worry, he hasn't told anyone else at the council about you, but he knew he could trust me."

Hayden frowned. He didn't know if he should believe the man, but he found himself edging closer and asking, "What is your name?"

"Oh, do forgive me," the man replied, closing the distance between them. "My name is Riley."

"Oh, you're Gregory's superior at the council."

"That's right, I am. So are you going to invite me in for a coffee?"

"Uh, okay, sure."

Hayden still wasn't sure he was doing the right thing but the man seemed harmless, despite his size. He led the way up the porch steps and pushed open the door. "Come in."

"Thank you." Riley followed him into the bunkhouse, through the living room and into the shared kitchen. He nodded in thanks when Hayden motioned for him to take a seat in one of the chairs around the table.

Hayden set about making coffee. Neither spoke while he worked. It was Riley that broke the silence.

"So how do you like it here on the ranch, Hayden?" he asked.

Hayden's smile was wide, genuine. "Very much. Everyone has been so welcoming to me since I arrived."

Riley nodded. "You came to a good place, and Kelan is a wonderful alpha. He looks after his friends and family."

Hayden nodded enthusiastically. "At first I thought he was only helping me out because he knew Gregory and I are mated, but, now that I've come to know Kelan more, I realise that he loves to help people. It makes him happy to do so. I guess it's in his nature."

Riley's eyes widened slightly as though this were a revelation to him, but he quickly recovered. "Well, yes, quite. I imagine it is. So tell me, Hayden, have you and Gregory been happy since you mated?"

That seemed like an odd question to ask. Hayden's stomach lurched. Had Riley picked up on Gregory's discontent? Or had his mate actually confessed his unhappiness to the wolf?

"Why do you ask? What has Gregory told you?"

"Oh, nothing, really," Riley said with a shrug of his shoulders. "It's just an impression I get from him."

Hayden gave up all pretence of making coffee and sat down opposite the large wolf. "Did he say he's not happy with me? Is he sorry we mated?"

Riley met Hayden's gaze head-on. The look he threw Hayden's way made him shiver. "What do you think?" Riley asked. "Do you think he's happy?"

Hayden dropped his gaze and began picking at a knot on the wood of the table. "No," Hayden whispered. "I don't think he is."

"And why do you suppose that is?"

All of Hayden's doubts and insecurities were suddenly in the forefront of his mind. There were probably myriad reasons why Gregory didn't want him. Hayden was too quiet, too shy. He wasn't clever. He'd done nothing with his life but wash dishes and clean up horse shit. Gregory was intelligent, clearly educated. He had a good job as an agent at the supernatural council. What could he possibly see in someone like Hayden? And then, of course, there was his scar. He knew it made him ugly. It didn't matter how often Gregory tried to convince him otherwise—he had eyes in his head, he knew how he looked in a mirror and he was too much of a coward to do anything about it. He was afraid to shift. He was pathetic. Gregory needed a strong partner, someone worthier. He would be better off without Hayden holding him back.

"Maybe it would be better if I left him," Hayden whispered.

Riley shrugged. "Only you know what's best for you both. But what I can tell you is that Gregory hasn't been himself in the past couple of weeks. He's been lying to his superiors, hiding things. Not doing the things I asked of him. That's not Gregory, not at all. He's changed since he met you."

Riley was right. Gregory had changed in the past couple of weeks, even Hayden could see that. Gregory had been getting more and more distant, more distracted. He wasn't the same man Hayden had met just two short weeks before. He clearly wasn't happy. Hayden swallowed down a lump in his throat and nodded his head, mind made up.

"I'll go," he said quietly.

Riley nodded. "That might be for the best. You know, you could always come back to council headquarters with me. I can assure you no harm would come to you there. I would personally see to it that we find you somewhere to live, a new job. Gregory would never have to know."

Hayden blinked back the tears that had begun to cloud his eyes and nodded. "Just give me five minutes to get my things."

* * * *

"Kelan!" Gregory pounded on the ranch house door, his heart hammering so hard against his ribcage he was afraid it would break free from his chest at any moment. "Kelan!"

The door opened and Kelan stepped out on to the porch. "Gregory, what's wrong?"

"He's gone," Gregory managed to choke out. "Hayden's gone." Bile rose in Gregory's throat but he swallowed it down and ran a hand through his hair. "What am I going to do?"

"Calm down. Have you spoken to Cary or Aaron? Maybe he's out in the north—"

"His clothes are gone!" Gregory said desperately. "There's nothing left. It's like he was never here at all."

Kelan frowned. "Did you guys have a fight? Is Hayden upset with you for any reason?"

Gregory shook his head. "No, things were going great between us—at least I thought they were. He wouldn't just run out on me like this. Something's wrong. I can feel it. What if it's Dean? What if he took him?"

"Look, we don't know that it's anything sinister yet. Let's try to keep a clear head, okay? I'll call Jared to come around and help us search. Don't worry, we'll find him."

Twenty minutes later Gregory sat in the bunkhouse kitchen with Kelan, Cary and Aaron. Kelan hadn't had any luck with Jared. The deputy had gone to the nursing home with Nate to visit Nate's father. Jared had promised to stop by the Crazy Horse as soon as he got back, but the nursing home was a couple of hours' drive from Wolf Creek. Gregory was so angry he was ready to tear the place apart to find his mate. He'd never felt so helpless in his entire life.

"I haven't seen him since breakfast this morning," Aaron said, looking to Cary for confirmation.

Cary nodded. "Aaron and I were out riding fence most of the day. We took sandwiches with us for lunch so we wouldn't have to come all the way back. When we got here at dinner time, we just assumed he was in the barn with the horses."

"Jesus, then he could have been gone all day," Gregory said desperately.

"Are you sure there isn't somewhere he would have gone?" Aaron asked. "His parents' place maybe, or any other family around here? Does he know anyone else in the area?"

Gregory was starting to lose patience with everyone, even though he knew they meant well. "He doesn't know anyone around here and he hasn't spoken to his family in five years. I'm telling you, something has happened to him. He wouldn't have just left like this—something's wrong."

"We don't know that," Kelan reasoned.

"If something has happened to him, I'll never forgive myself," Gregory whispered. It was becoming increasingly difficult to breathe through the pain in his chest.

"Hayden's not a kid, Gregory," Kelan said. "From what I know of him he's taken care of himself since he was sixteen years old."

"That's my point exactly," Gregory snapped. "Hayden looked after himself for five years, and then I bring him here to keep him safe from the council and something happens to him within two weeks of him being here. I failed him, Kelan! He'd have been better off without me."

"Isn't there *anyone* in the council you can trust to talk to about this?" Kelan asked. "The council has better resources than us. They would be better equipped to find him."

Gregory massaged the back of his neck while he thought about Kelan's question. "I don't know. I could maybe call Riley. I've worked under him for years and he's always seemed trustworthy. I thought about talking to him when I discovered Hayden was my mate, but I didn't want to take the chance, just in case."

Kelan put a hand on Gregory's shoulder. "I don't think you have any choice anymore."

Gregory let out a shaky breath. "I know. I'll make the call."

* * * *

When Hayden opened his eyes a strong sense of déjà vu washed over him and fear prickled along his spine. He was sitting in a chair in a small living room, his hands tied behind his back. His head hurt. He thought maybe he'd been hit and lost consciousness.

"Ah, you're awake, good."

Hayden looked around the room for the source of the voice. "Riley?"

The man chuckled. "I'm afraid I might have misled you. My name is Dean—Dean White."

"Dean?" The blood in Hayden's veins turned to ice when he realised the implications of that name. Dean was the person Gregory suspected was responsible for the deaths of all the shifters' mates in recent months.

Dean chuckled. "That's right. Your expression tells me you're familiar with my name. Why do you think I didn't use it earlier at the ranch?"

Hayden's gaze flickered around the small room, hoping for some clue as to his whereabouts. They appeared to be in some sort of cabin. "Where are we?"

"That's not important." Dean placed a dining table chair in front of Hayden and sat down in it, looking him directly in the eye.

"What am I doing here? What do you want with me?"

"Now you're asking the right questions," Dean said. "Let's just call you insurance. I asked Gregory to do something for me, but he's been...reluctant. I can't have that. I might even return you when he's done what I ask. I'll have to think about it."

Hayden flinched when Dean reached out and traced a finger down the line of his scar. "You're a very pretty kitty," he mused. "Shame about the scar. I wonder why you haven't shifted to get rid of it."

"That's none of your goddamn business!" Hayden spat. He refused to tell Dean any more than he already had. He feared he'd already said too much about his relationship with Gregory. And now Dean was trying to use him to get Gregory to do his bidding—the exact reason the council was against its members mating.

Dean shrugged. "It's not important. I'm sure I could…overlook it."

Dean's eyes filled with heat and Hayden's stomach lurched. "You'll never get away with this." His voice cracked.

Dean threw his head back and laughed and the coldness in his tone sent shivers prickling down Hayden's spine. "Don't you get it? I have been getting away with it, for some time now. Who's going to challenge me? *Gregory*?" Dean snorted. "Don't think your precious mate will save you. If he cared that much for you, he would have done what I asked already. Your life clearly isn't *that* important to him."

Hayden tried to ignore Dean's words, but they stung regardless, just as he knew Dean had intended them to. Then he took a moment to really think about what Dean had said. It was true that Gregory had changed over the past couple of weeks, especially the last few days. He'd seemed distant. Hayden had believed it was because Gregory regretted meeting him and was sorry they'd mated, but if what Dean said was true—if he'd really been blackmailing Gregory to do something for him—then that would explain why Gregory had been distracted. Maybe his aloofness had had nothing to do with Hayden and their bond after all, and everything to do with worry about what Dean might do if Gregory didn't do what he'd asked. Hayden felt his anger for Dean grow more and more pronounced.

"If you really believed I wasn't important to Gregory, you wouldn't have kidnapped me," Hayden argued. "You would have just killed me like you did the other council members' mates." As he spoke, Hayden concentrated on shifting his hands into claws so that he could slice through the ropes that kept him tied to the chair.

Dean shrugged. "I'm just making sure I cover all bases, nothing more. Besides, I didn't personally kill the other mates, you know. I didn't have to. I got other people to do it for me." The smile on his face was more of a sneer. Hayden shivered, even as a bead of perspiration trickled down his brow.

"But I don't understand why." Hayden tried to keep Dean talking so he could work on cutting through his bonds.

"Mating makes shifters weak!" Dean shouted. "We don't need weak men in the council. We need strong men that can lead by example. Men that are not afraid to do what it takes for the greater good."

Hayden finally managed to cut through his ropes, but he kept his hands behind his back and waited for the right time to make his move.

"And just what is the greater good?" Hayden asked his captor.

"Shifters have become spineless creatures. Only out for themselves. There's no pack mentality anymore, no community spirit and no common sense. You wouldn't believe some of the idiots I've had to deal with in the council lately," Dean ranted. "You be surprised how many shifters want us to reveal ourselves to humans. That can never happen! We'd be digging our own graves. I had to put a stop to it. I had to deal with those members that would see us discard our way of life. I had to—"

"You took away people's lives," Hayden said.

"This is a war!" Dean screeched. "Don't you understand that? There are always casualties. I did what I had to do. I took lives to save others."

"You played God is what you did. You used people to your own ends, killed people to get what you want. You want to talk about war? If this is a war, what does that make you? Tyrannical. A dictator and a monster."

Dean roared and struck out. Loose from his restraints, Hayden was able to dive to the ground before Dean's powerful blow landed on the top of his head. He recovered quickly and spun around. Dean shouted out in frustration at losing his prisoner and rounded on Hayden, his eyes instantly shifting to their wolf form.

Hayden looked around for something he could grab, but he wasn't fast enough. When Dean reached him he struck out and even though Hayden tried to dive out of the way to avoid the blow he didn't manage it. Dean's claws caught him, scraping along his back. The wounds were deep and Hayden tried not to cry out from the pain of it, not to show Dean any weakness, but he wasn't entirely successful. Hayden crawled along the floor to try to get away from Dean's imposing frame, but he only managed a couple of yards before Dean was on him again. Dean punched Hayden in the stomach, stealing his breath.

"Don't fuck with me," Dean roared. "Or I'll give you another scar to match the one you already have."

He dragged Hayden back across the room and threw him into the chair. "Sit!" he ordered. "And don't fucking move while I call your worthless mate."

Hayden's breath was coming in pants. He had to do something to get himself out of this situation, but he didn't know what. Dean was twice his size and incredibly strong. There was no way Hayden could fight him. His only chance to get out of this alive was to escape. Being smaller, Hayden had no doubt he would be lighter on his feet and much quicker than Dean. He could outrun him, he was sure of it. But he had to wait for Dean to be distracted enough so he could make his move. Dean fished out his cell, punched in a number then held the phone to his ear. He grinned manically at Hayden.

"Hello, Gregory," Dean said. "Guess who's here with me?"

* * * *

Gregory's heart hammered frantically in his chest, his stomach lurched and he had to fight with his gag reflex when he heard Dean's voice and had his suspicions confirmed. Dean had Hayden, although the fact that Dean was calling him was a good sign. It meant that Hayden was still alive, but for how long? And the question was, why? Why was Dean keeping Hayden alive? What did he want?

"Where are you?" Gregory asked.

Dean chuckled. "You don't honestly think I'd tell you that, do you? Now, about that little thing I asked you to do for me? You know, all of this could have been avoided if you had just killed Jared like I asked."

"*What?*" Gregory heard Hayden squeak in the background. His heart began beating even faster. "Don't do it, Gregory!" Hayden shouted.

Dean roared. He must have struck out, hit Hayden, because the next thing Gregory heard was Hayden crying out in obvious pain. Gregory was surprised he didn't throw up for real that time. It had been close.

"Leave him alone!" Gregory shouted. "Don't hurt him!"

"Are you going to do what I've asked?"

Gregory looked across the room to where Kelan was watching him warily. Panic engulfed him. He hoped this would work, it had to. He had to save Hayden. His mate was all that mattered.

"If I do it, how do I know you won't kill Hayden anyway?" Gregory asked. "What assurance do I have that Hayden will be safe?"

"I guess you'll just have to take my word for it, won't you?" Dean said. There was laughter in his voice and Gregory wished he was there to wipe the smile from the wolf's face. He wouldn't get away with this.

"Well, what'll it be?" Dean asked. "Are you going to do this little thing for me?"

"I'll do it," Gregory said. "But you'll have to give me a couple of hours. Jared is out of town. I'll do it as soon as he gets back."

Dean sighed happily. "I knew you'd come around. You're doing the right thing. Call me when it's done."

"Let me talk to Hayden," Gregory asked. He needed to hear from his mate's own lips that he was okay.

"I'm afraid that's not possible," Dean said. "I wouldn't want the little brat to try to talk you out of this. You have three hours. Call me when it's done and I'll tell you where you can find your mate."

Dean hung up before Gregory could say anything else. He closed his eyes and tried to get his breathing back under control. "You think that was long enough?" he asked Kelan.

In response his cell started vibrating in his hand. He immediately picked up the call. "Gregory."

"We have him," Riley said. "We can get to his location in about twenty minutes."

Gregory closed his eyes. "Please hurry, Riley. What if Hayden hasn't got twenty minutes?"

"I think he's safe for the time being. Dean isn't going to do anything to Hayden until he knows you've done what he asked. He'll want confirmation that Jared is dead."

"Unless Hayden provokes him," Gregory said. "And, knowing Hayden, he's likely to do just that."

"Yeah, I agree. Look, Dean's location is actually close to the Crazy Horse—you'd get there quicker than we could, but you need to be careful. You can't go in there guns blazing. I don't have to tell you that you could do more harm than good."

Gregory's reply was sharper than he intended. "Give me the location, Riley," he ordered his superior.

* * * *

Hayden cradled his throbbing face. It was painful. It seemed Dean had made good on his promise and slashed him with his claws, giving him a mark on the right side of his face that had to be close to identical to the scar on his left. The wound was deep and the blood trickled through Hayden's fingers and ran down his arm. Hayden seethed with anger. He had to do something. Dean could not get away with his blackmail attempt. Hayden couldn't live with himself if someone were to die because of him. He couldn't let Gregory kill Jared to save him. He eyed Dean warily as the wolf hung up the call and stuffed the cell back into his pocket.

"It seems Gregory has more sense than I gave him credit for," Dean said, "although threatening a shifter's mate usually inspires that level of obedience."

Dean turned his back to upright the chair he'd knocked over when he'd attacked and Hayden saw his chance. It was now or never. He might not get the opportunity again. He got to his feet quickly and used all his energy to charge at Dean and knock the large wolf to the floor. Dean screamed out his frustration. Hayden ran for the door only to find it locked, but he wouldn't let that stop him, he couldn't. He was dimly aware that Dean had recovered from his shove and was rounding on him. Hayden nimbly sidestepped the wolf and ran for the window. Shielding his face with his arm, he crashed through. The sound of the glass breaking was loud and surpassed only by Dean's roars of outrage at having lost his captive.

Hayden knew the glass had cut him quite badly in several places on his arms and head, but he ignored the pain and stood up on shaky legs. He didn't have much time. Dean was already climbing out of the window after him. He took a look at his surroundings for the first time and realised they were in a wooded area. He could see Dean's truck parked at the front of the cabin but there were no other vehicles in sight. The property seemed fairly cut off, at the end of what looked to be a private road. It was some sort of hunting lodge, probably one that Dean himself owned. Hayden didn't pause for thought. He ran for the only visible road and followed it, pushing his feet to work harder, ignoring the sting from his cuts, the throb in his cheek and the pounding of his head. As he ran, he could hear Dean keeping pace behind him. Hayden knew what he needed to do. It was the only thing he could do to ensure his survival. If Dean caught him, he would kill him.

Hayden had to shift.

He veered right, into the line of the trees, and snaked his way through the large elms, brushing branches aside that got in his way. He twisted and turned through the dense woods, constantly changing direction in the hope of losing his pursuer. When he'd been running for what seemed like hours, but couldn't have been more than a few minutes, he chanced a look over his shoulder. Dean was nowhere in sight, but that didn't mean he wasn't there, watching, waiting for the right time to attack.

Hayden had to do this now. He couldn't wait any longer. His body shook with anticipation, his cat exultant and excited at his release. Hayden stripped off his clothes, paying careful attention to the surrounding area. He used his cat senses to scan the woods for any indication that Dean was near. But he didn't pick up on any sounds or scents from the wolf so he continued undressing.

When he was naked, Hayden took a deep breath and knelt down. This was going to be difficult and it was going to hurt. Hayden tried hard to focus his mind, to concentrate on the shift, and eventually felt his cat rise to the surface and take over. He stretched out his limbs and felt them begin to elongate, felt the bones break and realign. His eyes shifted and incisors tore from his gums. His claws ripped through the skin on his knuckles. Hayden tried to ignore the pain and focus on his shift. His cat snarled and hissed as the change continued, as his body accomplished the thing denied to it for so long. It was both exhilarating and terrifying at the same time.

After long, excruciating minutes, Hayden lifted his head and looked around him with the sharp vision of his jaguar. He scented the air and growled. There was a wolf nearby. A fully shifted wolf. Hayden snarled. He took a tentative step forward and continued to scent the air, to find out where the wolf was hiding—and he was hiding, of that Hayden had no doubt. He was waiting for him, wanting him to make the first move.

It was then that the fog cleared in Hayden's mind and he knew who the wolf was. *Dean*. Dean had shifted to his wolf form. He followed the scent. The wolf appeared to be moving, back towards the road. Hayden followed. He wasn't sure where the wolf was leading him, but he was happy to oblige. When the road came into sight, Hayden lost the scent of the wolf. He froze and listened, waited.

A movement to his right caught his eye and he spun around, but not in time. The wolf careened into him, knocking him off his feet, huge jaws snapping inches from his neck. Hayden managed to use the force of the impact to his advantage and he rolled to his side, throwing off the large wolf, but Dean recovered almost at once and came for him again. The second time, Hayden was ready for it. When Dean pounced, Hayden dived out of the way and slashed out with his claws, cutting the wolf's throat, slicing deep. Dean threw his head back and howled. The sound was loud at first, but then it turned into a spluttering, choking gurgle.

The wolf fell to his side, trying to turn his head to get at the wound in order to clean it, but couldn't reach. He whined, the sound low and mournful.

Hayden watched, still on high alert, as the wolf lay there, panting, blood seeping from the open wound. Hayden looked around him, trying to get his bearings. They were right next to the road.

He left the wolf's side, keeping Dean in his peripheral vision as he crawled out onto the road. Hayden looked up and down the road, looking for the best way for him to get away, to escape. The wolf didn't look healthy enough to follow, but he could always heal from his injuries. Hayden was still deciding what direction to take when he heard the low rumble of an engine, the crackle of tyres on gravel. There was a car heading their way. He thought it best to hide. He couldn't afford to show himself to humans.

He was just about to duck back into the treeline when the wolf landed on his back and sank his canine teeth deep into Hayden's neck. The bite was excruciating and Hayden's cat cried out. Hayden was aware of the heat of his blood as it ran down his shoulder.

Hayden tried to move, but the wolf had pinned him to the ground. He was going to die like this, with Dean the victor, able to carry on with his reign of terror unchallenged. He felt bad that he hadn't been able to stop him. But Hayden's biggest regret was not seeing Gregory one last time, not being able to tell him how much he'd come to care for him. It was too late for that. Hayden could feel the energy seep out of his body along with his blood.

When he thought about Gregory, Hayden's cat hissed, infuriated at having to leave his mate. He roared and, with the last ounce of energy left in his body, managed to throw the wolf off and lash out with his own claws at the same time the wolf went for him. Dean caught him again and this time Hayden knew it was bad. He laid his head down, trying to catch his breath, and felt his eyes grow heavy. Just as he gave in to the need for the sleep his body craved, he saw the headlights of the truck speeding towards them.

* * * *

"There he is!" Gregory shouted. The sound was loud in the enclosed space. "Kelan, stop the truck!"

Kelan slammed on the breaks, but Gregory was out of the door and running before the pickup came to a complete stop.

"Hayden! Oh, shit."

Gregory ran to his mate's side. Hayden was lying in the dirt in his human form, naked and covered in dried blood. Gregory knelt beside him and began to assess his injuries. Hayden was breathing, but his breath was shallow, laboured. His eyes were closed and his long eyelashes were flickering, as though he were dreaming. Hayden had a few small cuts and welts on his face, neck and arms but none that looked life-threatening. They all looked as though they had been worse but had already begun to heal. The scar on Hayden's cheek had all but disappeared. Hayden had shifted. Gregory finally allowed himself to take a breath. He'd never felt more relieved.

"Hayden, can you hear me?"

A low moan tore from Hayden's throat but he didn't speak.

"I'm here, Hayden, you're safe now. You're going to be okay."

Kelan stepped up next to them. "How is he doing?" Kelan asked.

"Good. He's sleeping. Whatever happened to him must have used up his energy reserves, but I think he's going to be fine."

"Any sign of Dean?"

"I hadn't even thought to look," Gregory admitted, finally looking up from his mate's face. "You think he's still around here?"

"I think so... Look." Kelan indicated a spot on the ground a few feet away from them.

Gregory followed Kelan's finger to a patch of blood in the grass that trailed off into the woods. "He couldn't have gone far," Kelan said. "I'll follow the trail."

Gregory wanted to stay with his mate to make sure he was going to be okay, but a fury unlike any he'd known consumed him. When he thought about what could have happened to Hayden, what nearly *had* happened to him at Dean's hands, he wanted to tear the wolf apart. Wanting revenge might make him little better than Dean, but he didn't care. Dean had gone too far. He would pay for what he'd done to Hayden and for the other mates he'd killed, the families he'd destroyed.

"Will you stay and take care of Hayden for me?" Gregory asked.

"Gregory, I don't think that's—"

"Please, Kelan. This is important."

Kelan nodded. "Fair enough, but be careful. Dean is a powerful wolf and even injured he'll make a formidable opponent."

Gregory nodded. "I know. When Hayden wakes up, tell him—"

Kelan shook his head. "Oh no, I'm not telling him a thing. Hurry back and you can tell him yourself."

Gregory nodded solemnly. He bent to kiss Hayden's forehead then got up and followed the trail of Dean's blood into the woods. The first twenty yards or so the trail was clear and easy to track. Dean had lost a lot of blood. But then the blood on the ground disappeared altogether, indicating that Dean had shifted. Gregory wasn't sure if he had changed into a wolf or back to his human form.

He pulled his gun out of his shoulder holster and listened carefully, concentrating hard on the sounds of the woods. He couldn't hear anything that indicated Dean was near, so he cautiously walked deeper into the wood. His heightened cat hearing wasn't picking up any unusual sounds so he used his other senses to try to discover the wolf. He focused on the smells in the wood, hoping to catch a trace of Dean's scent. His eyes followed every leaf blowing in the wind and every beetle scuttling across the ground.

He didn't notice anything at first, but then rustling behind him caught his attention and he spun around and pointed his gun. He wasn't fast enough. Dean knocked him from his feet and landed heavily on top of him. In the tussle, the gun fell from Gregory's hand and landed on the ground out of reach. Dean roared and tried to get his hands around Gregory's neck to choke him, but Gregory's lighter weight made him more agile and he was able to grab Dean's arm, twist it and throw him off. He made a dive for the gun, but Dean grabbed him around the waist and dragged him back.

They scrabbled on the floor, each trying to gain dominance over the other. Gregory wasn't sure how much longer he could hold out against the much larger shifter. Dean's weight was heavy on top of him and, even though it was clear he was not in full health, he was still incredibly strong. Gregory managed to pull his arm back and throw a punch that landed right where he wanted it to. He heard Dean's nose crack under the pressure, broken. Dean growled and fell back, holding it gingerly and trying to stem the flow of his blood.

Dean's retreat lasted long enough for Gregory to stretch out and grab hold of the gun. The second Dean realised what he'd done, a low growl tore from his throat and he shifted his hand into a claw. Gregory had just managed to point the gun when Dean struck out with his claws, aiming them at his face. Gregory didn't have time to think before he reacted. He squeezed the trigger and shot Dean, the bullet hitting the wolf in the centre of his forehead. As Dean fell backwards and hit the ground with a thud, Gregory felt nothing but relief.

"That's for Hayden," he whispered. "And for Ashton and for Tania and for everyone else that died because of you."

* * * *

"Baby, wake up. Can you hear me?"

Hayden cracked his eyes open and tried to focus on Gregory's face. His mate was leaning over him, wearing a worried expression.

"Hey," he whispered hoarsely.

Gregory's features relaxed into a relieved smile. It took Hayden a moment to remember where he was and what had happened to him, but when his memories finally returned, his eyes widened and he sat up abruptly, searching the woods around him. "Dean…he got away."

"It's okay," Gregory soothed, stroking Hayden's cheek with the back of his fingers. "Dean is dead. I killed him. He can't ever hurt anyone again."

"He's…" Hayden couldn't believe what he was hearing. "He's dead? You mean, it's all over?"

Gregory nodded. "Yes, it's finally over."

"Where's his body?" Hayden asked, nervously looking past Gregory into the trees beyond. "I mean…are you sure?"

Gregory's face softened and his lips curved up into a tender smile. "You've been asleep for nearly two hours. The council has already been here to take Dean's body. Kelan got a lift back with them, but he left his truck so we can get home. I didn't want to wake you, because I knew your body would need the rest in order to heal, but when you didn't wake on your own, I started to worry."

When Hayden's hand lifted to feel his face, Gregory nodded, confirming, "It's healed. The scar is gone."

Hayden closed his eyes and drew in a long, deep breath, tracing the now smooth skin of his cheek. "Then you're right. It is finally over." He opened his eyes and met Gregory's gaze. "I thought I'd never see you again. I thought—"

"Shh." Gregory pulled Hayden into his arms and crushed him in an embrace. "I'm here."

"You're here." Hayden echoed. He pulled back, took hold of his mate's face and pressed their lips together gently. The soft kiss was meant to ease his mind. To reassure him that they were both alive, both safe, but as soon as their lips touched, the relief and tension poured from his body only to be filled with an insatiable, almost primal need.

When Gregory grabbed Hayden around the waist and hauled him closer, deepening the kiss, Hayden gasped, the sound somehow lost in the depths of his mate's mouth. Their bodies melded together, Hayden reached up and grabbed a fistful of Gregory's hair, holding on tight as though it were the only thing keeping him grounded. The kiss became frantic, a wild frenzy of teeth and tongue, of nipping and biting, licking and sucking. Hayden was so lost in the desperate need that filled him that he nearly missed the sound of Gregory tearing at the button and zipper on his jeans. But there was no way he could miss the cool air that hit his ass as they were pulled down his hips. Gregory wrapped his hand around his rock-hard cock.

"Fuck me," Hayden said against Gregory's mouth. "Please."

Hayden nearly groaned when the hand on his cock disappeared, but when he broke the kiss and looked down, he saw Gregory fighting with his own jeans and his heartbeat skyrocketed. His eyes had shifted to their cat form and immediately Hayden's shifted to match, his incisors scratching at his gums.

"Hurry," Hayden pleaded.

Gregory pulled his jeans down and began stroking his cock, but when his hand stilled and he met Hayden's gaze, there was disappointment in his eyes. "We haven't got anything."

Hayden turned and knelt, resting his forearms on the ground and pushing his ass towards Gregory. "Improvise," he said over his shoulder.

"Fuck."

Hayden's need was spiralling out of control. He worried at first that Gregory would back out, but then he heard his mate spit into his hand and a moment later his cock nudged at Hayden's entrance. He couldn't wait, couldn't remember when he'd been this desperate. Never. He pushed back.

"It's gonna be rough," Gregory warned.

"Good!"

No further words were needed. His mate pushed in and they both groaned when Gregory slid all of the way inside until his groin was pressed snugly against Hayden's cheeks.

"Do it," Hayden begged. His need thrummed through his body, so much so that he was barely aware of the small bite of pain. All he could feel was the intense pleasure, the relief, the absolute rightness of his mate filling him. Hayden had never felt so alive.

The fuck was brutal and without finesse. Gregory had a bruising grip on Hayden's hips and he used it to drive deeper, to push harder until they were both grunting and shouting out their pleasure into the otherwise quiet woods.

When Gregory's hand reached around to grab Hayden's cock, it was all over. It only took a couple of strokes before Hayden cried out, his orgasm barrelling through him in an endless wave of dizzying pleasure.

"God, yes!" Gregory shouted and Hayden felt the cock in his ass giving up its seed, filling him so deliciously with liquid heat.

Hayden's arms gave out and he collapsed to the ground, Gregory coming down heavily on top of him, his cock slipping free from his body.

"I'm here," Gregory whispered in his ear, "and I promise you, as long as I'm alive, no one will ever harm you again.

Epilogue

"Hayden, hurry up or we'll be late for dinner! Aaron and Cary are already on their way over."

"Be out in a minute!" Leaning forward with his hands resting on the white ceramic tiles, Hayden took a good look at his face in the bathroom mirror. He'd been doing that a lot in the past few weeks. And sometimes it still surprised him when he unexpectedly caught sight of his reflection, often doing a double take. He wasn't used to seeing himself without the scar. It was like looking at a stranger. He still frequently caught himself trying to hide the left side of his face from someone when he spoke to them. It was a difficult habit to break, but he was getting there.

Every day Hayden saw the changes in himself—changes for the better. He was becoming more and more confident, more outgoing and he was more receptive to meeting new people and making friends. For the first time since his parents had thrown him out, Hayden felt happy about putting down roots and calling somewhere home. Gregory had noticed the changes, too, and commented on them.

Hayden had moved out of the bunkhouse three weeks ago and into Gregory's house, and since then their relationship had gone from strength to strength. Now that Dean was dead and things had finally settled down at the council, Hayden and Gregory didn't have to hide their bond anymore. Riley hadn't been pleased with Gregory for lying to him about losing Hayden in Vegas, but in light of everything he'd learnt about Dean, he could understand why Gregory had done it.

"Hayden!"

Hayden grinned and pulled open the bathroom door. "There some reason you got your fur in a knot today?"

When Gregory lowered his gaze and walked back into the bedroom Hayden frowned and followed in his mate's wake. "Okay, spit it out. What is it? What's bothering you?"

Gregory lifted the legs of his pants so as not to crease them then took a seat on the edge of the bed. "It's been a stressful day today at work, that's all. The investigation into the corrupt council members has shaken the place up. Everyone is on edge."

"Well, if they're not guilty they have nothing to worry about, do they?" Hayden asked.

Gregory nodded. "Yes, but the wolves the elders brought in are ruthless. They questioned me about Ashton, Dean and Deveraux for three hours today. Three goddamn hours! I told them the same story over and over again, but they kept asking the questions like I was going to suddenly confess to knowing about Dean's game all along."

"I'm sure they just want to be thorough."

Gregory shook his head. "It's over the top. You know they have wolves working for the elders that can tell if you're lying? From what I understand they're like empaths that can sense shifters' emotions. They had one in the office today yet they kept going over the same damn questions like a broken record. It's ridiculous."

Hayden sat down beside his mate. "Well, they can tell you aren't lying, so hopefully that will be the end of it."

"Yeah, let's hope so."

"Has there been any news on Deveraux?"

"No. They haven't sentenced him yet. But it will go in his favour that he gave himself up and confessed after he found out Dean was dead. You wouldn't believe the number of people who have come forward and confessed to doing something for Dean. He was blackmailing a lot of people to get what he wanted. Most of them would have got away with what they'd done, too, but they couldn't live with the guilt.

"At least it's all out in the open now. There should be no more secrets at the council anymore."

"Yeah. It'll be a relief to go into work and know I can trust the people I'm working with. I haven't had that luxury for a long time. How was your day at the ranch?"

"It was good, but Nate has been a nervous wreck all day." Hayden giggled, but when he realised he'd just said something he shouldn't have, his hand flew up to cover his mouth.

"Hayden, what's going on?"

"Uh…nothing?"

"You know you're no good at lying. Why has Nate been nervous?"

"Aww, crap. Okay, fine, but you can't let on you know, okay?"

Gregory grinned broadly. "My lips are sealed. Unlike you, I can keep a secret."

Hayden scowled at Gregory, but he couldn't stay angry with his mate. Truth was he'd been desperate to tell Gregory ever since he'd found out. "Nate is going to propose to Jared tonight."

Gregory threw his head back and laughed.

"Hey! It's not funny!" Hayden said, poking Gregory in the side. "It's romantic."

"Well, sure, but...*Nate*? This I've got to see."

"Now I wish I hadn't told you. You're going to make fun of him."

Gregory looked as though he was trying not to laugh. "I promise I will not make fun of him, okay?"

"Fine."

"Did you talk to Mac today?"

Hayden couldn't stop the smile that formed on his lips at the mention of his former boss. "Yeah. I called just before you got home."

"How is he?"

"He sounded good. He was complaining about the new guy he hired to wash dishes. I think he keeps smashing plates. Mac said he's going to fire him."

"Damn. Poor kid."

Hayden chuckled. "Nah, the fact that Mac kept grumbling about him meant he likes him. He kept threatening to fire me for the first couple of months I worked there, too."

Gregory laughed. "So Mac bought the story about you having to go into the witness protection programme?"

"Yeah, but I hate lying to him."

"I know, but we're shifters, Hayden. Sometimes we have to lie to humans to keep our secret. It's not a pleasant thing to have to do, but it's necessary."

"I know. Doesn't mean I have to like it."

"You know you can go see Mac anytime you like, right? I know he's like a father to you."

Hayden nodded. "I was thinking about visiting him for Thanksgiving, maybe taking him a gift to say thanks for everything he did for me."

"I think that's a great idea." Gregory said, kissing Hayden softly on the lips. Hayden quickly deepened the kiss but the sound of a horn honking outside made him pull back, already breathless. "Aaron and Cary?"

"Sounds like it," Gregory confirmed. "Come on, let's get this dinner over with so we can come home and have dessert."

Hayden chuckled. "Could you be any cornier?"

Gregory grinned. "Apparently not."

Hayden followed Gregory to the door and felt in his pocket to make sure he had his key. He took a look around the now familiar living space then let Gregory take his hand and drag him from the house. There was a smile on his face as they made their way down the path. He was so happy to be finally home where he belonged.

About the Author

Lavinia discovered reading at an early age and could always be found with her nose in a book. She loved getting lost in a fantasy world even then. When her parents bought her a typewriter for Christmas at aged eleven, her fate was sealed. She spent hours dreaming up characters and creating stories. Not a lot has changed. Now when she is not writing you can find her enjoying a new release e-book.

Lavinia has lived all over the UK but currently resides in London, England. She has travelled extensively to places including Africa, Asia, Australia, America and most of Europe. Although some of her books are set in Texas she has never visited the state but plans to spend time there in the near future.

She is an avid reader and her favourite authors include J L Langley, Carol Lynne, Chris Owen and Andrew Grey. Lavinia particularly loves supernatural fiction and her favourite authors in this genre include Kelly Armstrong, Keri Arthur and Charlaine Harris.

Although Lavinia is a huge fan of the romance genre, she will admit to reading anything and everything. She loves horror, a good thriller and if a book has the capacity to make her cry, well, all the better. One thing she does insist on in a book however, regardless of genre is a happy ending, so you will always find one in the books she writes.]

Lavinia Lewis loves to hear from readers. You can find her contact information, website details and author profile page at http://www.total-e-bound.com

CPSIA information can be obtained
at www.ICGtesting.com
Printed in the USA
BVOW08s2153040117
472671BV00001B/8/P